I0599817

# FIRST RESPONSE

## Joyce Byers Hill

Yakima, WA

Lilac Hill Publishing
www.joycebyershill.com
joycebyershill@gmail.com

Printed in the United States of America

# Books by Joyce Byers Hill

## A PLACE CALLED HOPE
*Diamond in the Rough*
*JC's Hope*
*Building Dreams*
*Ryleigh's Rescue*
*Lenora Sue Comes to Town*

## Other Novels by Joyce Byers Hill
*First Response*

# DEDICATION

I want to dedicate this novel to all the first responders out there, and to the families who love and support them. First responders have dangerous jobs and often don't get the credit they deserve.

A special thanks to my many friends and family who are, or have been, first responders. Thank you for always running toward situations that everyone else runs away from.

I also dedicate this story to my brother, Gary Byers, who became permanently disabled as a result of fighting a fire. Rest in Peace, Bro.

# CHAPTER ONE

Shane Gallagher backed the fire truck into the garage at the station and shut down the engine. He removed his helmet, set it on the seat next to him, then rested his forearms and head on the steering wheel. A couple of the other firefighters jumped off the back of the truck and were already stowing their gear, respecting Shane's need to be alone with his thoughts.

Today's fire had been fairly easy, but they weren't always that lucky. This was a barn fire that involved a small section of the barn – no animals were in danger, and minimal damage was done to the structure. His crew could have handled this in their sleep. Shane loved fighting fires, but he would never consider himself an adrenaline junkie; he just loved knowing that what he was doing was making a difference. Simple structure fires weren't a big deal – it was the house and car fires that took a toll on his psyche. But he could never give it up; the work was too important.

Lost in his thoughts, staring out the windshield toward the road in front of the station, Shane had no idea how long he had been sitting in the cab of the fire engine. A middle-aged fireman approached the driver's door from the rear and tapped on the window. Shane knew without looking who it was, so he lowered the driver's window.

"Hey, Chief," Shane greeted his friend and commander.

"Hey," Doug Hart replied with a smile. "Cody said you guys got that barn fire knocked down quickly. I'm sure it helped that you didn't have to deal with frightened livestock. I always know I can count on you guys. You're my best crew; I hope you know that."

"That's what you keep telling me," Shane grinned as he ran his fingers through his dark red hair.

The chief walked around the front of the fire engine and climbed in on the passenger side, not saying anything for several minutes.

"You go through this at the end of every summer," Chief Hart began. "I don't know why you don't just join the department full-time. We could use you. There's not a person in the department who doesn't like working with you. What do you say, son? It would sure make my life easier."

Shane grinned at his mentor. "You know why, Doug. I'm a teacher. That's what I do. Fighting fires has always been a part-time gig for me. I've been a volunteer firefighter for over ten years. Key word: *volunteer.*"

"I know," Doug nodded. "You were the first cadet to sign up when I became the chief." Chuckling, he added, "You could un-volunteer and make it permanent at any time."

"But if I did that," Shane grinned, "we wouldn't get to have this conversation at the end of every summer."

The chief picked up Shane's helmet and turned it over in his hands before asking the question he didn't want to ask.

"School starts in a couple of weeks," Doug said. "When do you report?"

"Next week," Shane replied. "I need to get my classroom set up before students arrive."

"You're still going to be a volunteer during the school year, right?" Doug asked.

"Always, Chief," Shane replied. Staring out the windshield of the fire engine, he added solemnly, "I do miss it when I return to school. Every single year without fail. Especially the first few weeks. But I'm a teacher, and that's not going to change."

Chief Hart patted Shane's forearm and said, "I know, son. But you can't blame me for trying. The school and those kids are lucky to have you." After a brief pause, he added, "You're going to come by the station this weekend for your party, right?"

Shane laughed as he opened the driver's door. "You've been having cake and ice cream after my last fire every summer. Why do you keep doing that? You know I'm not going anywhere. Why do you insist on having a going-away party?"

Doug climbed out of the truck and walked around to join Shane, chuckling as they headed toward the office. "You know how you can stop the going-away parties, don't you?"

"Let me guess," Shane chuckled. "I could stop teaching and join the department full-time."

"You said it," Doug grinned. "Not me."

\* \* \*

After the staff meeting wrapped up in the gymnasium, Shane wandered down the hall to his classroom. Once inside, he wasn't surprised to discover the school's janitor had already set up all the desks. Everyone who worked at the small Christian school, whether they were teachers, administrators, or support staff, was like family. Everyone pitched in to do whatever needed to be done.

Mountainview Christian typically had around a hundred and twenty-five students in kindergarten through twelfth grade. Most of the teachers taught multiple grade levels, and Shane was no different. He taught junior high and high school math and science classes, as well as high school chemistry and physics. He didn't have a lot of prep work to do in his classroom, but he would have to set up the chemistry lab. After he finished that, he could concentrate on his lesson plans for each of his classes.

While setting up the chem lab, his thoughts returned to the earlier staff meeting. This year, there were two new teachers, one in the lower grades and one in the upper grades. He hadn't had a chance to talk to them after the staff meeting since the principal had cornered them for some additional instruction. He made a mental note to take the time to seek them out and introduce himself.

It took Shane most of the morning to set up the chem lab. He had just sat down at his desk to work on planning when there was a light tap on the classroom's open door.

The school principal poked his head into the classroom and said, "Don't forget about lunch, Shane. We're planning it every day this week in the cafeteria."

"Oh, right," Shane laughed, having already forgotten the announcement at the staff meeting. "Thanks, Mark. I'll head down there in a minute."

Fifteen minutes later, with a lunch tray in his hands, Shane looked around for a table, hoping to find the new teachers.

Another staff member walked up behind him, also holding a lunch tray.

"Trying to decide who to sit with on the first day of school takes me back to junior high," she chuckled, standing slightly behind him.

Shane turned toward the voice, finding it belonged to a young lady with long strawberry-blonde hair and a beautiful smile.

"Why don't I make it easy on both of us?" Shane grinned, nodding toward an empty table. "Would you care to join me over at that table?"

"I'd love to," she smiled. "Once I set my tray down, I can properly introduce myself. Otherwise, I run the risk of spilling half my lunch."

"Only half, huh?" Shane chuckled. "I'd probably upend my entire tray."

After their trays were safely on the table, Shane reached out his hand in greeting.

"Hi," he smiled. "I'm Shane Gallagher. You must be one of the new teachers."

"Well, they gave me a key to the school, so I guess so," she smiled. "I'm Taylor Wilson, the new English and literature teacher."

Shane nodded, smiling, "Yeah, you look like someone who enjoys books."

Taylor chuckled. "I'm choosing to take that as a compliment. Let me see if I can guess what you teach."

Grinning as she looked into his sparkling green eyes, she said, "If we had an Irish History class, that would be my guess. Between the red hair and the name…you can't get much more Irish than 'Shane Gallagher.' However, knowing we don't have an Irish History class, my next guess would be you're the math and science teacher. How'd I do?"

Shane shook his head and grinned. "Not bad. You get an 'A'. You're right; I teach junior high and high school math and science." He chuckled, adding, "For excitement, I also teach chemistry."

Taylor smiled and said, "I can't take credit for the 'A'. I have to admit I had inside information. Mark told me who you were earlier."

With a knowing laugh, Shane looked across the table at his co-worker and asked, "Are you new to town, or just new to this school?"

"New to the school," Taylor replied, smiling. "I've lived here my entire life. Well, not counting the four years I was away at college. How about you?"

"I moved here with my family the summer before I started high school," Shane replied. "So, I've been here for several years. I like it; it's a nice change from living in the city."

Guessing Shane was roughly her age, Taylor assumed they had both been teaching for a handful of years.

"How do you like teaching at Mountainview?" Taylor asked.

"I like it," Shane began, "it's a great school. Granted, I don't have anything to compare it to since it's the only place I've taught."

Taylor nodded. "This will be my second school. I think I'll like it; everyone is very friendly and helpful."

After a brief lull in the conversation while the two ate their lunch, Shane looked across the table at Taylor without saying anything.

"What?" Taylor asked, covering her mouth. "Do I have food stuck in my teeth?"

Shane chuckled. "No. I was just thinking that lunch is nearly over, and I haven't really learned much about you. Well, other than the fact you grew up here."

About that time, the school bell rang, and Taylor laughed.

"You know we don't have to head back to our classrooms right this minute, don't you?" Shane asked. "They're testing the bells so they're ready for the students next week."

Taylor grinned as she stood and grabbed her tray. "Bell or no bell, lunch break is over."

Shane grabbed his tray and began walking along with her. "So, saved by the bell, huh?"

Taylor smiled and shrugged. "Whatever works. It was nice meeting you, Shane. I'm sure we'll be bumping into each other in the hallway occasionally."

"You can count on it," Shane grinned. "See you around, Taylor."

\* \* \*

The moment Taylor walked into her house, a three-year-old bundle of energy ran and jumped into her arms.

"Mommy!" the little boy yelled happily. "You're home!"

Wrapping her son in a tight embrace before kissing his cheek, she replied, "Hi, sweet boy. I sure missed you. Were you a good boy for Grandma today?"

"Yep!" Connor replied. Turning to Taylor's mom,

he added, "I was good, Grandma, huh?"

Stephanie Matthews reached for her grandson and hugged him before placing him on the floor.

"Yes, little man," she said. "You were a very good boy today. And since Mommy's home now, and you were so good, I have a cookie for you. Eat it at the table so you aren't walking around scattering crumbs, okay?"

"Okay, Grandma," Connor replied as he ran toward the kitchen.

Stephanie smiled at her only grandson as he climbed into his chair at the table. Turning to her daughter, she took her by the hand and walked into the living room, where they sat on the sofa.

"You look tired, honey," Stephanie said as Taylor tipped her head back and closed her eyes. "How was the first day?"

"It was okay," Taylor replied, sitting up and looking at her mother. "Everyone at the school is nice. I think I'll like teaching there…once I get back into the swing of things. Starting at a new school would be easier if I hadn't taken the last year off."

Stephanie patted her daughter on the hand. "You know you needed that year off, Taylor. You wouldn't have been able to teach."

"I know, Mom," Taylor agreed quietly. "This week is mostly preparing lesson plans and stuff. The real test will be having a class full of students next week. At least they'll be new faces and not the same students who watched me go through the worst day of my life."

"Your old students were good to you," Stephanie reminded her daughter. "They were there when you needed them. I'm sure your new students will be just as understanding when they connect the dots."

"It's just hard hearing the whispers," Taylor said as tears gathered in the corners of her eyes. "I don't want people's pity."

Stephanie wrapped her arms around her daughter and pulled her close. "Just don't mistake sympathy for pity. What happened to Zach was all over the news. It's been a year, but most people probably still remember that day. You're going to be teaching high school students. I'm sure they've all heard about it. Give them a chance and let them be your friends. The same goes for the other teachers."

"I will, Mom. Thanks."

Stephanie stood and walked toward the door. "You and Connor can come over and have dinner with me and your dad tonight if you want. That way, you don't have to cook, and I know your dad would love seeing you both."

"Maybe another night, Mom," Taylor said as Connor jumped into her arms. "I think we'll probably order pizza tonight."

"Okay," Stephanie replied. "You know I'm always just a phone call away."

"I know, Mom. Tell Daddy hi from us. See you tomorrow."

\* \* \*

After tucking her son in for the night, Taylor curled up on the sofa and pulled out the photo album. She was glad that both she and Zach enjoyed taking pictures because that meant she had lots of memories to relive.

*It's true that pictures become more valuable when you know there won't be any more,* Taylor thought to herself as she flipped through the pages of the album. Their college days, their wedding, the day Connor was born, the day Zach joined the department. Tucked behind the pages of Connor's second birthday party was the newspaper clipping. It was a good thing her dad thought to have it laminated. Otherwise, she would have worn it out by now.

It was a great picture of Zach in his policeman's uniform. She'd always loved that picture of her handsome husband. Connor looked so much like his dad, with his dark hair and chocolate-brown eyes.

The newspaper headline sliced through her heart every time, but she couldn't stop seeing it. "Off-Duty Police Officer Killed During Bank Robbery." She let the tears fall, even a year later. "Officer Zachary Wilson was shot and killed protecting innocent people during a bank robbery yesterday. The off-duty policeman was standing in line with other bank patrons when a lone gunman burst through the door of the bank."

Taylor rarely read past the first couple of sentences, but they were etched into her memory. She pulled the laminated clipping to her chest, tipped her head back, and drifted off to sleep.

# CHAPTER TWO

Taylor headed out to the school's parking lot after the last prep day before classes were scheduled to start the following week. She was ready. Well, maybe not entirely ready, but her classroom was organized, and her lesson plans were finished. As she crossed the parking lot, she was drawn to a beautifully restored classic pickup. Looking around, she wondered who it belonged to. *Probably one of the older teachers*, she thought.

Walking up to the truck, she was careful not to touch it, respecting the owner's hard restoration work. She walked around the truck, admiring the beauty and even peeking inside the cab. *Wow*, she thought, *even leather upholstery. Dad would be impressed.*

"So," a voice from behind startled her. "Do you like my truck?"

Taylor turned to find Shane standing with his hands in his pockets and a grin on his face.

"This is *your* pickup, Shane?" Taylor asked.

"It is," he replied. "Do you like it?"

Looking back into the cab through the driver's window, she smiled. "Like it? I *love* it! What's not to love? A 1954 Chevrolet 3100. Good color choice; it's the perfect color of blue for it."

"Wow," Shane nodded his head, obviously impressed. "You know your pickups. I'm impressed."

"My dad restores classic cars," Taylor explained. "I learned to appreciate the classics from a young age."

Shane followed her as she began walking around the truck again. When he opened the passenger door, she looked inside, running her hand along the leather upholstery.

"Connor would love this," Taylor whispered, forgetting that Shane was behind her.

"Is Connor your brother?" Shane asked hopefully.

"My son," Taylor replied, stepping away from the pickup.

"Oh," Shane said, trying to hide his disappointment. "You can climb in and check it out if you want."

"Maybe some other time," Taylor smiled. "I need to get going."

"Rest up this weekend," Shane suggested. "The first day with students can get hectic around here."

Taylor just nodded, then headed toward her car.

Shane watched her walk away, get into her car, and drive out of the parking lot. He climbed into his pickup and stared across the nearly empty lot.

*She has an incredible smile*, Shane thought to himself.

*But, for some reason, it never seems to reach her eyes. I wonder why.*

"She was saved by the bell last time," Shane said aloud. "Maybe it's time to meet over lunch trays again."

\* \* \*

As was typically the case, the first day of school was chaotic. New students, new teachers, new class schedules, new locker combinations, and people seemed to be running everywhere. Several times throughout the day, Shane had looked for Taylor, hoping to have a few minutes to chat. But it never happened.

Midway through the first week, Shane walked down the hallway after his last class, ready to head home. As he passed Taylor's classroom, he caught a glimpse of her sitting at her desk with her head down, resting on her arms.

Going with his gut instincts, he tapped on the open door.

"Are you okay, Taylor?" he asked, stepping into the classroom. "Do you mind if I come in?"

Taylor raised her head slowly, then nodded. "Sure, come on in."

Shane walked to her desk, then lowered himself into the student desk directly in front of her.

"You look exhausted," he said sympathetically. "High school students can be a bit much at times, especially the first week. We didn't have much time to talk the other day before the bell let you off the hook."

Taylor smiled but said nothing.

"Is Mountainview larger than your last school?" Shane asked. "It can be overwhelming at times."

"No," Taylor began, "it's actually smaller, but I took last year off. I guess getting back into the swing of things isn't as automatic as I had hoped."

"Did you take the last year off to be with your son?" Shane asked. When Taylor didn't reply immediately, he added, "I'm sorry, I shouldn't have asked that. It's none of my business."

Taylor smiled weakly. "That's okay. No, Connor is a very energetic and healthy three-year-old."

Shane waited patiently while Taylor appeared to gather her thoughts. He had a fleeting thought that it would be easy to get lost in those light-blue eyes…the eyes her smile never quite reached.

"Do you have a few minutes to talk?" Taylor asked, having regained her composure. Then she smiled and added, "You know, without taking a chance of being interrupted by the bell again."

Shane grinned and said, "Absolutely. And if the bell rings, we can ignore it. Mark says I'm pretty good at that."

Taylor smiled as she picked up her cell phone and said, "Let me make a quick call first."

After tapping a number on speed dial, Taylor said, "Hi, Mom. Is everything going okay? Do you need to get right home, or can you stay with Connor for a little longer?" She was quiet while her mother responded, then she said, "Thanks, Mom. I won't be long. Love you."

Taylor set her phone on the desk, then stood and walked over to the window, staring out onto the school grounds. When she returned a moment later, she sat at the desk beside Shane.

"I don't know how much you know about me," Taylor began before Shane interrupted her.

"Almost nothing," Shane grinned. "Remember, you were saved by the bell."

"Yeah, right," Taylor smiled before her face clouded over. Knowing she desperately needed her co-workers to understand, and sensing Shane was genuinely concerned, she decided to go ahead with her story before she talked herself out of it. "Well…I'm a widow. I took the last year off work because my husband died."

Shane reached over and touched Taylor's hand. "I'm so sorry, Taylor. That had to be devastating."

"Unbelievably so," Taylor nodded. "I never expected to be a widow at twenty-six. I thought my life was just getting started."

"Was your husband sick?" Shane asked with compassion.

"No, he was the picture of health," Taylor replied before taking a deep breath and plunging ahead. "Zach was a police officer. He was killed in a bank robbery attempt a year ago."

"Oh!" Shane exclaimed. "Was he the off-duty police

officer who saved the others in the bank?"

Taylor nodded.

"I remember hearing about that," Shane said. "I'm really sorry, Taylor. I can't even imagine how horrible that would be."

"Thanks," Taylor replied quietly. "Yeah, everyone remembers hearing about it. That's one of the things that makes it hard."

"Do the other teachers know?" Shane asked.

"No, I don't think so," Taylor said, shaking her head. "Mark knows. We discussed it during my job interview. He said he would keep it to himself and let me handle it however I needed to. Sometimes I think I should just announce it over the P.A. system, so everyone knows. You know, get it over with, like ripping off a Band-Aid. But obviously, that's not going to happen. I guess the word will eventually get around and people will make the connection."

Taylor stood and said, "I should get going. I try not to take advantage of Mom's willingness to watch Connor while I work."

As they walked to the door, Shane said, "Just so you know, I'm a good listener if you ever want to talk."

"Thanks," Taylor said as she locked her classroom door.

"And if you ever want to bring Connor by to drool over my truck, figuratively speaking, of course," Shane smiled, "I'd be happy to take you both for a ride in it."

Taylor perked up. "Don't make promises you can't

keep, Shane. I've never ridden in a 1954 Chevy truck. Now, a 1956…"

"Of course, you have," Shane laughed as they went their separate ways in the parking lot.

\* \* \*

Once Taylor had been back in the classroom for a couple of weeks, she began to feel a bit more comfortable. She enjoyed teaching high school English classes but truly loved teaching literature. Getting lost in the books gave her a place to escape from reality, and she was fortunate to have a class of students who shared her love of reading. In fact, on this day, as she headed down the hall at the end of the day, one of her students walked along with her to continue discussing the book they were reading in class. Somewhere along the way, Shane had joined them.

"I could discuss *The Princess Bride* all day," the girl smiled. "Comparing the book and the movie would take me at least an afternoon. I often wonder how I would feel about the book if I hadn't seen the movie first. See, there I go again! But I need to get to choir practice."

Taylor laughed knowingly. "Have a great practice, Mia."

With the optimism of a teenager, Mia smiled. "Thanks, Mrs. Wilson, I will. See you tomorrow." Then, looking at Shane, she added, "Don't worry, Mr. Gallagher, I haven't forgotten about tomorrow's algebra test."

"See you in the morning, Mia," Shane grinned. "You'll be able to get that pesky test out of the way before lunch."

As they exited the building, Shane looked at Taylor and said, "It looks like you're starting to settle in. Are things going okay?"

"Yeah, I think so," Taylor replied optimistically.

Looking toward the parking lot, Taylor grinned as she spotted a yellow and black Chevy Chevelle beside her car.

"It looks like Dad stopped by," she said, pointing across the lot.

Shane glanced over to where he knew Taylor usually parked. "You mean that beautiful Chevelle parked next to your car belongs to your dad?"

"Yep," Taylor grinned. "Do you want to come check out the car? That means you also have to meet my dad, but he's a pretty nice guy."

Shane replied as he walked toward the car. "Well, yeah!"

Taylor was still laughing when her dad climbed out of the car.

"Hi, Daddy," Taylor greeted as she walked up and hugged her dad.

"Mommy!" A squeal came from inside the car.

Taylor's dad reached into the car, unbuckled Connor's seat belt, and lifted him out of his car seat. He then passed the bouncing boy over to his daughter.

"Mommy!" Connor yelled again. "Me and Grandpa came to school!"

"I see that," Taylor smiled as she kissed the little boy's cheek. "Let me guess. Did you talk Grandpa into taking you for ice cream?"

"Maybe," Connor grinned innocently. "But you get to come too, Mommy."

"Well, thank you!" Taylor laughed.

While this exchange was happening, Shane had been walking around the car, checking it out and nodding frequently. After making a full circle, he returned to stand next to Taylor.

"Shane," Taylor began, "this is my dad, Kenny Matthews. Dad, Shane Gallagher."

Kenny reached out and shook hands with Shane. "It's nice to meet you, Shane."

"It's nice meeting you too, Mr. Matthews," Shane replied before adding, "And your sweet car!"

Kenny laughed. "Just call me Kenny. And we'll discuss the car after you've met my grandson."

"This bundle of energy is my son, Connor," Taylor said, hugging her little boy.

Shane shook Connor's little hand and said, "I'm happy to meet you, Connor."

In an act of shyness, Connor buried his head in his mom's shoulder.

"Shane is the math and science teacher," Taylor explained to her father.

"So, you're a numbers guy, huh?" Kenny asked.

Shane chuckled. "It's a curse, I'm afraid."

Looking past Kenny, Shane grinned. "Speaking of numbers…is that a '68 or '69 Chevelle?"

"So, you know the classics, huh?" Kenny asked, impressed. "This is a '68."

"I love old cars and trucks," Shane replied. "Let me guess, does it have a 327 engine?"

"Is there any other?" Kenny asked, grinning.

"Daddy," Taylor began, "you should see Shane's restored pickup. It's gorgeous!"

Kenny pointed across the parking lot. "That '54 Chevy belongs to you?"

"Yep," Shane replied proudly.

"I had to restrain myself from stopping and drooling over it when we got here," Kenny laughed.

"Would you like to come take a look?" Shane asked, grinning. "Well, you know, without the drooling, of course."

"You bet!" Kenny exclaimed, already walking toward the truck. "Did Taylor tell you I restore classic cars?"

"She did," Shane nodded as he followed Taylor's dad around his truck. Unlocking the door, he said, "Go ahead and climb in and check it out, if you want."

"You don't have to tell me twice!" Kenny laughed.

The two men spent several minutes checking out Shane's pickup and talking cars. Taylor stood back, holding Connor's hand as he watched two birds fight over a discarded French fry.

Losing interest in the birds, Connor finally tugged on his mother's hand. "Mommy," he whispered, "can I sit in the truck with Grandpa?"

"Let me ask Shane," Taylor smiled. "Shane, Connor wants to know if he can sit in your truck."

"Absolutely!" Shane grinned. "Come here, little man. You can sit by your grandpa."

Shane lifted the boy into the truck, and he immediately crawled over beside his grandpa and put his hand on the steering wheel.

Finally, after about ten minutes, Kenny picked up his grandson and climbed out of the truck. "You did a great job restoring this truck, Shane. Thanks for letting us check it out. But, I seem to recall promising a little boy ice cream, so we should probably get going before it gets too close to his dinner time."

Resting comfortably in his grandpa's arms, Connor reached over and tapped him on the cheek. "Grandpa, can he come have ice cream too?"

Turning to Shane, Kenny said, "We don't want to interfere with any plans you might have, but you're certainly welcome to join us for ice cream."

"If you're sure I won't be imposing on family time," Shane began, "I rarely turn down ice cream."

Apparently deciding that Shane was okay, Connor abandoned his shyness and said, "You bring your truck too, 'kay?"

"You got it, little man," Shane chuckled.

"Should we meet over at Baskin-Robbins?" Taylor

asked. "It's the closest place for ice cream."

"Sounds good to me. See you there," Shane said, watching Kenny place his grandson on his shoulders.

As they walked back toward their cars, Shane could see Connor imitating steering a car and heard the unmistakable "Vroom, vroom" of a little boy.

# CHAPTER THREE

Shane was standing outside Taylor's classroom, waiting for the last of her students to leave. He was hoping to catch her before she headed home. She never stuck around long after her last class, and he now knew that was because her mother was watching Connor.

Stepping into her classroom the moment the last student left, Shane grinned. "Have you got a minute, Taylor?"

Taylor smiled as she looked up from her desk. "Sure. What's up?"

Shane walked over and sat at one of the student desks. "I hope you know you're quickly becoming one of the most popular teachers in the school," he grinned. "When the bell rings at the end of *my* classes, it's a stampede to see who escapes first. Your students hang around and visit. What's your secret?"

"It's no secret that reading books is more fun than math and science," Taylor grinned.

"Maybe," Shane agreed. "But I'd bet I could put one of my chemistry experiments up against your dangling participles and I'd come out the winner."

"I think I'd have to agree with you," Taylor nodded. "Literature is more exciting than learning proper sentence construction, but you need to know that to write great literature. I guess it's a trade-off."

Shane walked over to the window and looked toward the parking lot.

"Do you need to get home right away?" he asked hopefully.

"Actually, I'm not in a big hurry today," Taylor replied. "Mom took Connor to the park to watch the ducks and run off some energy. Why?"

"I thought maybe you'd like to go for a short ride in my pickup," Shane suggested. "Your dad and Connor have been in it, but so far you've been on the outside looking in. What do you say?"

"That sounds fun," Taylor agreed. "As long as we're not gone too long."

Ten minutes later, Shane drove his pickup out of the school parking lot with Taylor smiling from the passenger seat. They drove around town for about fifteen minutes before he stopped in the parking lot of a shopping center. When he turned off the ignition, Taylor opened the passenger door and started to climb out.

"Where are you going?" Shane asked in surprise. "I *do* plan to take you back to your car at school, you know."

Taylor looked across the cab at him and smiled mischievously. "Are you brave enough to let me drive your truck?"

Shane raised his eyebrow. "You want to drive *my* truck?"

Taylor simply grinned and nodded.

"Can you even drive a three-speed stick shift?" Shane asked.

"Three on the tree, four on the floor, I can drive them all," Taylor grinned. "My dad restores classic cars, remember?"

Shane laughed as he climbed out of his truck and walked around to the passenger side.

Handing Taylor the keys, he grinned and asked, "Do you think you can get us back to the school in one piece?"

Taking the keys from his outstretched hand, Taylor laughed. "Piece of cake. Let's go!"

Taylor purposely took the long way back to the school. By the time she pulled the pickup into the school parking lot and parked beside her car, she was grinning from ear to ear.

"That was fun!" she exclaimed.

Shane grinned. "I'm impressed. Your dad taught you well. You didn't grind a single gear."

"I told you," Taylor laughed. "Piece of cake. But seriously, Shane, thanks for letting me drive it. I know how protective guys can be about their classics. It's a beautiful truck, and it drives like a dream."

"One of these days," Shane began, "I should follow you home so we can give Connor a ride. I bet he'd love it."

"I know he would," Taylor agreed. "Unfortunately, he has to ride in a car seat, and there are only two seat belts in these old trucks. Hey, I'd better get going so I can rescue Mom. See you Monday, Shane. And thanks again for letting me drive your truck."

"Any time, Taylor," Shane smiled. "Have a good weekend."

\* \* \*

Football season was in full swing, and the students were gearing up for homecoming. Excitement filled the halls as students and faculty alike got into Spirit Week. If it weren't "Dress Like Your Favorite Bible Character" day at the Christian school, it would look like every other school in town. But at Mountainview, on this day, Moses and Jesus roamed the halls. Several students in the lower grades dressed as Moses, as did some of the high school students. It was an interesting sight, passing students in the hallway and seeing a nearly six-foot Moses high-five a three-foot Moses. Jesus, Mary, Ruth, and Sarah were other popular choices, and little shepherds seemed to pop up everywhere.

Dressed as a nondescript Biblical woman, Taylor stood in line beside Shane at the cafeteria. Most of the students had already filled their lunch trays and settled in at tables with their friends.

Taylor studied Shane's costume before asking, "Let me guess. You're Daniel today?"

"Very good," Shane smiled. "As you can see, I escaped the lions' den."

Taylor laughed. "I'm not so sure. You're teaching a bunch of teenagers. Some days that's kind of the same thing."

"You might be right!" Shane agreed as he looked around the cafeteria.

"I don't think I've seen so many shepherds in one place in my life," he laughed.

"I agree!" Taylor said. "One of my favorite costumes I've seen was when I spotted Jesus walking down the hallway wearing a football helmet and carrying a football!"

Shane laughed. "One of the boys does that every year. Usually, it's one of the football players. This year, it was Scott. He doesn't even play football. He's the center on the basketball team!"

"That's hilarious!" Taylor said as she found a table and set down her tray.

Shane sat across from her, then said, "If we have a few minutes at the end of lunch, I'd like to show you something in my truck."

"Okay," Taylor said, looking at her lunch without enthusiasm. "This shouldn't take long."

"Not a big spaghetti fan, huh?" Shane grinned.

"I can take it or leave it," Taylor smiled. "Today, I'd rather leave it. But I'll eat the garlic bread."

Twenty minutes later, they headed to the parking lot.

Shane unlocked his truck, stood back, and said, "Look."

Taylor looked inside the pickup but didn't see anything unusual. "Am I missing something?"

"Look on the seat," Shane smiled.

"You installed a third seat belt!" Taylor said excitedly.

"Yep," Shane grinned. "Now I can give Connor *and* his mom a ride in my truck."

"That's pretty cool, Shane," Taylor began. "But you didn't have to do that."

"Yes, I did," Shane said modestly. "I saw how much he liked sitting in the truck with your dad. I know he'd love to go for a ride. So, you just name the day when you'll have some free time, and we'll take Connor for a spin around the block."

Taylor smiled and said, "Well, since I didn't have much lunch, we could always go pick him up after school today and maybe get ice cream."

"Great idea!" Shane agreed. "However, maybe you could give me your address so I can run home and change out of this costume first."

"Yeah, me too," Taylor laughed. "I'm not crazy about showing up at the ice cream parlor dressed like this."

\* \* \*

Shane parked his pickup along the curb in front of Taylor's house. It was a nice, but modest home, in a good neighborhood. It was easy to see this was a family neighborhood, evidenced by all the toys and bikes scattered around the yards. A glance toward Taylor's back yard revealed the top of what appeared to be a large play structure rising above the fence. Shane got out of his truck, walked up the sidewalk to the front door, and rang the bell.

Taylor answered the door and had already changed out of the day's Spirit Week costume. She was now comfortably dressed in jeans, a graphic T-shirt, and tennis shoes, with her long hair pulled back in a ponytail.

"Boy," Taylor laughed, "you must have set a record for changing clothes and driving over here. I barely got changed."

Shane chuckled. "What can I say? I'm motivated by ice cream."

"Come on in and meet Mom," Taylor invited, pointing toward the living room.

The moment Shane entered the house, Connor burst into the living room.

"Hi," Connor greeted, having overcome his shyness around Shane. "I don't 'member your name. Did you bring your truck?"

Shane laughed. "As long as you remember my truck,

my name's not important." Then he leaned down and whispered to the little boy, "In case you need to know it, my name is Shane."

"Oh, yeah! Shane!" Connor exclaimed. "Can I sit in your truck again?"

Taylor grinned at Shane, then told her son, "Shane has a surprise for you, but first he needs to meet Grandma."

Connor jumped up and down and clapped his hands. He then pointed to Stephanie, who had been standing back watching the exchange, smiling.

"That's Grandma," Connor said. "Surprise time?"

Stephanie laughed as she joined the others in the living room. "I guess even grandmas aren't as important as a surprise."

"Mom," Taylor began, "this is Shane Gallagher. He's the math and science teacher at school. Shane, my mom, Stephanie Matthews."

Stephanie shook hands with Shane and said, "I'm happy to meet you, Shane. So, you're the man with the truck Connor's been talking about non-stop."

"Yes, ma'am," Shane grinned.

"I hope you know I'm going to have to check it out too," Stephanie smiled. "I've been hearing about it from Connor *and* my husband. Kenny was pretty impressed with your restoration job."

"Thanks," Shane replied. "That's high praise from a man who restores classics. Well, I happen to have my truck parked along the curb, so you can come check it out if you want."

In his excitement, Taylor had to remind Connor not to run into the street as they walked down the sidewalk toward the pickup. He hung back just long enough for Shane to open the passenger door of the pickup.

Jumping up and down and clapping his hands, the little boy asked, "Can I sit in your truck, Shane?"

Shane chuckled as he lifted the boy and placed him on the truck's seat.

Looking around the cab of the truck, Connor asked, "Where's my surprise?"

"Do you see that extra seat belt in the middle of the seat?" Shane asked as the boy looked around. "That's so we can put your car seat in the truck and take you for a ride."

Connor's eyes got as big as saucers. "I get to *ride* in your truck?"

"You sure do," Shane replied. "As soon as your mom gets your car seat, I can get it buckled in."

"Mommy, hurry!" Connor said with excitement, literally bouncing in the seat.

Taylor laughed as she headed over to her car to get his car seat. Shane immediately got to work securing the seat, under the supervision of an anxious three-year-old.

While all this was happening, Stephanie had been walking around the pickup admiring it. "Kenny was right, Shane. You did a great job restoring this truck. It's beautiful."

"Thanks," Shane said proudly. "As you

undoubtedly know, restoring vehicles is a labor of love."

"It certainly has to be!" Stephanie laughed. "It sure isn't a money-making hobby."

"Mom," Taylor began, "Shane is going to take us for ice cream. Obviously, there's only room for three people in his truck. If you want to follow us over in your car, we'd love to have you join us."

"Let me grab my purse," Stephanie said, "then I'll be right behind you. Make sure you have your license, Taylor, because you're driving my car back. I'm going to ride with Connor in Shane's truck."

As she buckled her son into his car seat, Taylor laughed. "As you can see, my family is a wee bit obsessed with classic cars and trucks."

Shane put the truck in gear and pulled away from the curb. "There are worse obsessions to have," he grinned, looking at the little boy seated next to him.

Connor was having the time of his life. He sat in his car seat and imitated Shane's every move. He was steering an imaginary steering wheel in front of him and reached up to shift gears whenever Shane did.

"That little man is going to know how to drive long before he turns a key in the ignition," Shane laughed.

"Don't remind me!" Taylor exclaimed.

Once Stephanie met them at the ice cream shop, they went inside, and Shane said, "This is my treat. Get whatever you want."

"I want chocolate," Connor announced. "With the candy inside."

Shane gave Taylor a questioning look. "Chocolate with candy inside? Is that something new that I've been missing?"

Taylor chuckled as she pointed to a tub of ice cream in the cooler. "It's chocolate ice cream and has little peanut butter cups mixed in."

"Oh!" Shane exclaimed in surprise. Turning to the clerk, he said, "This little guy and I will each have a scoop of that. Then whatever the ladies want."

After getting their ice cream, Connor followed his mom to a table, looking back frequently to make sure Shane was still with them.

"Mommy, can I sit by Shane?" the little boy asked hopefully.

Taylor smiled as she grabbed a booster seat and situated it on a chair before helping her son into it.

"I don't see why not," she agreed as Shane approached the table.

Pointing to the chair beside Connor, Taylor announced seriously, "This little man has requested that you sit beside him."

Shane looked at the boy seriously and rubbed his chin in thought. "You don't plan to steal my ice cream, do you?"

Connor laughed. "Your ice cream is same as mine!"

Shane looked at his bowl of ice cream, turning it around to inspect it from every angle, much to the delight of the little boy.

"By golly, I believe you're right," Shane replied,

smiling. "In that case, I think it's safe for me to sit beside you. Besides, that'll make it easier to talk about cars and trucks and other important things."

Connor nodded as he shoved a spoonful of ice cream into his mouth.

The small group visited for more than half an hour over ice cream. They talked about classic cars and trucks, discussed Connor's visits to the park, and talked about Spirit Week at the school. Connor had barely swallowed his last bite of ice cream when he announced it was time to ride in the truck again.

Stephanie handed Taylor her car keys and said, "Okay, Connor, it's Grandma's turn to ride in the truck with you."

"Just 'member to be careful, Grandma," Connor cautioned. "It's a 'stored truck. Just like Grandpa's 'stored cars."

Stephanie smiled as she climbed into the pickup. "Got it. I'll be very careful."

With his hand on the gear shift, Shane looked at Connor and smiled. "Ready to go, buddy?"

Connor reached for his imaginary gear shift and replied seriously, "Yep. Ready to go!"

# Chapter Four

Taylor usually spent her free period at her desk in the classroom, grading papers or doing prep work for the following day. This afternoon, she decided to relax in the teacher's lounge. As she passed Shane's classroom, she glanced in the door's window and saw him, with his back to the class, working out an algebra problem on the whiteboard. She smiled when she noticed a couple of kids in the back of the class passing notes. *Some things never change,* she thought to herself, remembering she used to do the same thing when she was a teenager.

After grabbing a bottle of juice and a candy bar from the vending machine, Taylor looked around for a comfortable chair to relax in for the next forty-five minutes. Expecting to be the only one in the lounge, she was surprised to find one of the elementary teachers curled up in an easy chair, reading.

"Hi, Sue," Taylor smiled. "I didn't see you when I came in. If you'd rather be alone to enjoy your book, I can head back to my classroom."

Sue was a few years older than Taylor, probably in her mid-thirties, and taught first and second-grade students.

She looked up from her book and smiled. "Don't be silly, Taylor. Grab a chair and get comfortable." Then she laughed and added, "I'm just seizing the opportunity to read something other than a picture book."

Taylor laughed. "I know what you mean. I spend most of my evenings reading to Connor. He usually chooses books with pictures of police cars, fire trucks, and race cars. If I'm lucky, he pulls out a book that has a horse or two. So, reading a grown-up book can be a luxury."

"You *do* understand!" Sue laughed.

"How did you manage to escape all the little munchkins?" Taylor asked. "The elementary teachers don't often get a free period."

"The gods smiled on us this afternoon," Sue grinned. "All the kids from first through fourth grade are in the gym watching a movie."

"Nice!" Taylor replied as she curled up in a chair and put her feet on an ottoman.

"How old is your son?" Sue asked. "I think I saw him in the parking lot a while back with a middle-aged man."

"Yeah," Taylor smiled. "That was my dad. Connor convinced Grandpa they needed ice cream, and he was sure I needed some too."

Sue laughed. "It's nice that he was looking out for your needs."

"Like I *needed* ice cream," Taylor chuckled. "Oh, and Connor's three. A *very* active three-year-old. He runs me ragged at times. I don't know how my mom can keep up with him."

"Your mom watches him during the day?" Sue asked.

"She does," Taylor nodded. "She's an absolute lifesaver."

The two settled into a comfortable silence while Taylor drank some of her juice and started on her candy bar.

Sue closed her book and laid it on the chair beside her. Glancing at Taylor, she wondered if she should ask the question on everyone's mind.

"Can I ask you something, Taylor?" Sue asked hesitantly.

Taylor stared at the half-eaten candy bar in her hand and sighed as she suspected what was coming.

"Sure, go ahead," she replied.

"You don't have to answer if you don't want to," Sue said, knowing she would be treading into personal space.

Taylor simply nodded.

"Was your husband the police officer killed in that bank robbery attempt last year?" Sue asked compassionately.

Taylor continued staring at her candy bar, then took

a small bite and chewed it slowly before looking at her fellow teacher.

"Yes, he was," Taylor answered quietly.

"I'm so sorry, Taylor," Sue said. "I can't even imagine."

"Thanks," Taylor replied. "Do the other teachers know?"

"Several of them suspected it was your husband," Sue said with a shrug. "This may not be a super small town, but that was pretty big news. A lot of people around town still bring it up occasionally. People remember his wife was a school teacher, and he had a young son."

Again, Taylor nodded without saying anything.

"Do you want to talk about it?" Sue asked. "You don't have to. I'm sure you're probably tired of explaining it to people."

"Actually," Taylor began, sitting up in the chair, "it might be nice to just get it out in the open, so everyone knows. That way, maybe the rumors would stop.

"There's really not that much to tell since it was all over the news," Taylor continued. "Zach was off duty that day, running errands. One of those errands was going to the bank. There were quite a few people in the bank that afternoon. When the gunman rushed in, luckily, one of the tellers was able to push the emergency button right away, so the police were there quickly. Before the police arrived, Zach tried to talk to the gunman – he was just a young kid, maybe early twenties

– trying to convince him to put down the gun. Zach did a good job of stalling and getting everyone else to back away as far as possible. But, ultimately, it wasn't enough. As soon as the police showed up, the kid shot Zach. Then the gunman was shot and killed."

Taylor took a long breath. "Zach died on the way to the hospital."

By the time Taylor finished, Sue's eyes had filled with tears.

"I'm so very sorry, Taylor," Sue whispered. "Your husband was a hero. He saved a lot of lives that day."

Taylor nodded. "I know. That's what we always tell Connor when he asks about his dad. Even though he's too young to understand fully, he knows his daddy died saving other people, and he's a hero."

"Do any of the other staff members know the story, and know that the police officer was your husband?"

"Mark and I talked about it at my job interview," Taylor replied. "And I told Shane Gallagher about it not long after school started."

"Shane's a great guy," Sue said. "He never said a word to anyone. Do you want me to keep it quiet, too? I will if you want me to."

After a few moments, Taylor said, "No, that's okay. At this point, it will be a relief to have everyone know. I just don't want people's pity."

"It's not pity, Taylor," Sue said quietly. "It's friendship. Every member of the staff here likes you. And you have quickly become one of the students' favorite teachers! We're your friends. We just want you to know we're here for you if you need anything. Anything at all."

"Thanks, Sue," Taylor sighed heavily.

Suddenly, there was a loud commotion in the hallway.

"Uh-oh," Sue laughed. "It sounds like a munchkin invasion. The movie must be over, so I have to go."

"If you hurry and get to your classroom first," Taylor laughed, "maybe you can hide under your desk."

"Smart thinking!" Sue chuckled as she headed to the door. "Wish me luck!"

\* \* \*

A week later, the final school bell hadn't stopped ringing when Taylor heard loud footsteps pounding down the hallway. As her students gathered their books and backpacks, she rushed to the door and looked in the direction of the noise. She saw several other teachers peek their heads out of classroom doors just as Shane burst open the exterior door and dashed into the parking lot.

She held the classroom door open as students wandered into the hall. Mixed in with the usual end-of-day banter, she overheard several comments like "there he goes again" and "off and running." As soon as the last student left her classroom, Taylor closed the door and quickly headed toward the other hall where the elementary classrooms were located. The door to Sue's classroom was standing open, and she was helping a little girl with her backpack.

"Don't forget to show your mom and dad the picture you drew today, Charlotte," Sue reminded the little girl as she helped adjust her backpack.

"I will, Mrs. Jensen," Charlotte smiled. "And Daddy said he'll read with me again tonight."

"That's great!" Sue smiled. "Work on your reading every day. You're really improving."

"Thanks!" Charlotte beamed at the praise. "I can't wait to read the *big* chapter books like Zoe reads."

"You'll be reading bigger books before long," Sue grinned. "Then you'll need another backpack to carry all those books!"

"I know!" Charlotte laughed as she waved, then started down the hall toward the gym to wait for her mother.

Turning to Taylor, who was waiting patiently off to the side, Sue asked, "How's it going, Taylor? Only one more day until the weekend."

"Busy as usual," Taylor grinned. "Hey, did you see Shane rush out of the building a few minutes ago? When I saw him running toward the exit, the final bell hadn't even stopped ringing. I hope everything's okay."

"I didn't see him," Sue replied. "But I heard someone slam the door open. That must have been him. He's probably heading to a fire."

"What?" Taylor gasped, a little louder than

necessary. "What do you mean he was heading to a fire?"

"Yeah," Sue replied nonchalantly. "He's a volunteer fireman."

Sue watched as some of the color drained from Taylor's face.

She reached out and put her hand on Taylor's arm. "Are you okay, Taylor?"

Taylor shook her head to bring her thoughts back to the present. "Yeah, I'm fine," she said weakly.

"You didn't know Shane was a fireman?" Sue asked quietly.

Taylor shook her head without replying.

"He works for the fire department full-time when school isn't in session," Sue explained. "Once school starts back up, he reverts to being a volunteer firefighter. Chief Hart has been trying to convince him to give up teaching and join the department full-time. Shane keeps turning him down. So far."

Taylor leaned against the classroom door and shook her head.

"Another first responder," she whispered. "I can't believe it. Another first responder."

Sue ushered Taylor into her classroom and motioned for her to sit at her desk. She then pulled a chair over and sat down in front of Taylor.

"You like Shane, don't you?" Sue asked compassionately.

Taylor nodded, then shook her head in confusion.

"I don't know," Taylor replied, looking at Sue. "I

do. Maybe. I did. But I can't."

She was talking in spurts as she gathered her thoughts and attempted to understand the feelings she had not yet acknowledged.

"Another first responder," Taylor shook her head again as tears tugged at the corners of her eyes. "I can't do that again. I just can't."

"You haven't dated since Zach died, have you?" Sue asked gently.

Taylor shook her head slowly.

"But you and Shane have been spending a little time together," Sue began, "getting to know each other. Why don't you give it a chance and see where it goes? It may not turn into anything, but you never know." She hesitated before adding, "Shane really is a great guy."

"But a first responder…" Taylor said, her sentence trailing off as she stood and walked toward the door. "I can't…"

* * *

Taylor did everything she could for the next week to avoid running into Shane. She stopped going to the cafeteria for lunch, instead packing a lunch and eating in her car in the parking lot. She avoided the teacher's lounge and left school immediately after her last class. She knew she wasn't being rational, but she had to protect her heart. She wasn't even sure she was ready to date again. After all, it had only been a year since Zach was killed. In her mind, she had long ago written off any future relationship with a first responder. That was too bad because Shane really did seem like a nice guy. But she knew in her heart that she couldn't go down that road again. It was just too painful.

As she sat in her car eating lunch, there was a light tap on the driver's door window. Taylor looked up to see her friend Sue standing there holding up a lunch cooler.

Taylor lowered the window and smiled.

"Do you mind if I join your picnic?" Sue asked, grinning.

"Not at all," Taylor chuckled as she unlocked the passenger door.

Once Sue was settled in the passenger seat, Taylor asked, "How did you find me?"

Sue opened her cooler and pulled out a sandwich. "I've been watching you disappear every day at lunchtime. At first, I checked the teacher's lounge. When I didn't find you there, I figured you were escaping to your car."

The two young teachers sat in silence for several minutes as they ate their lunch.

Finally, Sue looked at Taylor and said honestly, "You don't need to hide from Shane. He asked me the other day if I knew why you were avoiding him. I wasn't sure what to tell him, so I just said I didn't think you were. Talk to him, Taylor. Just because you talk to him and you're friends doesn't mean you're going to marry the guy."

Sue reached over and put her hand on Taylor's arm. "I know you've been through a lot. I can't even imagine what the last year was like for you. But you can't stop living. I didn't know Zach, but I can't imagine he'd want you to give up on life. It's not fair to you, and it's not fair to Connor."

She grinned before adding, "I happen to know Shane likes you and was hoping to get to know you better. Don't shut him out, Taylor. Give him a chance."

"But he's a first responder, Sue," Taylor said quietly. "They have such a hard job, and you never know if they'll be coming home at the end of the day."

"That's certainly true," Sue nodded. "I have a lot of respect for first responders. They run toward situations that everyone else is running away from. They're a special breed. But most of them, Shane included, do it because they know someone has to. And because they want to make a difference. And…first responders or not, none of us has any guarantee we'll be going home at the end of the day."

Taylor stared at the half-eaten sandwich in her hand, wrapped it up, and returned it to her lunch cooler.

"Thanks, Sue," Taylor began. "I'll think about what you said. You're right, of course. I'm just not sure if I'm ready." Then she smiled and added, "Connor certainly is. He's always asking me when Shane will take him for another ride in his truck. I'm not sure if he likes Shane or just his truck!"

"Well, it *is* a pretty sweet truck," Sue agreed. "And, honestly, Taylor, if your son already likes Shane, that's half the battle."

Taylor chuckled. "You should have seen Connor imitating Shane when we went for ice cream the other day. Connor sat in his car seat and watched Shane the entire time. Whenever Shane reached up to shift gears, Connor grabbed his imaginary gear shift to do the same thing."

Sue grinned as she gathered the remains of her lunch. "See, the battle is already half won. Why don't you put this battle in God's hands where it belongs? You know He's always got your back."

Taylor smiled. "Once again, you're probably right. How did you get so smart?"

Sue laughed, "I spend my days with first and second graders. They know *everything!*"

# CHAPTER FIVE

Shane stood beside his desk while the students passed their chemistry tests to the front of the room. Once he gathered the tests, he placed them in a neat pile on his desk and then turned back to his class.

"How do you think you did on today's test?" Shane asked his students. "I noticed a few of you sped through it pretty quickly." Then he smiled and added, "I didn't make the test too easy, did I?"

Several of the students chuckled, but most shook their heads.

"Okay, that's good. Since you had a test today," Shane began, "I'm not going to give you an assignment for tomorrow. If you get bored, you can begin reading Chapter Four because that's where we'll be headed next."

Just as the bell rang, he added, "Remember, we have lab tomorrow."

Since chemistry was his last class of the day, Shane

had intended to begin grading the tests before he headed home. As he flipped over the top test paper, he heard one of the students outside his classroom.

"Hi, Mrs. Wilson. When did you say our lit paper is due?"

"It's due on Friday, David," Taylor replied. "So, you still have a couple of days."

"That's great!" David said. "I'm almost finished."

"I'm sure it'll be a great paper," Taylor said. "But don't forget to get outside for some fresh air occasionally, too."

"I will! See you tomorrow."

Shane listened to the conversation and fought his desire to walk into the hallway, hoping to see Taylor. *No,* he thought to himself, *it's obvious she's been avoiding me. I wish I knew why. I thought we were getting along great.*

He returned to the task at hand just as there was a light knock on the classroom door. When he looked up, Taylor was standing in the open doorway.

"Do you mind if I come in?" Taylor asked quietly.

Shane stood and walked toward the door. "Of course not," he smiled. "Did you come to help me grade chemistry tests?"

Taylor smiled. "Since my knowledge of chemistry is limited to my one high school chem class, I'd probably just give all your students an 'A' and be done with it."

"I'm sure they wouldn't mind," Shane chuckled, pointing to one of the desks. "Have a seat."

Taylor sat down and placed her hands on the desk. For a moment, she simply stared at her hands.

"I thought maybe we could talk," she began, looking up at Shane.

"I'd like that," Shane replied, never taking his eyes off Taylor.

"A friend pointed out to me that maybe I wasn't being fair to you," Taylor began quietly. When Shane didn't respond, she continued. "It wasn't right for me to suddenly start avoiding you."

Trying to lighten the mood, Shane grinned and said, "Oh, so you *were* avoiding me. I thought I was imagining things."

Taylor smiled. "No, it wasn't your imagination. I was purposely avoiding you. It was wrong, and I'm sorry."

"It kind of took me by surprise," Shane admitted. "I thought we were getting along great, and I couldn't think of anything stupid I'd done to chase you away. So, I didn't understand what the problem was. I still don't know where we went sideways."

Taylor stood and walked to the window that overlooked the schoolyard. Off to the side, she could see a small portion of the faculty parking lot. Shane's pickup was parked in his usual spot.

"Connor really likes your truck," Taylor sighed.

"He's got good taste," Shane replied, joining Taylor at the window.

Shane put his hand on Taylor's shoulder and said,

"Remember when I told you I was a good listener?"

Taylor nodded.

"It's one of my few redeeming qualities," Shane grinned. "Talk to me, Taylor. I want to know what happened that made you pull away."

Taylor glanced at the clock on the wall. "Do you have time to go get a smoothie or something so we can talk? My treat."

"You don't have to get right home?" Shane asked.

"No," Taylor replied. "Mom took Connor to the park."

Heading toward the door, Shane said, "Let's go."

They decided it would make sense for each of them to take their own vehicle so they wouldn't have to return to the school. A short time later, after ordering smoothies, they sat down at a small table on the patio where they could talk without interruption.

Taylor didn't know where to begin. She needed Shane to understand, but wasn't sure she could explain her feelings. She wasn't even sure she could explain them to herself.

After taking a drink of her smoothie, she looked up at Shane. "You didn't tell me you were a fireman."

"I didn't?" Shane asked, not sure where she was heading with that statement.

"No," Taylor replied. "Why didn't you tell me, Shane?"

Shane shook his head. "I guess it didn't occur to me. Everyone at school knows. I guess I assumed you knew too."

"I didn't know you were a first responder…" Taylor whispered, her voice trailing off.

Shane reached across the table and covered Taylor's hand with his own.

"Is that what this is all about?" he asked.

Taylor nodded.

"I honestly never gave it a thought, Taylor," Shane began. "I wasn't trying to hide it from you. It just never occurred to me to mention it."

"I saw you rush from the building that afternoon," Taylor said quietly. "I asked Sue about it because I was afraid something had happened. She told me you were a fireman. It sucked the air out of me."

"Because of Zach," Shane nodded, suddenly understanding. "So, you decided to put some distance between us."

Neither said anything for several minutes. Shane looked into Taylor's eyes, trying to see past the hurt and pain, and decided to put all his cards on the table.

"I have to tell you, Taylor," Shane began slowly. "I like you. I like you a lot. And unless I was reading you completely wrong, I thought you liked me too. Was I wrong?"

Taylor shook her head, almost imperceptibly.

"I'm glad," Shane sighed in relief. "Okay, so we have something to work through. But, Taylor, I want you to know something. You can always talk to me. I *want* you to talk to me. Believe it or not, I understand your concerns. I've been fighting fires since I was a senior in high school. My mom still struggles with it. I understand the risks first responders take. But I also know it's an important job and someone has to do it."

"That's what Zach used to say all the time," Taylor agreed. "He never promised he'd be home at the end of his shift. He always promised he would try – unless God had other plans. So, every day when he walked out the door to go on duty, I put him in God's hands. He wasn't on duty that day. He was just going to the bank…"

Shane squeezed Taylor's hand. "Zach didn't go home that day, and nothing will ever change that. But a lot of other people, including a couple of young kids, *did* go home that day because of Zach and his training. Don't ever forget that."

"Thanks," Taylor replied quietly.

Shane still held Taylor's hand across the table. They were quiet for several minutes, each thinking about their conversation. Shane finished the last of his smoothie, then tossed the empty cup into a nearby trash bin.

As they headed to the parking lot, Shane put his hand on Taylor's back.

"I realize it's not easy getting involved with a first responder," Shane began, "and I'll never take your concerns lightly. But promise you'll talk to me. Don't shut me out, okay?"

"I promise to try," Taylor replied with a small smile.

"That's all I can ask for," Shane smiled, holding the car door for her. "See you at school tomorrow."

Taylor nodded, got into her car, and then drove out of the parking lot.

Shane climbed into his pickup and stared out onto the road. *It would make things easier to just give up fighting fires and stick with teaching,* Shane thought. He shook his head and voiced what was in his heart. "Someone has to do it. It might as well be me."

\* \* \*

Taylor was sitting cross-legged on the floor in her living room with a picture book in her lap, spending a relaxing Saturday afternoon with her son. Connor sat beside her, snuggling in close, while he pointed to all the pictures. As usual, they were looking at his favorite book, a book filled with fire trucks, police cars, and ambulances. Connor "read" the book, making up his own stories, complete with all the appropriate sound effects.

Taylor glanced down at her phone when she received a notification of a text message. The text from Shane made her smile. "If you're not busy, do you and Connor want to get some ice cream?"

She sent a reply text, "Come on over. We're just hanging out reading books."

Twenty minutes later, the doorbell rang. Connor jumped up and ran toward the door.

"I get it, Mommy!" Connor exclaimed.

Taylor smiled as she watched her little boy go through all the proper rules he had been taught before opening the door.

"Who's there?" he asked with his hand on the locked doorknob.

The reply from the other side of the door made the little boy smile.

"It's Shane."

Connor smiled. "Did you bring your truck?"

"I sure did," Shane replied through the closed door.

"What color is your truck?" Connor asked, grinning at his mom.

Taylor stifled a laugh.

"Uh," Shane replied in confusion. "My truck is blue."

Connor opened the door and looked past Shane to see his truck parked along the curb.

"Why did you ask me what color my truck is?" Shane asked with a smile.

"To know it's really you," Connor shrugged.

"That's smart thinking, Connor," Shane grinned, tousling the boy's hair.

"Wanna look at my book?" Connor asked.

"Of course!" Shane replied as Connor took his hand and led him to the book lying on the floor.

As they passed Taylor, Shane grinned and said, "Hi."

"Hi," Taylor laughed, joining the boys on the floor.

Connor immediately began pointing to pictures in the book and telling Shane all about them.

He pointed to a police car and said, "My daddy had

a police car. He took me for a ride in it. But he died. Daddy saved a bunch of people at the bank."

Shane glanced at Taylor, then turned back to Connor. "I heard about that. Your daddy was a real hero."

"I know," Connor nodded. "Police always save people."

Then the little boy abruptly turned the page and pointed to a big red fire truck.

"I didn't ride a fire truck," Connor said matter-of-factly. "I want to."

Shane shot a questioning look at Taylor, who responded with a nod.

"Do you want to ride in a fire truck, Connor?" Shane asked.

The little boy nodded, then said, "I don't know a fireman."

"Well," Shane grinned, "I just happen to be a fireman."

Connor's eyes grew large. "Do *you* have a fire truck?"

"It's not mine," Shane replied. "But there are fire trucks down at the station."

"Can you drive it?" Connor asked, completely captivated.

"Yep," Shane grinned. "If it's okay with your mom, we can go down to the station, and I can give you a short ride in a fire truck. Then maybe we can go get ice cream. How does that sound?"

Connor jumped up and clapped his hands. "Come on, Mommy!"

Taylor laughed as Shane helped her up from the floor. "Okay, buddy, we need to grab your car seat from my car. We'll need that in Shane's truck."

"And the fire truck!" Connor yelled. "Don't forget about the fire truck!"

* * *

Connor was straining the confines of his car seat all the way to the fire station. Bouncing as much as the restraints allowed, he could hardly contain his excitement. The little boy was so excited that he forgot to imitate Shane as he shifted gears. A few minutes later, Shane pulled his pickup into a parking space alongside the fire station, then unbuckled the boy's seat restraint. Taylor reached over to grab Connor as he scrambled out of the car seat.

"Come on, Mommy!" Connor said as Taylor lowered him to the ground and took his hand.

"Slow down, buddy!" Taylor laughed as they walked toward the office with Shane.

Once inside the office, Shane introduced Taylor and Connor to Chief Hart and got the okay to give Connor a short ride around the block. The chief chuckled when Connor tugged his mom's hand as he tried to pull her toward the parked fire trucks. The wide-eyed little boy inspected all the trucks and sat behind the wheel of each truck before announcing that he wanted to ride in the "biggest" fire truck. Shane transferred Connor's car seat to the passenger seat of the fire engine and buckled him in. Within minutes, Shane pulled out onto the street with a very happy little boy sitting beside him, imitating his every move.

Less than ten minutes later, Shane backed the fire truck into the station's garage and unbuckled Connor's seat restraint. Taylor opened the passenger door, lifted her son from the truck, and placed him on the ground.

"Did you have fun, Connor?" Taylor asked her grinning son.

"Yeah!" Connor yelled. "Shane let me honk the horn!"

"So *that* was the loud noise I heard a few minutes ago!" Taylor laughed.

"There's just something about fire trucks and little boys," Chief Hart laughed. "I haven't met a kid yet who didn't enjoy climbing around on fire trucks."

Turning to grab something from the table behind him, Chief Hart patted Connor on the back. "I've got something for you, little guy. How would you like your very own fireman's helmet?"

"Really?" the little boy asked. "For me?"

The chief placed the red plastic fireman's helmet on Connor's head and said, "It's all yours, and it's a perfect fit."

Shane knelt in front of Connor and pulled something from behind his back. "And you also get a badge," he said as he pinned the silver badge to the front of the little boy's shirt. Tapping the badge, he added, "Now it's official. You're an honorary fireman."

With one hand on his helmet, Connor looked down at the badge. "Wow! Thanks, Shane! Thanks, Chief! We're going to get ice cream now. Can you come too?"

Chief Hart chuckled and said, "I'd love to, Connor, but I need to stay at the station."

"'Cause there might be a fire, huh?" Connor asked knowingly.

"Yep, just in case there's a fire," the chief nodded. "But you guys enjoy your ice cream."

"Okay," Connor smiled. He walked over to the fire truck and ran his hand along the bottom of the door. Then, running his finger along the front bumper, he traced the number twenty-four that was painted on the bumper and quietly said, "Be safe."

Shane and the chief looked at Taylor and nodded, amazed by the little boy who was wise beyond his years.

Suddenly, Connor clapped his hands and announced, "Time for ice cream!" Then he grabbed Shane's hand and started toward the parking lot, imitating the loud screaming sound of a fire truck's siren.

# CHAPTER SIX

Time may not heal all wounds, but it has a way of marching on while you figure out how to deal with life's changes. Taylor was learning how to accept that reality when she realized the school year was rapidly approaching Christmas break. But she had to admit she was beginning to settle into her new life. A life that no longer included Zach, but a life where Shane was starting to fill that void. She loved her job and her students and had made several friends at the school. It was no longer a secret that she and Shane were spending a lot of time together, and their friends at school were supportive of their budding relationship.

She still struggled with the possibility of being hurt again and tried to protect her son's young heart. Connor was barely two years old when his father was killed, so it was easier for him to accept Shane into their lives. Shane had become a regular fixture in their home on the weekends, and Connor asked about him frequently throughout the week.

Sitting on the floor of her living room surrounded by toys, Taylor smiled as Shane helped Connor build a large structure out of blocks.

"Are you building a garage for your cars, Connor?" she asked, knowing that's what he typically did.

"Nope," the little boy grinned as he looked up from the building project. "A castle!"

Taylor chuckled. "You're building a castle? Why do you need a castle?"

"So I can fight dragons," Connor replied with a shrug.

"Oh," Taylor laughed, "Silly me. Of course, you need a castle if you're going to fight dragons."

Taylor pointed to blocks that seemed to form a bridge of sorts, and asked, "What's this?"

"A bridge," Connor replied without looking up.

"And why do you need a bridge?" Taylor asked, smiling.

Connor looked at Shane in confusion and asked, "What's the water for?"

"The water makes a moat that surrounds the castle," Shane reminded the little boy.

"Oh yeah! Water is around the castle so the dragons can't get in," Connor smiled.

"That's good! You don't want dragons getting into the castle!" Taylor agreed.

"Nope. I cross the bridge to fight dragons," Connor nodded. "No dragons in the castle."

In the middle of the castle building, the doorbell rang.

"I'll get that," Taylor said, standing. "You boys keep building that castle."

Taylor looked through the peephole and saw a policeman standing on the porch holding a gift bag. She smiled before opening the door.

"Hey, Pete," she greeted the officer. "Come on in."

As soon as the policeman stepped inside, Connor jumped up and ran toward the door.

"Uncle Pete!" Connor yelled excitedly as he launched himself into the man's arms. Suddenly noticing the gift bag, Connor asked, "Did you bring me something, Uncle Pete?"

Lowering the boy to the floor, Pete handed him the bag and said, "You bet, I did."

Connor immediately dug into the bag and pulled out a large police car and a wooden puzzle with farm animals.

"Wow! Thanks, Uncle Pete!"

Pete reached into his jacket pocket and pulled out a pack of batteries. "Let me borrow that car for a minute, and I'll put the batteries in it."

After installing the batteries, Pete handed the car back to Connor and said, "Push this little button right here."

Connor pushed the button, causing a loud siren to blare. "Wow! Thanks!"

"Yeah, thanks," Taylor laughed as Connor made

good use of the siren.

Pete laughed and said, "I haven't been over in a while, so I thought it was time for a special gift."

Shane had joined the others near the front door shortly after Connor launched himself into Pete's arms.

"Pete," Taylor began, "this is Shane Gallagher. Shane, this is Pete McDonald."

The two men shook hands, and Taylor continued. "Pete was Zach's sergeant and partner."

"It's nice to meet you, Sergeant," Shane said.

"Just call me Pete," the forty-year-old officer said with a smile. "I try to stop in and check on these two occasionally to see if they need anything and make sure they're doing okay. I've been over at the academy working with some of the recruits, so I haven't had a chance to stop by."

"Thanks for checking on us, Pete," Taylor said. "You're a good friend, and it's always great to see you."

"It's the least I can do, Taylor," Pete replied. "Well, I'd better get back on patrol. Oh, all the guys down at the station said to tell you hello."

"Tell them hi," Taylor smiled. "Connor, come tell Uncle Pete bye. He needs to leave."

Connor ran over and hugged the policeman. "Thanks for the police car and puzzle, Uncle Pete."

"You're welcome, buddy," Pete smiled. "Well, gotta go."

"Bye, Uncle Pete," Connor said. "Be safe."

"I will, little man," Pete replied.

Pete hugged Taylor, then shook Shane's hand. "It was nice meeting you, Shane. And, Taylor, you be sure to let me know if you need anything."

"I will," she replied.

After Pete left, Shane and Taylor sat on the sofa and watched Connor play with the police car.

Taylor laughed. "I wonder how long it will take for him to wear out the batteries?"

"You may need to pull them out occasionally," Shane chuckled, "just for your own peace of mind."

With a police siren wailing across the room, Shane smiled and turned to Taylor. "I keep forgetting to tell you something. Mom has been asking when she and Dad get to meet you. She seems to think I'm hiding you from them."

Taylor grinned. "You're not, are you?"

"Of course not," Shane chuckled. "I just didn't want to spring the whole 'meeting the family' thing on you too soon."

"It's fine, really," Taylor smiled. "You've already met my parents. You know, I don't know their schedule, but it's almost lunchtime. If you want, and they're available, maybe they could meet us somewhere for lunch."

"That's a great idea!" Shane said enthusiastically. "I don't think they had any specific plans today. Let me text Mom and see."

After a few texts back and forth with his parents, everyone decided to meet at a local diner for lunch. It took some convincing, but Connor reluctantly agreed to leave his new police car at home, with the promise of a cheeseburger for lunch.

\* \* \*

Shane pulled his pickup into the parking spot beside his dad's SUV, then quickly unbuckled Connor from his car seat.

"I get a cheeseburger, right, Mommy?" Connor asked as he scrambled from the car seat.

"Yes, Connor," Taylor grinned. "You get a cheeseburger. You know, you've already asked me that three times."

Connor reached for Shane's hand before replying, "Just making sure."

Shane laughed as he held the door open for Taylor, then looked around for his parents. He found them seated in a corner booth, then led the way over to join them. As they neared the booth, Shane's dad stood to greet them.

"Dad, Mom," Shane began, "this is Taylor Wilson and her son Connor. Taylor, my parents, Owen and Mary Gallagher."

Owen shook Taylor's hand, then bent to shake Connor's hand. "We're happy to finally meet you two. We've heard a lot about you."

"It's nice to meet you as well, Mr. and Mrs. Gallagher," Taylor smiled.

"Please," Owen waved his hand dismissively. "It's Owen and Mary."

After everyone was seated, Mary smiled and said, "Let's look at the menus and decide what we'd like to order. The waitress said she'd be back in a few minutes. Then we can visit and get to know each other."

Owen looked across the table at Connor, sitting in a booster seat, and smiled, "I bet you like hamburgers, don't you?"

"Yes, sir," Connor replied shyly before adding, "Mommy said I get a cheeseburger 'cause I left my police car at home."

"That sounds like a fair trade to me," Owen chuckled. "Should we get you some fries to go with that cheeseburger?"

Connor nodded. "And a chocolate milkshake, please."

"Gotta appreciate a man who knows what he wants," Owen chuckled. "And lunch is on me, so order whatever you want."

Taylor tapped Connor on the arm and nodded toward Shane's dad.

"Thank you, Mr. Owen," Connor said quietly.

"You're welcome, son," Owen smiled before leaning toward Connor and whispering, "I happen to know they make the *best* milkshakes in town here."

"*Really?*" Connor asked, as his eyes got big.

"Yep," Owen confirmed. "In fact, I'm going to order one too."

Connor tapped Shane's hand and proclaimed, "I like your daddy, Shane."

Shane smiled. "That's good to know. I kind of like him, too."

They all enjoyed lunch and visited for a little over an hour, getting to know each other. Mary chuckled every time Connor slipped a French fry onto Shane's plate. The little boy was concerned because Shane didn't order fries, so he decided to share his secretly.

"Taylor, we've had so much fun getting to know you and your little boy," Mary said. "It's too bad we have to cut our visit short, but I'm sure they're going to want to kick us out soon."

"I have an idea," Taylor smiled. "That is, if you two don't have plans for the rest of the day."

"You've got my attention," Owen chimed in. "We're completely open. What do you have in mind?"

Taylor looked at Shane and smiled, knowing how much he wanted them to get to know his parents.

"Why don't you come back to my house, and we can continue our visit?" Taylor suggested. "If you happen to like pizza, I promised Connor we could order pizza for dinner. You can join us."

"That's a great idea!" Owen exclaimed. "We love pizza!" Turning to Connor, he said, "A cheeseburger and pizza all in the same day. What's your secret, little guy?"

Connor shrugged. "I'm cute!"

Owen roared with laughter. "Cute *and* honest.

That's a winning combination! I think I'm going to like this kid."

Shane laughed at Connor's response as they walked to the parking lot. "Taylor, why don't you text your parents and see if they're able to join us? We could all hang out for the afternoon, then have a pizza party for dinner."

"I can show people my police car!" Connor exclaimed.

Shane chuckled as he held the door to his pickup open for Taylor. "I see disappearing batteries in Connor's future."

\* \* \*

Taylor's parents quickly agreed to spend the afternoon with their daughter and grandson. Having the opportunity to meet Shane's parents was a bonus. Shane had just parked his pickup along the curb in front of Taylor's house, with his parents right behind him, when Kenny and Stephanie pulled into the driveway. Everyone gathered on the front porch while Taylor unlocked the door, saving the introductions until they were inside.

They had no sooner shed their coats and hung them in the coat closet in the entryway when Connor ran to retrieve his new police car. Taylor intercepted him before he pushed the siren button.

"Wait until Grandma and Grandpa meet Shane's

parents," Taylor began, "then you can show everyone your police car. Okay?"

"Okay, Mommy," Connor agreed, patiently waiting for his turn.

"Okay," Shane began, "let me get the introductions out of the way, then we can visit."

Connor tapped Shane on the leg. "And Connor can show everyone his new police car," Shane chuckled.

"Dad and Mom," Shane began, "this is Kenny and Stephanie Matthews, Taylor's parents. And this is Owen and Mary Gallagher, my parents."

Kenny and Owen shook hands, then led their wives to the sofa and loveseat in the living room.

As everyone found a seat, Connor walked over to his mom and asked, "Now, Mommy?"

Taylor and Shane chuckled. "Yes, Connor, now you can show everyone your new police car," Taylor agreed.

Connor immediately pushed the button on top of the car, and the blare of a siren filled the room. Stephanie and Mary jumped back in their seats in surprise.

"Oh," Taylor smiled. "I guess we should have warned you!"

"What have you got there, Connor?" Kenny asked his grandson.

"Uncle Pete gave me a police car!" Connor exclaimed proudly. "It has a siren!"

"Yes, we heard," Kenny laughed. "That was awfully nice of Pete."

"Oh, don't worry," Taylor chuckled. "I plan to get

even with him. A siren, Pete? Really?"

"Is Pete your brother, Taylor?" Mary asked.

"No," Taylor replied. "Pete was Zach's sergeant and partner on the police force. He still stops by occasionally to check on us. And to spoil Connor."

"Shane told us about your husband," Mary said sympathetically. "I'm so sorry, Taylor."

"Thanks," Taylor replied quietly, just before the siren wailed again.

After Connor showed everyone his car, demonstrating the siren for each person, Kenny pulled the little boy onto his lap. "Why don't we let the siren rest a while, buddy? Then maybe you can use the siren later to announce the arrival of pizza for dinner."

Connor's face broke into a smile as he scrambled from Kenny's lap. "Good idea, Grandpa!"

"Yes, Dad," Taylor grinned. "Good idea. I may be sending the batteries home in your coat pocket!"

Hoping not to end up with a police car stuffed into his coat, Kenny quickly changed the subject.

"What line of work are you in, Owen?" he asked.

"I'm an engineer," Owen replied, immediately getting Connor's attention.

"Do you drive a train, Mr. Owen?" Connor asked.

"Sorry, Connor, no train," Owen replied sadly. "I'm a different kind of engineer. I design roads and bridges and stuff."

Pointing to the block structure on the other side of the room, Connor said, "Me and Shane builded a castle.

It has a bridge."

Owen nodded. "Bridges are important for castles. It helps keep the dragons out."

"I know," the little boy nodded. "You can play with my castle, Mr. Owen."

"Thanks, buddy," Owen smiled. "I'll check it out in a little while."

Anxious to get to know Taylor's parents, Owen turned to Kenny and asked, "What do you do for a living, Kenny?"

"I earn a living as an attorney," Kenny replied. Laughing, he added, "Then I restore classic cars to spend all that hard-earned money."

"That would do it!" Owen agreed. "Shane told me you restore cars. I know how much time and money he put into restoring his truck." Turning to Stephanie, he asked, "How about you, Stephanie? What do you do to stay busy?"

"I'm a happily retired school teacher turned full-time grandma," Stephanie smiled. "Being a full-time grandma is more fun. Although I truly loved teaching."

"You followed in your mother's footsteps, huh, Taylor?" Mary asked. "Teaching is a noble profession. I admire anyone who has the patience to teach."

"I agree, Mary," Taylor said. "I love it. I'm not sure I have the patience to teach elementary students like Mom did, but I love the challenges of high school."

"Do you work outside the home, Mary?" Stephanie asked, already liking both of Shane's parents.

"Yes, I do," Mary replied. "I work at the opposite end of the spectrum. I'm the activities director at one of the nursing homes in town, so I spend my days with senior citizens."

"Wow!" Taylor exclaimed. "Talk about noble professions! I'm not sure that's something I could do."

"It's a lot of fun," Mary explained. "The only requirement is loving people and helping them have fun and enjoy life. I basically get paid to play all day."

"That's my kind of job!" Kenny proclaimed. "Where do I go to sign up?"

The four older adults spent the afternoon getting to know each other while Taylor and Shane split their time between their parents and Connor. Before long, Kenny and Owen were stretched out on the living room floor playing with Connor and checking out the castle. Mary and Stephanie ended up sitting side by side on the sofa, thoroughly enjoying each other's company.

At some point, as dinnertime approached, Shane announced it was time to order pizza. Conversation and play halted long enough to decide what to order, then the castle renovation began. With an engineer on the team, a few minor changes were required to bring things up to code.

The moment the doorbell rang, a police siren blared across the room. And blared…and blared…and blared. Just before a little boy announced, "Pizza's here!"

# CHAPTER SEVEN

Not quite sure how the seasons had transitioned so quickly, Taylor found herself putting the final touches on decorations around her home. There was only another week before students got out for Christmas break, with Christmas Day being less than two weeks away. Taylor and Shane's parents had become close friends, with the four of them even going out to dinner occasionally without their adult children. The big holiday dinner was going to be held at Taylor's house, and Shane's parents were invited to join the festivities for the day.

Taylor's parents had offered to take Connor to a movie to give her a chance to finish wrapping his Christmas presents. As was the case most weekends, Shane spent as much time as possible with Taylor. They had finally finished wrapping all the presents, so Taylor made some hot chocolate and joined Shane on the sofa to relax.

Taylor appeared to be deep in thought as she sat with her hands wrapped around the warm mug of cocoa.

Shane glanced in her direction and asked, "What are you thinking about so intently?"

Taylor turned to face him and smiled. "I was just thinking how much life has changed. This is only the second Christmas without Zach, and it's so much different than last Christmas."

"I was thinking about that the other day," Shane began. "I wondered how you might be dealing with the holidays."

"It was hard to put on a happy face for Connor last Christmas," Taylor admitted. "Everything was still so new. I honestly didn't even want to celebrate Christmas. I wouldn't have if it hadn't been for Connor. This year isn't as hard, and you're a big part of the reason why."

She sat quietly for a few moments before adding, "Thanks for making my life a little easier, Shane. And thanks for accepting Connor. He really likes you, you know."

Shane grinned. "I think he just likes my truck."

"He definitely likes your truck," Taylor chuckled. "But you've become pretty important to him, too. He likes it when you hang out with us on the weekends, and he drives me crazy asking about you during the week."

"He's a great kid, Taylor," Shane said seriously. "You can be proud of him."

"Thanks," she nodded, leaning back against Shane with her hands still wrapped around the mug of cocoa.

The doorbell rang suddenly, jarring Taylor out of her relaxed state.

"I wonder who that can be?" she asked, handing her mug to Shane as she started toward the door.

Shane set both mugs down on the coffee table and stood while Taylor answered the door. She peeked through the peephole, and Shane watched some of the color drain from her face.

"Oh no," Taylor said quietly.

Shane was behind her in an instant. "Who is it?"

Taylor looked like she had seen a ghost. "It's Zach's parents."

* * *

The doorbell rang a second time while Taylor worked to compose herself. She finally took a deep breath and opened the door to find a middle-aged couple standing in the cold, looking like they had just come from a night at the opera.

"Mr. and Mrs. Wilson," Taylor greeted, forcing a smile.

Zach's mother wrapped Taylor in a one-sided hug as they pushed past her into the house. "Taylor, dear, how many times have I told you to call me Janet?"

"What are you doing here?" Taylor asked in confusion. "I didn't know you were in town."

Zach's parents were the polar opposite of Taylor's down-to-earth parents. They lived back East and lived a pretentious lifestyle of high-society New Yorkers. Who showed up, uninvited, in a relatively small town in the Pacific Northwest wearing a mink stole?

Janet began walking around the living room, with her husband following behind, as Taylor and Shane remained near the front door.

"Where's little Zachie?" Janet asked, looking around.

"My son's name is Connor," Taylor replied, as her fists tightened involuntarily.

Janet waved her hand dismissively. "I always thought you should have named him after his father."

"His name is Connor," Taylor reiterated. "And, again, why are you here?"

"We thought we'd come out for Christmas," Janet replied, suddenly noticing Shane standing beside Taylor. "Who's this?"

Taylor took a deep breath. Then another. "This is Shane Gallagher. Shane, this is David and Janet Wilson, Zach's parents."

Shane shook hands with David and nodded at his wife, who had not made a good first impression in Shane's mind.

Janet glared at Shane, not bothering to acknowledge him, then turned her attention back to Taylor.

"Well," Janet began as she tightened her stole around her shoulders, "I see it didn't take you long to replace my son."

Taylor knew Janet's snide comment didn't deserve

a reply, so she opted to silently count to three before saying anything.

"Let me see if I understand you," Taylor began, barely keeping her emotions under control. "The last time you were in town was for your son's funeral. You were the first to leave the cemetery – even before the hearse. I haven't heard from you since that day. And now you suddenly appear on my doorstep, unannounced, and proclaim you 'thought you'd come out for Christmas'? What part of that makes any sense to a rational mind?"

Shane could sense that Taylor was just getting started, and he was secretly rooting for her, when there was a commotion at the door. Taylor's parents had just returned from the movie with their grandson. They walked into the room and immediately sized up the situation.

"Stephanie," Kenny began, barely glancing at his wife, "why don't you take Connor down to his room and read him a story?"

Taylor's mother nodded and pointed Connor down the hallway toward his bedroom.

Shane heard Connor ask, "Grandma, who are those people?" as they left the living room.

"David. Janet," Kenny greeted the couple. "Taylor didn't mention you were in town."

"That's because I didn't know," Taylor replied with frustration.

"We wanted to surprise her and little Zachie," Janet

said, smiling.

"You come clear across the country from New York," Kenny began, "not knowing anyone would even be home, to simply drop in? And, by the way, my grandson's name is Connor."

*You go, Kenny!* Shane thought to himself, trying to hide a smile.

"We thought we'd surprise them and come out to have Christmas together," Janet replied as she adjusted her mink stole. Glaring at Shane once again, she added, "I wasn't aware she'd already forgotten about her husband."

Suddenly remembering how difficult Janet could be, Kenny took a deep breath.

"Have you even called Taylor once since Zach's funeral to see how she was doing?" Kenny asked, his fatherly instinct in high gear. "Did you bother to send a single birthday or Christmas gift to your grandson in the past year?"

Janet waved her hand as if the question didn't deserve a response. "We've been busy. You know how it is in New York City."

"No, Janet, I *don't* know how it is in New York City," Kenny said evenly. "And if it would mean ignoring my grandson's existence, I don't *care* to know what it's like. Let me ask you something, Janet – and, David, feel free to chime in if your wife has a memory lapse – how many times have you seen Zach or Taylor since their wedding?"

Looking flustered, Janet stammered, "Who can remember how often you see a person?"

"I can," Kenny replied, clearly not willing to let her off the hook. "You saw them the day of their wedding. That's one. And you left before the reception. You saw them again when Connor was born. That's two. You didn't stick around long enough for my daughter and grandson to get out of the hospital. And you saw them at your son's funeral. That's three. Now you show up out of the blue, more than a year later, and expect a red-carpet welcome?"

"Maybe we should leave, Janet," David suggested, the first words he had uttered since their arrival.

Kenny quickly ushered them to the door. "I think your husband has a good idea."

"I'm not leaving without seeing my grandson," Janet stated emphatically.

"What's your grandson's name, Janet?" Kenny asked.

"Zachie," she replied with confidence.

"Nope, wrong answer," Kenny said, urging them to the door. "Have a nice day."

"You mean we came all this way, and we don't even get to see our grandson?" Janet asked incredulously.

"That appears to be the case," Kenny replied without remorse. "When you can remember the boy's name and figure out how to call ahead, then you might stand a chance. Until then, as I said, have a nice day."

David took his wife by the elbow and started for the

door. Janet lingered in the doorway and stared at Shane as if she were sizing him up.

"How long have you known Taylor?" she asked judgmentally.

Before Shane could reply, Kenny said, "He doesn't owe you an explanation, and neither does my daughter. Drive safe."

Then he promptly shut the door behind them and immediately pulled his daughter into his arms.

"Are you okay, honey?" Kenny asked Taylor.

"I think so," Taylor replied. "That was certainly a surprise. Thanks, Daddy."

Shane shook his head in admiration. "Wow! That was really something, Kenny! You didn't hold back."

"The nerve of that woman," Kenny stated, shaking his head. "Ignoring her own son and grandson, not to mention her daughter-in-law, then thinking she can waltz in here like there's nothing wrong with her actions."

About that time, Connor ran down the hallway toward the living room, with his grandma close on his heels. Then he launched himself into Kenny's outstretched arms.

Kenny hugged his grandson tightly, then asked, "Have I told you recently how much I love you, buddy?"

"About a hundred times today," Connor giggled.

"Okay," Kenny laughed. "Then I only have about another hundred to go today."

"Silly Grandpa," Connor said, then kissed his

grandpa's cheek. "Grandpa, who was that man and lady?"

Kenny looked at his daughter to see if she wanted to field the question.

"Go ahead and give it your best shot, Daddy," Taylor shrugged.

Kenny sat on the sofa and pulled his grandson onto his lap, not quite sure how much to explain.

"You know I'm your mommy's daddy, right, Connor?"

"Yep," the little boy nodded. "You're Grandpa."

"And your grandma over there is your mommy's mommy, right?" Kenny asked.

"Yep," Connor nodded again.

"Well," Kenny explained, "that man was your *daddy's* daddy. And the lady was your *daddy's* mommy. Do you understand?"

"Maybe," Connor replied, not really understanding. "My daddy died."

"Yes, he did," Kenny agreed, as he watched the little boy struggle to understand.

"He still has a daddy and mommy?" Connor asked in confusion.

"Yes, he does," Kenny answered.

Seeming to have all the information he needed at the moment, Connor slid off his grandpa's lap and announced, "I don't know them, so they can't play with my police car."

"Fair enough," Kenny grinned as he watched his

grandson run across the room to get his police car.

* * *

Several days passed with no further word from Zach's parents. Taylor's mom tried to convince her daughter to put their visit out of her mind and not let it spoil the holidays. Easier said than done, but Taylor made an effort. School was out for Christmas break, so Shane spent most of his days with Taylor and Connor. They made several trips to the park to go sledding. There was a large hill at the park that became a popular sledding spot, and Connor was determined to make it down the hill without falling off his saucer. Shane's parents stopped by to drop off gifts for everyone, and then his mother returned on her day off to help Taylor and Stephanie make cookies and fudge.

All in all, Taylor was beginning to feel like it was a normal Christmas. Almost. But there was no doubt in her mind that it was a huge improvement over last Christmas.

The Saturday before Christmas, Shane and Taylor's parents gathered at Taylor's house to spend the afternoon watching Christmas movies. Most of them were animated children's movies, but they thoroughly enjoyed them. Connor bounced between the adults and the floor, giggling at his favorite parts of the movies and trying to convince Grandpa that he needed another cookie.

At the end of one of the movies, Connor announced they needed to have pizza for dinner because "you can't watch movies without pizza." None of the adults could come up with a convincing argument against pizza, so they started discussing what to order. In the middle of their pizza discussion, the doorbell rang.

"I'll get it," Kenny announced. "I'm already up."

He opened the door and hesitated a moment. "David," he greeted, looking past Zach's father to see Janet in their car.

"May I come in for a minute?" David asked hesitantly as Taylor and Shane approached the door.

Kenny looked at his daughter. "It's your house, honey. It's up to you."

Taylor shot a glance back at her mom, who nodded slightly.

"Okay," Taylor said quietly.

"Thank you, Taylor," David said, relieved. "I won't take up too much of your time."

"I didn't know you were still in town," Taylor mentioned.

David's shoulders sagged like a man exhausted by battle. "Janet was ready to hop on the first plane back to New York. I told her we weren't going anywhere until we fixed this. I have no intention of being absent from my only grandson's life. I have to admit, we had the biggest knock-down drag-out we've ever had in thirty-five years of marriage. But I wasn't backing down on this one. I finally told her that if she planned to return to

New York without fixing this problem, she could go without me. Truth is, I hate New York."

Kenny put his hand on David's shoulder in support as the dejected man struggled to continue.

"I've already lost my only son," David explained with tears in his eyes. "I can't stand to lose my grandson, too." David took a deep breath before continuing. "I finally got through to Janet. She told me about all the phone messages you left, Taylor. I had no idea you had been calling to check on us. Thanks for doing that. I wish I had known. Janet and I have done a lot of soul-searching in the past few days. We're going to leave New York and move back out here. And I really hope – we both hope – that you'll let us be a part of Connor's life. Before we leave, I'd like to have Janet come in and apologize to you, if you'd allow it, Taylor."

"Absolutely," Taylor replied quietly.

When David walked out to the car to get his wife, you could have heard a pin drop in Taylor's living room. A couple of minutes later, David and Janet stepped into Taylor's house with tears in their eyes. Gone were the mink stole and the haughty attitude. Both had been replaced by genuine remorse.

Without saying a word, Janet walked over and pulled Taylor into her arms, sobbing openly.

"Can you ever forgive me, Taylor?" Janet asked as she released Taylor from her embrace. "There's no excuse for my behavior, and I'm truly sorry."

David tapped his wife on the arm and nodded

toward Shane.

Glancing at Shane, Janet sighed audibly. "I'm sorry, young man, but I've forgotten your name."

Trying to gauge the sincerity of this woman he had only met one time, Shane simply replied, "It's Shane."

Janet took a deep breath. "I owe you an apology, too, Shane," she said sincerely. "I'm very sorry for the way I acted the other day."

"Apology accepted," Shane replied as he pulled Taylor close.

Janet looked across the room to where her grandson was playing near what appeared to be a castle, knowing full well she didn't deserve to see the boy.

Taylor followed her gaze, then sighed in relief. "Janet, why don't you and David come over and say hi to your grandson?"

"Really?" Janet asked quietly.

Taylor took her mother-in-law by the hand and led them both across the room.

Connor looked up as they approached.

Janet looked to Taylor for reassurance, and the young mother nodded.

Surprising everyone, Janet sat on the floor beside her grandson. "Hi, Connor," she began, unable to continue.

David joined his wife on the floor beside Connor. "That's quite a castle you have there. Did you build it?"

The little boy nodded. "Shane helped me."

David glanced at Shane, then turned back to

Connor. "That was nice of Shane to help you. You guys did a great job." Hesitating just a moment, he added, "You look so much like your daddy, Connor."

"He was cute too," Connor smiled, with his mother standing behind him, trying to stifle a grin.

"He sure was," David chuckled.

Connor studied David's face, then said, "You and the lady were here before. Grandpa said you're my daddy's daddy." Then, pointing to Janet, he added, "And she's my daddy's mommy."

"That's right, Connor," David replied, looking at Taylor hopefully. "We're your grandparents."

Taylor joined David and Janet on the floor and pulled her son onto her lap. "Connor, this is your Grandpa David and Grandma Janet. They came a long way to see you."

"Oh," the little boy replied, still considering this new information. He looked back and forth between David and Janet, then said, "We're gonna have pizza. Can you have pizza with us?"

Janet burst into a fresh round of tears, unable to answer.

"We'd love to have pizza with you, Connor," David replied. "As long as it's okay with your mom."

"Yes," Taylor nodded. "Please stay."

Connor suddenly jumped from his mom's lap and grabbed David's hand. "Wanna see my police car, Grandpa David?"

"I can't think of a single thing I'd rather do," David

smiled as a lone tear made its way down his cheek.

As they started across the room, Connor turned back and asked, "Coming, Grandma Janet?"

"Right behind you, Connor," she managed to choke out between sobs.

# Chapter Eight

Christmas Day at Taylor's house was proving to be more chaotic than she had initially expected. It was a stark contrast to last year's subdued holiday that included only Taylor and Connor, along with her parents, all simply trying to hold things together after Zach's death. This year, Shane was a big part of her life. And in a few short weeks, his parents had found a special place in her heart as well. Shane and his parents would be part of this year's holiday festivities. Added to that was the unexpected arrival of Zach's parents in town. They would all be arriving shortly to spend the day. Taylor was eternally grateful her parents had come over early Christmas morning to help with last-minute preparations and try to keep a little boy distracted until everyone arrived.

When Taylor was sure she couldn't keep Connor out of the pile of Christmas gifts another minute, the doorbell rang. The arrival of Shane and his parents distracted the little boy long enough for Zach's parents to show up a few minutes later. Everyone came bearing gifts.

"Wow!" Connor exclaimed as the additional gifts were scattered around the tree. "Are these all for me?"

Shane laughed as he tousled Connor's hair. "Don't you think your mommy might want some Christmas presents too?"

"Oh, yeah," Connor nodded. "And you, Shane!"

Kenny walked over, scooped his grandson into his arms, and headed to the sofa. "Why don't we go sit over here and wait until the presents get passed out? I'm pretty sure there'll be something for everyone."

Before long, it became obvious that Connor was a happily spoiled, almost four-year-old. He sat in the middle of the living room, surrounded by an assortment of toys, books, and puzzles, oblivious to the chatter of adults around him. Everyone else had exchanged gifts, and Zach's parents were pleasantly surprised to have received something from both Taylor and her parents.

While the others were visiting, Taylor slipped over to Connor and whispered into his ear. He grinned and nodded, then they both disappeared down the hallway, returning a few minutes later with more packages. Taylor handed him one of the packages and nodded toward her parents.

Connor walked over and handed them the sloppily, but lovingly, wrapped gift.

"I wrapped it, Grandpa and Grandma," the little boy said proudly. "It's for you."

Kenny and Stephanie accepted the gift, and Stephanie patted Connor on the back. "You did a wonderful job wrapping it, Connor. I can't wait to see what it is!"

"Open it!" Connor exclaimed in his excitement. "Hurry!"

Together, Taylor's parents unwrapped Connor's gift, revealing a framed picture hand-drawn by a little boy.

Connor pointed to a yellow and black object with wheels. "That's your 'stored car, Grandpa."

"Well, it sure is!" Kenny agreed. "And it's yellow and black, just like my Chevelle."

"I know!" Connor beamed. "I made it just like your car."

Pointing to two brown and yellow objects with sticks protruding from the bottom, Connor added, "And that's the ducks we feed at the park, Grandma."

"I knew that right away, Connor," Stephanie grinned. "And this blue circle over here in the picture is the lake, isn't it?"

"Yep!" Connor grinned. "Do you like it, Grandma and Grandpa?"

"We love it, Connor!" the proud grandparents replied. "It's a wonderful picture."

After Connor received hugs from her parents, Taylor handed him a second gift and pointed him toward Shane's parents.

Connor handed them a similar package, and Mary

asked, "Did you wrap this gift, too, Connor?"

The little boy nodded.

"You did a great job, buddy," Owen said, patting the boy on the back.

Connor jumped up and down and clapped his hands. "Hurry! You have to open it!"

Chuckling, Owen and Mary unwrapped the gift together. Holding the framed drawing in their hands, Mary said, "I hope you drew this picture for us, too."

"Yep!" Connor beamed. Pointing to two brown oblong circles with a skinny yellow line between them, Connor explained, "That's the cheeseburger you got me. I ate the real one. This is just a picture."

"I'm glad you explained that last part, Connor," Owen grinned. "I was confused for a minute because I was pretty sure you ate that entire cheeseburger."

Mary pointed to three long yellow rectangles on the drawing. "These are your French fries, aren't they?"

"Yep!" Connor nodded. Then he whispered, "But not the ones I sneaked to Shane."

"Oh, of course not," Mary whispered.

Taylor handed her son the remaining gift and gently nudged him over to Zach's parents. He placed the gift in their hands and smiled.

David and Janet accepted the gift with tears in their eyes. "Did you draw a picture for us, too, Connor?" David asked as he and his wife began opening the present.

Connor smiled and nodded.

"When did you have time to do that?" David asked curiously.

"I made it the other day," Connor said proudly.

Their drawing showed two large stick figures and one much smaller stick figure. In the middle of the three stick figures was a blue object with black wheels and a red circle on top.

David pointed to the object in the middle. "This looks like your police car. Am I right?"

Connor nodded, then pointed to the stick figures in his drawing. "See, Grandpa David. That's you. And that's Grandma Janet."

Janet pointed to the small stick figure and explained. "And this is you, isn't it, Connor?"

"Yeah, 'cause I'm littler than grandmas and grandpas," Connor explained.

Zach's parents hugged their grandson tightly. "Thank you so much for the present, Connor," David said. "I don't think we've ever gotten a nicer gift."

Once the mess of wrapping paper was cleaned up, the adults settled in to visit while Connor played with his new toys. Shane followed Taylor into the kitchen to help her get mugs of hot chocolate for everyone to enjoy while dinner was cooking.

Shane pulled Taylor into his arms and asked, "How are you holding up? This is probably a lot different than you envisioned for today."

"It is," Taylor agreed. "But, you know, I think it's okay. I honestly never thought I'd see David and Janet again. But I think after David had what Dad calls a 'come to Jesus meeting' with Janet, things will be different. And there's no reason they shouldn't be a part of Connor's life."

"You're an amazing woman, Taylor Wilson," Shane grinned. "But I think we should get this tray of hot chocolate out there before I forget about it and just decide to kiss you instead."

Leaving Taylor with her mouth open in surprise, Shane grinned, grabbed the tray of hot chocolate, and walked into the living room.

\* \* \*

Most of Christmas Day was spent inside with the adults visiting, enjoying each other's company, and getting to know David and Janet. Zach's parents made the most of their visit and joined Connor on the floor to play with some of his toys. Even the favored police car was pulled out and added to the new toys. The siren blared frequently throughout the house until the batteries mysteriously wore out. After a couple of hours of racing cars around grown-ups, Connor jumped up and announced it was time to build a snowman in the back yard.

"I'm not sure there's enough snow to make a snowman, buddy," Kenny explained as they looked into the yard. "It doesn't look like more than a couple of inches."

Taking Kenny by the hand and leading him to the coat closet in the entryway, Connor suggested, "That's okay, Grandpa. We can make a little snowman."

Kenny laughed. "Okay, Connor, one little snowman coming right up."

"Do you mind if we come help you make a snowman, Connor?" Janet asked hopefully.

As Taylor helped her son into his coat, boots, and gloves, Connor nodded. "Everybody come! We can make lots of snowmans!"

True to the little boy's expectations, the back yard was soon dotted with little snowmen everywhere. When Connor decided to climb up the play structure so he could go down the snow-covered slide, Shane had an idea he knew the boy would love.

"Wait just a minute, Connor," Shane said, grinning. "Let me put a couple of these little snowmen at the bottom of the slide. That way, when you slide down, you can crash into the snowmen!"

"Yay!" Connor yelled excitedly. "Good idea, Shane!"

While David brushed off the steps to the slide, Shane quickly put together two snowmen and lined them up at the bottom of the slide.

"Okay, Connor," Shane grinned. "Ready when you are!"

The little boy scampered up the steps to the top of the slide, under the watchful eyes of Grandpa David, then sat down on the platform.

"Here I come!" Connor yelled, then launched himself down the slide.

He crashed into the little snowmen, completely demolishing them, then jumped up and wanted to do it again. Everyone joined in the fun, and soon there was a line of miniature snowmen waiting to be moved into place at the end of the slide.

After Connor had wiped out most of the miniature snowmen, and the back yard showed more grass than snow, Taylor suggested it might be time for hot chocolate and cookies.

It turned out that the hot cocoa and cookies were the perfect appetizer for dinner. Taylor and her mom were joined in the kitchen by Shane and Zach's mothers as everyone pitched in to get Christmas dinner on the table. They all enjoyed the traditional Christmas feast. Zach's parents smiled as they watched their grandson eat.

"Connor seems to have a hearty appetite," David chuckled. "It's been ages since I've seen a small boy enjoy his food like that."

Once everyone finished eating, Kenny suggested they could make short work of the cleanup if all the men jumped in to take care of the dishes.

"Since the women fed us," Kenny rationalized, "it's only fair for the men to do the cleanup."

"I think I like that rule, Kenny," Mary laughed as she quickly vacated the kitchen.

The women settled in to relax and visit in the living

room while the guys took care of the kitchen cleanup. In the meantime, Connor was digging around in his pile of Christmas goodies and pulled out one of his new books.

He walked over to Janet, seated on the sofa, and asked, "Grandma Janet, will you read me my book?"

"Of course, Connor," Janet smiled. "Crawl up here beside me and let's check out your book."

When the guys finished in the kitchen and returned to the living room, David found his wife sitting on the sofa with her grandson snuggled in close as they read a book together. David caught Taylor's eye, nodded, and smiled before joining his wife and grandson on the sofa.

Before anyone was ready for the day to end, David mentioned he and Janet had an early flight back to New York the next morning, so they should probably call it a day. By then, Connor was fading quickly and would soon be heading off to bed.

"Come here, Connor," David patted the seat beside him, then pulled his grandson up onto his lap. "Your Grandma Janet and I have sure had a great time getting to know you. It's been a long time since we've had a chance to play in the snow. We have to go home in the morning, so we'd like to say goodbye before you need to head to bed. But I promise, we'll be back to see you soon, okay?"

"Okay," Connor said sleepily. He hugged both his grandparents, then said, "Bye, Grandpa David. Bye, Grandma Janet. Thanks for playing with me."

Connor went around the room, passing out hugs to

everyone and telling them goodnight.

As Taylor started pointing her tired boy toward the hallway, he asked, "Mommy, can Shane tuck me in?"

"If he'd like to," Taylor smiled, looking at Shane.

Shane picked up the tired boy and started down the hallway. "Come on, buddy, let's get you to bed before you fall asleep standing up."

Connor laid his head on Shane's shoulder and said, "Silly, Shane. I can't sleep standing up."

When Shane returned to the living room, Zach's parents were putting on their coats, and his parents were also preparing to leave.

"Taylor," David began, "thanks so much for allowing us to share Christmas with all of you. We're going home and listing our condo for sale, then we're moving back out here. We've already missed almost four years of our grandson's life. We're not going to miss any more."

Taylor hugged her in-laws, then said, "Stay in touch and let us know when you're headed back this way. You're always welcome."

"We're going to head out too, Taylor," Owen added as he helped his wife into her coat. "Thanks for everything."

"Maybe we can meet up for lunch in a few days," Mary began, "before you kids have to go back to work."

"Sounds good," Taylor replied. "Maybe I can convince Dad and Mom to join us."

Kenny laughed. "If there's food involved, just tell

me when and where to show up."

* * *

After everyone left, Shane and Taylor sank onto the sofa and put their feet up.

"Well," Taylor smiled, "that was unlike any Christmas I've ever had before. But it was nice. A little overwhelming at times, but nice."

"It looked like everyone enjoyed themselves," Shane commented. He then added with a smile, "The food was fantastic! It's nice to know you're a good cook."

Taylor grinned. "I'll have you know, I'm an excellent cook. But after that Christmas dinner, I don't plan to cook anything for a week."

"I guess that means I'll have to take my favorite little guy and his mommy out to eat," Shane grinned. "I'm okay with that."

Shane stood and pulled Taylor into his arms. "I can tell you're dead on your feet, so I'm going to head home and let you call it a day."

He then lowered his head and placed a light kiss on Taylor's lips. She responded with a smile, then pulled him into a more meaningful kiss.

Shane gave her another quick peck on the cheek as he grabbed his coat from the entryway closet.

"Merry Christmas, Taylor."

"Merry Christmas, Shane."

"I'll call you tomorrow, okay?" Shane asked.

"You'd better," Taylor smiled. "You're going to have to feed us, remember?"

Taylor smiled as she listened to Shane's laughter all the way down the sidewalk until he climbed into his truck and drove off into the night.

# CHAPTER NINE

Christmas break was nearly over, and everyone would be heading back to school soon. Shane had spent all his free time with Taylor and Connor and suddenly felt at loose ends. He found himself alone in his apartment on New Year's Eve. Normally, he would be spending the day with Taylor, but she and her family had driven to Oregon to visit her grandparents for a couple of days. Things had even been relatively quiet at the fire station. If he admitted the truth to himself, he was bored.

*Maybe I'll see if Dad wants to go to lunch,* Shane thought to himself as he picked up his cell phone.

"Hey, Dad," Shane began when his father answered the call. "What are you doing today?"

"As little as possible, Shane," Owen laughed. "You're not over at Taylor's today?"

"No," Shane said, sadness showing through his voice. "They all went to Oregon to spend a couple of days with Stephanie's parents."

"So, you're bored, right?" Owen chuckled.

Shane laughed. "Yeah. Do you want to grab some lunch with me?"

"That sounds like a great idea," Owen replied. "Your mom's working today, so I could use the distraction. Besides, then I won't have to figure out what to feed myself."

"You'll still have to decide what to have for lunch," Shane chuckled.

"True," his father agreed. "But, at least I won't have to cook it. You know my cooking skills. I'd probably starve if your mother didn't take pity on me and feed me occasionally."

"Yeah, Dad," Shane laughed. "You have such a rough life! I'll be over in a few minutes."

\* \* \*

The Gallagher men decided to have lunch at a popular rib place in town. Since Mary didn't care for barbecue, they didn't go there very often. Shane and his dad smiled when the waiter set the rather large platter of barbecued ribs down in front of them. Baked beans, corn on the cob, and cornbread muffins rounded out their feast.

As they prepared to dig in, Owen grinned. "After this lunch, I can tell your mom she doesn't have to fix dinner tonight."

They ate in silence for several minutes, savoring the tender ribs. When they were nearly finished with the meal, Shane looked up at his dad and asked, "Can I talk to you about something, Dad?"

"Always," Owen answered. "What's up, son?"

Shane suddenly began second-guessing himself and hesitated.

"Spill it, Shane. You know you can talk to me about anything."

"I know, Dad. I'm just trying to figure out how to put it into words."

"When I have that problem, I just jump in with both feet," his dad suggested. "Then we can figure it out as we go."

"Okay," Shane agreed. "I know Mom has always struggled with me being a firefighter, but I don't think you've ever expressed an opinion about it one way or another. Does it bother you, Dad?"

Owen Gallagher looked across the table at his only son and pondered his answer.

"That's a tough question, Shane," Owen began. "On a superficial level, no, it doesn't bother me. On a very real and personal level, as a parent, I never want my son to be in harm's way. However, I also understand your passion for helping people. Fighting fires is the way you do that; it's what works for you. You help people when they're most vulnerable, when their lives are potentially altered drastically. That passion is what makes you a great firefighter. Do I wish you didn't put your life in danger every time you respond to a fire? Absolutely. But I also know you've got a good head on your shoulders, that you're properly trained, and that you don't take unnecessary chances."

"Thanks, Dad," Shane replied. "That helps." Then he added, "I don't think Mom will ever be okay with it, on any level."

"You could be right, son. But I also think she's come to terms with it and has accepted it the best she can."

Shane didn't say anything for several minutes as they finished their lunch. He looked up and noticed his dad was staring at him.

"What?" Shane asked, grabbing a napkin and wiping his face. "Have you been letting me sit here with barbecue sauce on my face?"

Owen smiled. "No, although that sounds like something I would do. I was just wondering when you were going to get around to your real problem."

"What do you mean?" Shane asked in confusion.

"Son, I've known you your entire life," Owen began. "I know your question was an ice breaker, just testing the waters. What's really on your mind?"

"It's Taylor," Shane began, unsure how to continue.

Owen grinned at his son. "You know, son, for a teacher, you sometimes have trouble putting your thoughts into words."

Shane chuckled. "I'm a numbers teacher, Dad, not a words teacher."

Owen sat back in his chair. "Okay, just tell me what's going on with Taylor. Your mother and I already know you have pretty strong feelings for both Taylor and Connor. So, what's the problem?"

Shane grinned and lowered his voice. "Just between us guys, I love her and want to ask her to marry me."

Owen grinned back and also lowered his voice conspiratorially. "It's not a secret, Shane. Your mom and I have already figured that out. In fact, Kenny and Stephanie have it figured out, too."

"She's really struggling with me being a firefighter," Shane said quietly. "It stresses her out to the point we have a hard time even discussing it."

"That's understandable, son," Owen replied. "You don't lose a spouse the way she lost Zach without having some emotional fallout. It can't be easy being married to a first responder.

"Let me ask you something, Shane," Owen continued. "Have you told Taylor how you feel? Have you told her you love her?"

"Not yet," Shane admitted quietly.

"You need to do that," his dad suggested. "You need to find out how she feels about you, then you can wade into the deep waters. If you love each other, God will help you find a way to make it work. Ask God to lead your discussion. But you can't move forward until you find out if you're both on the same page."

After settling the lunch tab, the two men stood up and began moving toward the door.

"Thanks, Dad," Shane said. "I don't know why I didn't come talk to you sooner."

Owen chuckled. "It's because you're a numbers guy, not a words guy."

* * *

Taylor and her family had returned from Oregon after a wonderful visit with her grandparents. Now, she still had the weekend free before she had to go back to work. She smiled as she thought about how much she had missed Shane in the short two days they were out of town. But he was coming over to spend the day with her and Connor, and she was nearly as excited as a certain little boy glued to the front window watching for him.

"Mommy!" Connor yelled from the living room. "He's here!"

By the time Taylor got from the kitchen to the living room, Connor was jumping up and down, with his little hand on the doorknob, waiting to open the door. Shane was halfway up the sidewalk when Connor opened the door and ran out to meet him.

Shane scooped the little boy into his arms and asked, "Why didn't you wait for me to ring the doorbell?"

Connor laughed. "I knowed it was you. I looked out the window."

Shane walked into the house carrying Connor, then leaned in and kissed Taylor. "Hi. I missed you two. Do you realize that two days is a very long time?"

Taylor smiled and replied, "We missed you, too.

And we missed your truck. Connor told me this morning that it's been *forever* since he's had a ride in your truck!"

"Well," Shane chuckled, "we'll just have to fix that later when we go to lunch. But first things first. I need to see how things are going at the castle. Have you had any trouble with dragons?"

"Nope!" the little boy replied confidently. "No dragons in the castle."

"I'll go get a plate of cookies while you boys check out the castle," Taylor grinned. "Then maybe we can relax and catch up a bit."

"I thought I smelled freshly baked chocolate chip cookies when I walked in," Shane chuckled.

After sharing a couple of cookies, Connor climbed onto the sofa with his favorite book and talked Shane into reading it with him. Taylor looked down at her son, snuggled between her and Shane, and felt at peace. *Shane would make a great dad*, she thought. *And Connor adores him.*

They turned the page in the book, and Connor pointed to the big red fire truck.

"That's your fire truck!" Connor exclaimed.

"It sure looks like it, doesn't it?" Shane agreed.

Still pointing to the fire truck, Connor said, "I love you, Shane."

Taylor and Shane looked at each other in surprise before Shane replied. "I love you too, buddy."

Connor suddenly jumped from the couch, oblivious to the bombshell he had just dropped, and asked, "Can

I have a cheeseburger for lunch, Mommy? I'm hungry."

Taylor laughed and shook her head. "Sure, one cheeseburger coming up."

A few minutes later, the trio walked down the sidewalk toward Shane's pickup. Connor was walking between his mom and Shane, holding each of their hands.

"I keep forgetting to ask you something," Taylor began. "When did you get a car seat for your pickup? I just noticed at some point that we weren't shuffling his car seat between vehicles anymore. You never mentioned it."

Shane shrugged. "It just made sense. It makes it easier on everyone."

As Shane was buckling Connor into his car seat, Connor announced, "When I'm bigger, I'm gonna drive Shane's truck."

Taylor raised her eyebrows and smiled. "Don't you think that's up to Shane? He might not want you to drive his truck."

"He'll let me," Connor replied with the confidence of a little boy.

"What makes you so sure?" Taylor asked.

Connor smacked his forehead with his hand and giggled. "He loves me, Mommy. 'Member?"

"Silly me," Taylor laughed. "That must settle it, then."

Taylor looked at Shane and shrugged. He simply grinned in return.

\* \* \*

Later that evening, after Connor had exhausted himself and had been tucked in for the night, Taylor joined Shane on the loveseat. He put his arm around her shoulder and pulled her close. She snuggled in and got comfortable, realizing how much she had missed him.

"I hope Connor didn't shock you with what he said," Taylor said quietly. "I'm not sure where that came from."

Shane turned to look at Taylor. "It came from his heart. Kids are so young and innocent. They say what they feel. They don't have to waste time overanalyzing everything. Life would be a lot less complicated if we all did that."

"I suppose," Taylor replied, looking across the room at a picture she and Zach had taken shortly after he joined the police force. "Life being less complicated would sure be nice."

The two were silent for several minutes, each lost in their thoughts.

Shane reached for Taylor's hand before taking a deep breath. "I'm going to borrow a page from Connor's playbook."

Taylor looked at him in confusion.

"I love you, Taylor," Shane professed. "I've loved you for a few months now, and it's time I told you. I was being honest when I told Connor that I love him. He's a great kid. So, now you both know how I feel about you."

"Oh," Taylor whispered as she gathered her thoughts. "I hope you know I love you, too."

"I do now," Shane smiled.

"But…" Taylor continued.

Shane put his finger on Taylor's lips and said, "No buts. For now, all I need to know is that you love me too." With that, he stood and started for the door. "We'll talk more later."

Taylor followed him to the door, her mind in a fog.

Shane leaned over and kissed her tenderly, then said, "Get some sleep, Taylor. I'll see you tomorrow."

All Taylor could do was nod as Shane walked out the door.

* * *

Even though they saw each other every day, Shane and Taylor didn't continue their discussion from a few days ago. Life was busy at school after Christmas break, so they didn't have much quality time together. That was just fine with Taylor. She was still processing everything and trying to sort out her feelings. Being completely honest, she knew in her heart that she loved Shane. She just wasn't sure she could handle everyday life with a firefighter. She also knew she could never ask him to choose between her and fighting fires. The result was that her mind and her heart were at odds with each other. Maybe it was time to talk to someone with experience in that area.

"Hi, Mary," Taylor greeted Shane's mother on the phone. "I hope I didn't catch you at a bad time."

"Of course not, Taylor," Mary replied. "It's always nice hearing from you. How are you doing?"

"I'm doing fine," Taylor said. "Well, maybe not totally fine. But fine."

"Is there anything I can help you with?" Mary asked.

"I hope so," Taylor replied. "Is tomorrow still your day off?"

"It is," Mary confirmed.

"Would you have time to meet me tomorrow afternoon around three?" Taylor asked. "We could grab coffee, or a smoothie, or something. My treat. I'd like to talk to you about something."

"I'd love to!" Mary gushed. "We've never had one-on-one girl time. It'll be nice."

"How about three o'clock at the little coffee shop over on Division?" Taylor suggested.

"I'll see you there!" Mary replied. "I'm looking forward to it."

After hanging up the call, Taylor sat back and sighed. *I sure hope Mary can give me some advice because I don't have a clue what to do.*

Across town, Shane's mother set her cell phone down on the table and glanced at her husband working at his desk in the corner of the room.

"That was Taylor," Mary explained to her husband.

"She wants to talk to me tomorrow afternoon."

"Did she give you any idea what she wanted to talk about?" Owen asked.

"No," Mary replied. "But I'd bet it has something to do with Shane fighting fires."

"Probably," Owen agreed, walking across the room to his wife. "If so, tread lightly. She's undoubtedly looking for a woman's perspective. Be honest with her, but don't scare her off. We both know they love each other. It's obvious."

"Love can be so hard," Mary said, shaking her head.

Owen bent down and kissed his wife on the cheek. "Yes, love can be hard. But it's worth it. God will help them work it out."

# CHAPTER TEN

Taylor struggled to concentrate during her last class of the day. She knew it wasn't fair to her students – they deserved her undivided attention – but thoughts of her upcoming visit with Mary weighed heavily on her mind. She still wasn't sure she could communicate her concerns about Shane fighting fires. But hopefully, a mother's insight would help.

She pulled into the parking lot at the coffee shop and took a deep breath before going inside. She found Shane's mother standing off to the side, looking at the menu board.

Taylor walked over and hugged Mary. "I'm glad you could meet me. Let's place our order, then maybe we can find a table in a quiet corner to talk."

After getting their drinks and settling in, Mary began, "So, Taylor, what's on your mind?"

Taylor hesitated a moment before she said, "I'm not sure where to begin. And what's worse is I don't know if I can articulate my feelings and concerns."

Mary placed her hand on Taylor's and said compassionately, "Then just talk to me. Don't worry about the right words."

Still, Taylor hesitated.

"Let me see if I can help you, Taylor," Mary smiled. "I'm going to assume it has something to do with Shane."

Taylor nodded.

"I'm also going to assume," Mary continued, "since you're having a hard time putting things into words, that it probably has to do with Shane's firefighting. Am I right?"

Taylor sighed in relief. "Yes." She then smiled weakly before adding, "You'd never know I teach English for a living."

Mary smiled. "I'm sure you're a wonderful English teacher. You're struggling with a lot of tough emotions right now. It's often hard to put emotions into words. I see that a lot with the seniors I work with at the nursing home. So why don't we start with the easy stuff? It's obvious to the rest of us that you and Shane care deeply for each other."

"I love your son, Mary," Taylor confessed quietly.

"Now that wasn't so hard, was it?" Mary smiled. "I know you do. You know Shane loves you, too, don't you?"

"Yes," Taylor nodded. "He told me a few days ago. After Connor told Shane that he loved him. That kind of took us both by surprise."

"He told us about that," Mary replied, smiling. "Connor is a very sweet little boy."

"How do you do it, Mary?" Taylor asked. "How can you be okay with your son fighting fires? Doesn't it make you worry about him constantly? That has to be exhausting."

Mary thought a moment before replying. "Let me ask you something, Taylor. How did you cope with Zach being a police officer?"

"Not very well, I'm afraid," Taylor smiled. "Maybe it was easier because I knew him in college. We fell in love before he became a police officer. After he joined the force, I did a lot of praying. A *whole lot* of praying! Then I put him into God's hands every day when he walked out the door to go on duty. I didn't know what else to do."

"That's the best thing you *can* do," Mary agreed. "I can't say I've ever reached the point of being okay with Shane fighting fires, but I have to be; it's what he does. I'm a mother – I always want my child to be safe. You know how that is, Taylor, you'd do anything to keep Connor safe. That's easier when they're young, but when they grow up and start making their own decisions, you have to let them go. They need to live their own lives, and you have to trust God to watch over them."

Taylor smiled. "So, what you're telling me is that it never gets any easier."

Mary smiled the knowing smile of a mother with

experience.

"And I just have to accept that," Taylor added.

"Do you know what you'll say when he asks you to marry him?" Mary asked. "Because you know he's eventually going to ask you, right?"

"I know he will," Taylor nodded. "And I have no idea what I'll tell him. But at least now, after talking to you, I don't have any wild notion that I'll wake up some morning and suddenly be okay with it. At least during the school year, he's only a volunteer rather than a full-time firefighter."

"He could just as easily be injured fighting a fire as a volunteer," Mary reminded her honestly. "A fire is a fire. Some of them are easier to fight than others, but the potential for danger is always there."

As the two women stood to leave, Mary hugged Taylor tightly.

"I want you to know that you can talk to me anytime, Taylor," Mary told the younger woman. "Don't ever hesitate, okay?"

"Thanks, Mary," Taylor replied. "I'll remember that."

Taylor hugged Mary again before she got into her car. "Thanks again for meeting me."

"It was my pleasure," Mary smiled. "Next time, you should invite your mother along. It would be great to have some girl time. And, of course, you'd have to bring that sweet Connor. No party would be complete without his perspective."

Taylor laughed. "His entire perspective involves police cars and fire trucks. Oh, and Shane's truck. Did Shane tell you the other day that Connor announced he would be driving Shane's truck when he was bigger?"

"That little boy sure has some big dreams!" Mary laughed.

"He certainly does!" Taylor replied. "I'm sure he'll also talk his grandpa into helping him restore a classic car someday. That boy had better find a good-paying job!"

* * *

As if being a working single mom wasn't busy enough, Taylor's life seemed to get busier by the day. She was beginning to plan for Connor's fourth birthday party, and Zach's parents were due to arrive in town any day. They had sold their condo in New York and purchased another one across town from Taylor. They were driving out ahead of the moving truck, and Taylor wanted to make them feel welcome. So, she had many legitimate reasons to avoid having the firefighter discussion with Shane. She understood the conversation could only be avoided for so long. Eventually, it would have to happen. Luckily, Shane wasn't pushing her, knowing she needed to work through her emotions, and that wasn't something he could help her with.

Taylor had just gotten home after school when her cell phone rang. She quickly hugged Connor and waved at her mom before answering the call.

"Hi, Janet," Taylor greeted Zach's mother. "How's the driving going?"

She was quiet while Janet replied, then said, "You're running ahead of schedule. That's great! What time do you think you'll get to town?"

After several minutes of conversation, Taylor hung up and hugged her son again.

Turning to her mom, she said, "David and Janet will be in town in about an hour. They made good time. Apparently, the moving truck is still a couple of days out, but they have hotel reservations here in town. She said David insists on picking up pizza for everyone for dinner. They'd like you and Dad to come over for pizza."

"We're having pizza for dinner?" Connor asked excitedly.

Stephanie laughed. "It sure sounds like it, Connor. Your Grandpa David and Grandma Janet are going to bring it over. Should we call Grandpa and tell him to come help us eat pizza?"

"Yeah! Me call him, Grandma, please!"

Stephanie pulled up her husband's number on her phone, handed Connor the phone, and had him push the call button.

Kenny answered on the first ring.

"Hi, Grandpa!" Connor yelled into the phone.

"Hey, buddy," Kenny replied. "Does Grandma know you have her phone?"

"Silly Grandpa," Connor giggled. "Grandma gived it to me. You need to come help us eat pizza."

"I do, huh?" Kenny asked, chuckling. "Is your Mommy ordering pizza for dinner?"

"Nope!" the little boy replied. "Grandpa David and Grandma Janet are bringing it."

"Okay," Kenny began, "you tell Grandma and Mommy I'll be right over. I can't let you guys eat all that pizza without me!"

"Hurry, Grandpa!" Connor instructed, then handed the phone back to Stephanie without disconnecting the call.

It wasn't long before everyone was gathered around Taylor's dining room table, enjoying pizza and garlic bread, and hearing about David and Janet's cross-country trek.

"Did you see any bears, Grandpa David?" Connor asked.

David laughed. "As a matter of fact, Connor, we *did* see a few bears when we came across the Rockies."

"Wow!" the wide-eyed little boy responded. "What's a 'Rockie'?"

"They're really big mountains," David explained with a chuckle as Connor had already turned his attention back to the pizza.

After eating his fill of pizza, Connor disappeared into a corner of the living room to play with his toys, and the adults settled in for a visit. Eventually, the conversation got around to Shane and his parents, and

Janet asked how Taylor and Shane were doing.

"We're doing okay," Taylor replied honestly. "But I'm struggling with him being a firefighter."

"As a mother of a first responder," Janet began gently, "it might not be a bad idea to talk to Shane's mother."

Taylor smiled. "That's good advice, Janet. I did talk to her recently, and she gave me some good insight. But it's still not easy."

"Kenny and I have talked to Taylor quite a bit about it, too," Stephanie added. "Having watched her go through everything with Zach, it's a big decision to consider getting involved with another first responder."

"Again, Taylor, we're so very sorry we weren't here to help you when Zach died," David said regretfully. "That wasn't fair of us."

"Taylor," Janet began hesitantly, "I know you haven't asked for my opinion, but would you mind if I provide a little insight?"

"Please," Taylor sighed. "I need all the help I can get right now."

Janet sat back in her seat and began relating a story Taylor had never heard before. "As a mother, as any parent, we were concerned for Zach's safety when he joined the police department. We knew he had gone through the police academy and was properly trained, but that's not necessarily enough to satisfy a parent's concern. We let fear get in the way. Well, mostly my fear, to be honest. So, when Zachary graduated from the police academy, we ran away to New York. I didn't want to be around and be constantly afraid for my son's safety."

Janet took a deep breath and continued her story. "Running away from our fear didn't fix anything. It didn't remove any of the danger from Zachary's job. And it obviously didn't prevent him from being killed. The only thing it accomplished was that it removed us from his life. We missed the last few years of our son's life. We missed the opportunity to get to know you better. And we missed the first nearly four years of our grandson's life. That wasn't fair to Zach, it wasn't fair to you and Connor, and it wasn't fair to us."

With tears in her eyes, Janet continued. "So, Taylor, if I can offer you any advice at all, it would be to not let fear rule your life. If there's a chance for you to find happiness again with Shane, and you love each other, don't let that slip through your fingers because of fear."

Taylor walked over and pulled Janet into her arms as her eyes filled with tears. "Thank you, Janet. Thanks for sharing your story with such heartfelt compassion."

Connor chose that moment to walk up to his mom. He looked up at her and tapped her on the arm.

"Why you cry, Mommy?" the little boy asked.

Taylor smiled and pulled her son into a hug. "I'm okay, Connor."

"You know what always makes my tears better?" Connor asked with a smile.

Taylor grinned as she wiped her eyes. "What makes

your tears better, Connor?"

"Ice cream!"

Kenny stood and said, "The boy's not wrong. Ice cream fixes all kinds of things. Why don't we all go get some ice cream? My treat. It can be dessert after pizza, and a welcome to town for David and Janet."

After enjoying ice cream, David and Janet headed to their hotel while Kenny took his family home. Connor insisted it was Grandma's turn to read him a bedtime story and tuck him in. So, Kenny and Taylor settled in on the sofa.

Kenny pulled his daughter close and said, "Can I make a suggestion, Taylor?"

"Sure, Daddy," Taylor replied.

"I know you're having a tough time accepting Shane's firefighting," Kenny began. "You've talked to me and your mom about it, you've talked to Shane's mom about it, and now you've heard Janet's story. It seems to me you're talking to everyone except the one person you *should* be discussing it with. Talk to Shane, honey. You know your mom and I just want to see you happy. And you're happy when you and Shane are together. Talk to him. After all the advice, the decision will come down to the two of you. You're the only ones who can decide if taking the chance is worth it."

"Thanks, Daddy," Taylor said. Then she grinned and asked, "How did you get so smart?"

Kenny stood as his wife walked back down the hallway from Connor's room. "I'm married to your mother," he grinned. "Her smarts rub off on me."

\* \* \*

At the end of school the next day, Taylor walked down to Shane's classroom. After the last student left, she tapped on the open door.

"Can I come in for a minute?" she asked with a smile.

Shane stood and grinned. "You can come in for however many minutes you want."

He hugged Taylor briefly, then pointed to a desk. "Have a seat and tell me what's on your mind."

Taylor looked down at her folded hands on the desk. "As you might have guessed, I've been dodging our discussion about your firefighting."

"You have?" Shane asked with raised eyebrows. Grinning, he added, "I hadn't noticed."

Taylor smiled and said, "Well, I have been, and that's not fair. Although I appreciate your patience with me more than you know. So, I wanted to make a deal with you."

"Oh? This could be interesting," Shane chuckled.

"I'm in the middle of trying to plan Connor's birthday party," Taylor began. "And Zach's parents arrived in town a few days early, so life has gotten busy. I really need to focus on Connor's birthday party."

"You know I can help you with that, right?" Shane offered.

"I know," Taylor grinned. "I fully intend to take you up on that offer. Anyway, as soon as I can put Connor's birthday party behind me, let's make some time to talk. Daddy said if we want to choose a day, he and Mom will come over to the house and stay with Connor so we can go out to dinner and talk."

"That sounds good to me," Shane agreed. "In the meantime, let me know what I can do to help with Connor's party. Just so you know, I've already picked up a special gift for him. I think he'll like it."

"You could give him an empty box, and he'd be thrilled," Taylor laughed. "As long as he also gets a ride in your pickup, he'll be a happy four-year-old."

"I can make that happen!" Shane happily agreed.

# CHAPTER ELEVEN

With the arrival of Zach's parents back in town, Connor's birthday party quickly became a family event. David immediately put himself in charge of rounding up a bouncy castle for the back yard, which Kenny helped set up. Connor was excited to invite a few of his little friends from church, along with a couple of kids from the neighborhood. Stephanie took on the task of making a special birthday cake, while Janet and Mary helped Taylor put together party favors.

When the big day arrived, Shane pulled up along the curb in front of Taylor's house with a surprise. As Connor and his friends watched from the living room window, a clown (also known as Owen Gallagher), complete with a big red nose and huge floppy shoes, climbed out of Shane's pickup. The clown's big shoes slapped the concrete sidewalk loudly all the way to the front door. Instead of ringing the doorbell, he honked a horn he pulled from his baggy pants. Shane followed the clown carrying a large gift-wrapped box and wearing a huge smile.

Connor ran to meet Shane at the door. "Where did you find a clown, Shane?" Connor asked, giggling.

"At the clown store, of course!" Shane chuckled. "I brought the very best clown they had."

"Thanks, Shane!" Connor exclaimed.

Before long, the pandemonium of a four-year-old's birthday party filled the house and spread into the back yard. There were games, roughhousing in the bouncy castle, gifts, cake, and ice cream. At one point, Connor asked Shane where his daddy was, and Shane explained that he had some work to do and would be over later. Sure enough, not long after the clown had to leave to go to another party, Shane's dad arrived.

"Mr. Owen!" Connor yelled excitedly. "You almost missed my party! We had a clown!"

"You don't say!" Owen exclaimed. "Clowns are the best! Was he a good clown?"

"Yep!" Connor explained. "Shane got the best clown from the clown store!" Shifting gears as quickly as a typical four-year-old, Connor added, "I saved cake and ice cream for you."

Connor took Shane's dad by the hand and led him through the house to the back yard, where the remaining birthday cake and ice cream were on the picnic table.

Owen leaned over and kissed his wife on the cheek and hugged Taylor.

"Your house looks like a war zone!" Owen laughed.

Taylor laughed. "Yeah, that's what the aftermath of half a dozen four-year-olds looks like! Grab a plate with some cake and ice cream and have a seat."

Owen looked around the yard and asked, "Where are the other kids?"

Stephanie smiled and said, "You just missed them. Their parents came to rescue us a few minutes ago and took them home."

"So, you loaded them up with cake and ice cream, then sent them home," Owen nodded. "Good plan. I bet their moms appreciated that!"

Once everyone had a chance to catch their breath and gather what was left of the cake and ice cream, they returned to the house. Suddenly, Connor realized he had *more* presents to open.

"Grandpa," Connor began as he walked toward another pile of gifts. "Are these for me too?"

"Must be," Kenny said, scratching his head. "I don't think there's anyone else around here who has a birthday today."

"Yay!" Connor yelled.

When the remainder of the gifts had been opened, Connor looked around in amazement and said, "Wow!"

Taylor had given her son a large fire truck and some books. Her parents gave him a bike with training wheels. He received a complete set of construction toys from Shane's parents and a racecar set from Zach's parents. Shane had found a large castle for Connor that came equipped with a drawbridge, knights, horses, and dragons.

Once most of the chaos had died down, and Shane and his dad were helping Connor set up his castle, the other adults relaxed to visit for a bit.

"Taylor," David began, "that little racecar set wasn't the only thing we got Connor for his birthday. Since we've already missed enough of his birthdays and Christmases, we wanted to do something a little special. So, we've set up a college fund for Connor, and we'll be contributing to it regularly."

Taylor looked at her parents, then back at Zach's parents.

"You didn't have to do that, David and Janet," Taylor began. "But thank you so much! That will come in handy, and I know when he's older, Connor will appreciate it."

David stood and reached for his wife's hand. "Well, everyone, we're going to head out. Since the moving truck finally arrived yesterday, we have a lot of unpacking to do."

"Let us know if you guys need help," Kenny offered. "Stephanie and I are good at unpacking boxes."

"Shane and I can help if you need it, too," Owen offered. "Just let us know."

"Thanks, everyone," David said. "I'll be sure to let you know once we have a chance to assess the situation. And, Taylor, thanks for letting us be part of Connor's birthday celebration."

"You're family," Taylor smiled. "You two are always

welcome."

Connor jumped up and ran over to David and Janet. "Are you leaving?" he asked.

"Yeah, we need to get home, Connor," David replied. "I hope you had a great birthday."

"I did!" Connor exclaimed. "Thank you, Grandpa David and Grandma Janet."

"We're going to head out too," Owen said. "Happy birthday, Connor."

"Thanks, Mr. Owen and Mrs. Mary," the little boy said. "Too bad you didn't see the clown, Mr. Owen. He was funny!"

Owen patted Connor on the back and chuckled as they headed toward the door.

Soon, only Taylor, her parents, Shane, and Connor were left. Connor talked Shane into playing knights and dragons at the castle. Kenny and Stephanie helped Taylor clean up the last of the party remnants, then settled in to visit in the living room.

"Talk to Shane when you have a minute," Kenny suggested to his daughter. "Decide when you'd like to have a night out to enjoy dinner and talk. Your mom and I will come over to entertain Connor."

"Thanks, Daddy. I will," Taylor replied. "I'll see when he's free and let you know."

* * *

Taylor and Shane were enjoying a rare night out

together, just the two of them. Life had become so busy that even at school, passing each other in the hallways was their only interaction. With Connor's birthday behind them and Zach's parents settling into their new condo, Taylor finally felt she could take a breather. They accepted her parents' offer to watch Connor, allowing the young couple to spend some quality time together. They chose a local Italian restaurant for an early dinner and then planned to walk to a nearby park to find a reasonably quiet place to talk.

Walking hand in hand along the sidewalk, Shane pointed to a gazebo a few yards away. "The gazebo happens to be empty. Do you want to go over there to talk?"

Taylor smiled. "That's a great idea. I love that gazebo."

They leaned against the gazebo railing for several quiet minutes and looked out over the park.

"It's so peaceful here," Taylor sighed. "It almost seems wrong to dig into a serious discussion. But at least the solitude will allow us to think."

She took Shane's hand, led him to one of the benches, and sat beside him.

"So, here we are," Taylor smiled.

Shane looked around and grinned. "Yep, here we are."

"I want you to know how much I appreciate you giving me some time to think," Taylor began. "It would be nice if everything in life were easy, but that's not how it works."

"Not very often," Shane agreed.

He looked into the face of the woman he loved with every fiber of his being and knew he needed to say what was on his mind.

"Taylor," Shane began quietly, "this may not be the ideal way of doing this, but we don't have an ideal situation. So, I'm just going to jump in with both feet." He took a deep breath, then said, "I love you, Taylor, and I can't imagine my life without you. Will you marry me?"

"I love you, too, Shane," Taylor whispered. "But I'm not sure I can live life in a constant state of worry."

"Then don't." Shane rushed to continue, "I don't want you to think I'm taking your concerns lightly, because I'm not. But you can choose not to worry. Or, at least not to worry constantly. Turn it over to God."

Still, Taylor hesitated and was quiet.

"Let me ask you something," Shane began, taking her hand. "If you were to put your fear aside, and not enter that into the equation at all, what would your first response be?"

"I would say yes," Taylor replied. "I love you and would love to marry you."

Shane smiled. "Then the answer is clear. Don't live your life in fear because of what happened to Zach. You know he would want you to move on and be happy. And I'm quite sure you have a little boy who'd like his mommy to be happy too."

Taylor sat quietly, wringing her hands together. Shane didn't press her, knowing this was difficult for her.

"I don't know, Shane," Taylor said quietly. "I just don't know if I'm strong enough to do it again. What if you got hurt fighting a fire? I don't know that I could handle that."

"I can't make any guarantees, Taylor," Shane began compassionately. "None of us can. You know that. As a first responder, all I can do is rely on my training and the training of my fellow firefighters, along with a certain amount of gut instincts. The rest I have to put in God's hands. It's the only way to retain any sanity at all."

Again, Taylor sat quietly for several moments, deep in thought.

"What do you say, Taylor?" Shane asked several minutes later. "Are you going to trust God with your happiness?"

Shane watched, mesmerized, as a smile slowly took over Taylor's face – a smile that reached her eyes for the first time since he'd known her.

Taylor stood and pulled Shane into her arms. She hugged him tightly, then reached up and kissed him lovingly.

"Yes, Shane," Taylor smiled. "Yes, I'll marry you."

Shane looked into the eyes of his future wife and smiled. He sighed audibly as all the tension melted from his shoulders. Then he kissed her tenderly before reaching into the pocket of his jeans.

Opening a ring box, he pulled out a stunning engagement ring with a large diamond in the center and a smaller diamond on each side.

He slipped the ring onto Taylor's finger, not releasing her hand, and grinned. "You *did* say yes, right?"

Taylor chuckled. "Yes, Shane, I *did* say yes."

She fingered the ring as a grin broke out on her face. She looked at Shane and said, "You know Connor and I are a package deal, right?"

"I wouldn't have it any other way," Shane replied as he sealed the deal with another kiss. Grinning sheepishly, he added, "That's why there's a small diamond on either side of the large one on your ring. One for you…and one for Connor."

Taylor stared at her ring, cherishing the special meaning, then took her fiancé's hand as they started back to the pickup.

* * *

Shane parked his pickup along the curb in front of Taylor's house, then glanced at his fiancée as she checked the time on her cell phone.

"If we hurry," Taylor began, "we'll be able to catch Connor before his bedtime."

"Then let's go!" Shane said, jumping out of his truck and hurrying around to help Taylor.

The moment Stephanie saw her daughter's face when they walked into the house, she gasped and covered her mouth with her hands.

Taylor nodded, then rushed over to hug her mom. Kenny stood, smiling, and shook Shane's hand knowingly.

Suddenly, Connor, engrossed in a battle with dragons, noticed his mom and Shane standing in the living room.

"Shane!" Connor yelled, jumping up from the floor while knocking out a dragon at the same time.

Shane reached out his arms and captured the happy little boy. "I saw you wipe out that dragon when you jumped up. Good job, Connor."

Connor wrapped his arms around Shane's neck and squeezed tightly. "I missed you, Shane."

"How could you miss me, buddy?" Shane asked. "We weren't gone that long."

"You were gone forever!" the little boy insisted.

Taylor stepped up beside Shane, with her hands on her hips, smiling. "What about me?" she asked her son. "Am I chopped liver?"

Connor giggled. "I don't know chopped liver, Mommy." Then he reached for his mom, and she pulled him into her arms.

"Let's go sit on the sofa," Taylor suggested. "Shane and I want to talk to you."

"Grandpa helped me fight dragons, Shane!" Connor exclaimed.

"Did you keep all the dragons out of the castle?" Shane asked, grinning.

"Yep!" Connor answered proudly. "Grandpa is a good dragon fighter."

Kenny laughed with his grandson and proclaimed, "I've been fighting dragons for a long time, Connor."

With her four-year-old son settled on her lap and Shane sitting beside her, Taylor took a deep breath and looked at her parents.

"Connor," Taylor began, "you like it when Shane comes over to visit, don't you?"

"Yep," Connor replied. "I miss him when he isn't here, and I don't get to ride in his truck."

Shane laughed at the honesty of the little boy. "Would you still miss me, even if I didn't have my truck?"

"Silly Shane," Connor giggled. "How could you come see me and Mommy if you didn't have your truck?"

"Good point," Shane laughed in agreement.

"You like Shane, don't you?" Taylor asked her son.

"Yep!" Connor replied enthusiastically. "Shane's the bestest!"

Taylor looked to her father for encouragement. Kenny smiled and nodded.

"Connor," Taylor began, "would you like it if Shane and I got married?"

Connor rubbed his chin like he had seen his grandpa do when he was thinking, and thought a minute before replying.

"Can Shane live here so he doesn't have to go

home?" Connor asked, trying to get all his facts straight.

"Would you like it if I lived here with you and your mommy?" Shane asked.

"Yep," Connor replied. "Then you can play with my toys whenever you want to."

"Thanks, buddy," Shane smiled. "I'd like that a lot."

Taylor nodded at Shane, who looked at the little boy and smiled.

"Would it be okay if I were your new daddy?" Shane asked carefully.

Connor looked at Shane, then looked over at his grandma and grandpa.

"My daddy died," Connor said sadly as he was working through the process. "So, I don't have a daddy."

"I know," Shane replied compassionately. "And I would never try to replace your daddy."

"So…you could be my new daddy…then I'd have a daddy like all my friends?" Connor asked, trying to understand.

"That's right," Shane agreed. "I would be your daddy, and we could do all the things your friends do with their daddies."

"My friends' daddies can't drive a fire truck," Connor said, smiling. "But you can."

Shane chuckled. "That's right. So, Connor, will you let me be your daddy?"

Connor smiled as he climbed onto Shane's lap. "Yep. You can be my Daddy Shane."

Shane hugged the little boy tightly and said, "I

would love to be your Daddy Shane."

Connor climbed from Shane's lap and took him by the hand to lead him across the room. "That's good, 'cause you have to know lots of stuff. You have to know how to work the siren on my police car – it's different from your fire truck – how to fight dragons...race cars with me...build a garage for my cars...help Grandpa work on his 'stored cars...feed ducks at the park..."

"That *does* sound like a big job!" Shane laughed. "I'd better get started!"

"Yep," Connor agreed knowingly. "Lots of 'portant stuff."

# CHAPTER TWELVE

Over the next several days, Shane and Taylor shared the news of their engagement with their families and friends. Everyone was genuinely excited and happy for the newly engaged couple. Shane's mother immediately offered to help Stephanie and Taylor with wedding plans. Kenny and Owen wisely chose to stay out of the planning, opting instead to 'simply keep their wallets open.' Taylor was hesitant to inform Zach's parents about her engagement, but she was pleasantly surprised to find her fears unfounded. David and Janet were thrilled for the young couple and offered to treat Taylor, Shane, and their families to dinner at a popular local steakhouse.

As everyone settled in at the restaurant after placing their dinner orders, David tapped a fork on his water glass to get people's attention.

"First of all," David began, "I want to thank you for allowing Janet and me to host this dinner. Taylor and Shane, we wish nothing but the best for you, and sincerely pray you have a long and happy life together."

David seemed to struggle a bit with his emotions before continuing.

"The past couple of years haven't been easy for many of us," David continued. "But we're both thrilled to be back in your lives – and the life of our precious grandson. We've had a wonderful time getting to know Shane and his parents. Owen and Mary, you have a son you can be proud of. He appears to be an amazing young man."

Owen nodded in acknowledgment.

David looked across the table at Taylor and Shane and smiled.

"Taylor," David began quietly, "you'll soon be gaining a new set of in-laws. So, Janet and I will pass the torch over to Owen and Mary. Hopefully, they'll get off to a better start than we did."

Taylor smiled as she watched David take his wife's hand in his.

"What's this 'passing the torch' nonsense?" Taylor asked, grinning. "You two aren't getting off that easily. David and Janet, you will always be my father and mother-in-law."

Looking at Shane's parents, Taylor continued. "How lucky can I possibly be to have *two* sets of in-laws? Mary and Owen are joining the family as my new mother and father-in-law, but they aren't replacing David and Janet. Shane's the math teacher in the family, so correct me if I'm wrong, but one set of in-laws plus one set of in-laws equals *two* sets of in-laws. Correct?"

"I believe you're right, honey," Shane grinned.

"Well, there you have it, then," Taylor stated emphatically. "I'm the luckiest girl around. I have one set of fantastic, and irreplaceable parents. And I also have two sets of wonderful in-laws. And Connor has *six* grandparents! What a lucky little boy he is!"

Upon hearing his name, Connor looked up from the paper he was coloring and asked, "What do I have, Mommy?"

"You have six grandparents," Taylor explained. "Isn't that great?"

"Six?" Connor asked in confusion.

Pointing around the table, Taylor explained. "You have Grandpa and Grandma. Then you have Grandpa David and Grandma Janet. And now, after Shane and I get married, you'll also have Grandpa Owen and Grandma Mary."

Connor looked confused for a moment, rubbing his chin. "So, Mr. Owen and Mrs. Mary will be Grandpa Owen and Grandma Mary?"

"That's right," Owen nodded to his future grandson. "Is that okay with you, Connor?"

"Can I call you Grandpa Owen now?" Connor asked.

"You can, if you want to," Owen smiled.

"Six grandmas and grandpas, huh?" Connor asked to confirm. "I'm okay with that."

Then the little boy went back to coloring his picture.

He suddenly looked up, crayon in his hand, and stated, "But Mommy gets this picture. I can't color *six* pictures!"

* * *

Shane wanted to stop by the fire station to inform Chief Hart about the engagement in person. Over the years, Doug had become one of Shane's closest friends and had gone out of his way to welcome Taylor and Connor at the station. He always enjoyed the youthful energy the little boy brought into the building and sensed something special about Connor.

Connor loved visiting the fire station with Shane and quickly became friends with many of the firefighters. By the time Shane parked his pickup alongside the building, the four-year-old honorary fireman was bouncing in his car seat with excitement.

"Hurry, Daddy Shane!" Connor exclaimed as he tried to unbuckle the seat belt on his car seat. "Come on, Mommy!"

Although Connor preferred to roam freely around the station, he knew to stick close to either Shane or his mom because of the possibility of moving vehicles. Holding Shane's hand tightly, the little boy practically dragged him into the fire station.

Chief Hart was talking to one of the firefighters when Connor hurried Shane and his mom into the station.

"Hi, Chief! Hi, Cody!" Connor greeted the two men loudly like they were his best friends.

"Hey, Connor!" Cody replied, reaching out his arms for the little boy. "What have you been up to, buddy? We haven't seen you in a few days."

"We been busy getting 'gaged," Connor explained.

"Getting 'gaged?" Chief Hart asked in confusion.

"Yep!" Connor replied happily. "Shane is going to be my Daddy Shane!"

Taylor chuckled as she squeezed Shane's hand. "It's a good thing you didn't want to tell Doug yourself."

"It's more fun to watch Connor make the announcement," Shane whispered.

"You don't say!" Chief Hart exclaimed.

He walked over to Shane and Taylor and shook Shane's hand before hugging Taylor.

"Well, that certainly *is* news!" the chief grinned. "When did that all happen?"

"A few days ago," Shane smiled.

"Congratulations, Shane and Taylor!" Cody said as he gave them both a hug. "You're a lucky lady, Taylor. You're getting a great guy."

"I'm the lucky one," Shane chuckled. "I'm getting a package deal!" Pointing to the little boy already inspecting the closest fire truck, Shane added, "And they're both cute!"

Chief Hart and Cody chuckled and nodded in agreement.

"When are you tying the knot?" Cody asked.

Shane looked to Taylor for a reply. She smiled and shrugged.

"We haven't talked about a date yet," Shane said. "We have plenty of time. We're both going to be pretty busy for the next few weeks as the school year winds down."

"Hey, Cody," Connor began, tugging on the firefighter's hand. "Can you take me for a ride in your fire truck?"

"Not now, buddy," Cody explained. "I was just about to pull the small truck out to wash it."

"Oh," Connor replied sadly.

"But, you know," Cody smiled, "I could sure use some help washing it if you're going to be here for a few minutes."

The little boy instantly perked up at the possibility. "Daddy Shane, can I help Cody wash the little fire truck?"

"Sure," Shane chuckled. "Your mom and I will just visit with the chief for a few minutes."

"Yay!" Connor exclaimed. "Talk real slow. We have to wash the whole truck."

Chief Hart laughed as he pulled a pint-sized fireman's coat from a peg near his office.

"Here, Cody," the chief said, handing the coat to his fireman. "Connor can wear this, so he doesn't get his clothes wet. And grab a pair of those little boots from the closet for him. They should fit him okay."

Cody helped Connor pull on the yellow waterproof

coat and boots as the little boy beamed proudly.

"Look, Mommy, I'm a real fireman!"

The little boy took hold of Chief Hart's hand and waited for Cody to pull the small truck out of the garage. Once it was safely parked alongside the building at the wash station, the fireman came and retrieved his little assistant.

"Ready for your first job, Connor?" Cody asked.

"Yep! We'll make the fire truck shine!"

* * *

The school year was sprinting toward the finish line as students wrapped up projects and studied for final exams. The end of the school year was busy for students and faculty alike, but the graduating seniors were extra busy. They not only had to finish all their projects and exams, but they also needed to plan their graduation program, coordinate picking up caps and gowns, and handle seemingly a million other little details.

Shane and Taylor were sitting with Sue at one of the tables in the cafeteria, enjoying lunch. Sue was trying to help them narrow down a timeframe for getting married. They all knew this summer was out of the question – it was too soon for proper planning. The next logical choice seemed to be during Christmas break. They were mulling over that possibility when one of the graduating seniors approached their table.

"Hey, Mr. Gallagher. Hi, Mrs. Wilson, Mrs. Jensen,"

Scott greeted the teachers. "Would I be bothering you if I asked you a couple of questions? I don't want to interrupt."

"Not at all, Scott," Taylor replied, smiling. "Have a seat."

Scott sat across the table from Shane and Taylor.

"I don't think I've had a chance to congratulate you guys on your engagement," Scott began. "That's pretty cool. Do you know when you're getting married?"

Taylor grinned. "We're still working on that, but we've got plenty of time."

"But not before graduation, right?" Scott asked anxiously. "You'll be here for graduation, won't you?"

Shane chuckled. "We'll be here, Scott. I'm told a lot of planning is involved in a wedding."

"Yeah, I bet!" Scott laughed.

Turning to Taylor, Scott began, "As president of the senior class, I was unanimously chosen – meaning I missed that meeting – to find a faculty speaker for graduation."

"Some things never change," Taylor laughed. "That's how people were nominated when I was in high school, too."

Scott grinned. "I think it's a pretty universal principle. It never pays to miss a meeting! Anyway, Mrs. Wilson, I was wondering if you'd be our graduation speaker?"

"Me?" Taylor asked. "Are you sure? I've only been a teacher here for a year. I'm sure there are better choices."

"We're sure," Scott stated emphatically. "As soon as I mentioned you as a possibility, the entire class agreed. What do you say? Please say yes."

Taylor smiled. "I'm flattered, Scott. Yes, I'd be honored to speak at your graduation. Is there a particular topic I need to address?"

"Whatever you want, Mrs. Wilson," Scott said as he stood. "Thanks! You'll be awesome!"

"That was a surprise," Taylor said after Scott walked away to join some friends.

"That's why I stick to math and science," Shane laughed. "No one wants a math and science teacher to be a speaker. They always want the English teachers. You know, the people who can string two sentences together and have it make sense."

Taylor picked up her lunch tray and stood, smiling. "Is this the type of humor I can look forward to when we get married?"

"Probably," Shane laughed. "But I may get some new material from Connor."

"Oh, lucky me!" Taylor replied, stacking her lunch tray on top of Shane's. "In that case, you get to empty my tray along with yours."

Shane picked up their trays, added Sue's tray to the stack, and laughed all the way to the trash bin.

* * *

Taylor survived the first year back teaching after taking a year off and made lots of new friends at Mountainview Christian. Graduation was over, and the seniors were embarking on their new adventures, while she hoped to settle in for a relaxing summer break. As he did every year, Shane took a few days off to decompress before heading back to the fire department as a full-time firefighter. And Connor was thrilled to have his mommy home with him every day. He wasn't nearly as thrilled to find out he wouldn't be seeing as much of Shane as he did during the school year. Shane would be spending some long days at the station, but he made a point to spend time with Taylor and Connor when he had a couple of days off.

Chief Hart told Taylor that she and Connor were welcome to stop by the station occasionally to say hi to everyone. When she initially hesitated, he laughed and assured her that most of the time they were sitting around playing cards and waiting for the fire alarm to go off. The chief also subtly hinted that they wouldn't object if she brought pizza once in a while to save them from the firemen's less-than-stellar cooking skills.

About three weeks into the summer break, Connor was having severe Shane withdrawals.

"Mommy," Connor began as he climbed onto Taylor's lap. "I miss Daddy Shane. Can we take the guys pizza? The chief said we could."

Taylor hugged her little boy and smiled. "Do you think everybody would like that?"

"Yeah!" Connor exclaimed excitedly.

"Okay," Taylor agreed. "Let me text Shane and make sure they're not out on a fire, then we'll take them some pizza."

Within an hour, Shane and Cody met Taylor and Connor in the parking lot to help carry in pizza.

Grabbing two of the pizza boxes, Cody shook his head and laughed. "Boy, Gallagher, you'd better take care of those two. There aren't many people who stop by with pizza for the whole crew!"

"What can I say, Cody?" Shane chuckled. "I have good taste."

With a small bag in one hand, Connor reached for Cody's hand and whispered, "We brought garlic bread, too."

"No way," Cody whispered. "Good job, buddy!"

After everyone ate their fill of pizza and garlic bread, they sat around swapping stories. Since this station only had two female firefighters, neither of whom was currently on duty, the firefighters took advantage of getting a woman's perspective on various issues. And, of course, Connor chimed in with the wisdom of a four-year-old. The guys were beginning to gather the remnants of lunch and put the leftover pizza in the refrigerator when the screeching sound of the fire alarm blared throughout the station.

As firefighters rushed to don their gear, the dispatcher poked his head out the office door and shouted, "It's going to take the entire crew. A house fire over on Lincoln."

Shane kissed Taylor quickly and then ran to his truck. Within seconds, the fire engines left the station with lights flashing and sirens blaring and sped down the road.

Taylor looked around the now-empty garage as she held Connor tightly in her arms. The only other person remaining was the dispatcher, relaying instructions over the radio.

As Taylor slowly walked toward the parking lot, a little boy whispered, "Be safe, guys."

# Chapter Thirteen

The main portion of the single-story house was fully engulfed in flames when several fire engines filled the streets. Firefighters sprang into action immediately as water shot through the air to extinguish the flames. Police cars blocked both ends of the street to keep traffic out of the area. Chief Hart remained busy coordinating his crews while firefighters quickly dragged hoses from the trucks. The fire started rapidly and gained a strong foothold, making it more difficult to control than anticipated, but the firefighters persevered.

A man, a woman, and two young children stood on the sidewalk several feet away. The woman was trying unsuccessfully to calm her children, who were screaming hysterically.

A police officer hurried over to the family and asked if everyone was accounted for and out of the house.

"Yes," the distraught man replied. "We all made it out, thank God!"

Suddenly, the little girl began screaming. "Toby! Daddy, Toby's still in the house!"

"Is Toby another child?" the officer asked with concern.

"No," the woman replied with tears streaming down her face. "He's their eight-week-old golden retriever."

Manning a fire hose with Cody nearby, Shane overheard the conversation.

"Can you handle the hose alone?" Shane asked, already releasing it to his partner. "I'm going in after the puppy."

Shane made a mad dash toward the burning house, adjusting his face mask as he ran. He quickly disappeared into the flames and smoke and began a frantic search for the little puppy.

Chief Hart ran over to Cody and asked, "What's Gallagher doing?"

Cody shook his head and replied, "He went in to see if he could find the puppy."

Chief Hart immediately got on the bullhorn and started relaying instructions.

"Keep the water going! We've got a man in the building! Don't let the flames get ahead of you!"

Inside the smoke-filled structure, Shane worked quickly and methodically as he searched for the puppy. After several minutes, he located the terrified animal huddled in a corner. He grabbed the puppy and tucked him inside his coat to protect the little guy from as much smoke as possible.

From the front yard, the firefighters suddenly heard the unmistakable creaking of timbers seconds before an entire section of the roof collapsed.

Without a second thought, Cody handed off his fire hose and rushed into the still-burning building, followed by two other firefighters. As he searched for his friend, he was knocked to the ground by a falling timber. He pushed it aside and scrambled to his feet.

Looking toward what appeared to be the living room, his heart sank as he noticed a leg protruding from underneath a pile of rubble. He signaled to the other firefighters, who were at his side instantly. With flames swirling around them and smoke filling the air, they began pulling timbers and debris off their friend. They tugged him free, then two men grabbed his upper body while the third took hold of his legs. They dodged falling timbers as they worked their way to the front of the building and out the door.

An ambulance was waiting on the street, and EMTs were ready with a gurney for the downed fireman. As Shane was loaded onto the gurney, Cody heard a whimper and noticed a slight movement in the front of Shane's turnout coat. He lifted the opening of the coat and found the frightened puppy tucked safely inside. He retrieved the small animal and tucked it inside his turnout coat before placing his hand on his friend's chest as the EMTs loaded the gurney into the ambulance.

Cody turned around to find Chief Hart standing

directly behind him.

"How is he?" the concerned chief asked.

Cody shook his head sadly. "I don't know, Chief. All I can say is he was breathing."

"That's a start," the chief said, bowing his head in a heartfelt silent prayer. "I see he found the puppy. Let's go give him to those kids over there. After the day they've had, they're going to need some good news."

By the time Chief Hart and Cody walked across the front lawn toward the sidewalk, most of the flames engulfing the house had been extinguished, and the crew was beginning the mop-up duties.

Cody walked over to the family whose lives had just been shattered. He reached into his coat and pulled out a squirming puppy.

"Toby!" two small kids yelled in unison.

"I think this little guy belongs to you," Cody smiled.

As his children reunited with their smoke-covered little friend, their father looked at Chief Hart and Cody.

"Is the firefighter going to be okay?" the concerned man asked. "That was a brave thing he did."

"We don't know how badly he's injured yet," the chief replied. "He was trapped under the collapsed roof. Hopefully, he'll be okay."

A police officer walked over to get some information from the family. He patted the chief on the back and said, "I'll be praying for your firefighter, Doug. Which man was it?"

"Shane Gallagher," Chief Hart replied somberly.

"I'd better head up to the hospital to see what I can find out."

* * *

Owen Gallagher looked at the caller ID on his cell phone and wrinkled his brow in concern.

"Hey, Chief," Owen greeted as he answered the call. "What's up?"

Owen listened to the chief for a couple of minutes as his wife walked over and stood beside him.

"What's going on, Owen?" Mary asked her husband anxiously.

"Okay, Doug," Owen began, taking his wife's hand. "I'll call Taylor, then we'll head up."

"What's wrong?" Mary asked the moment her husband disconnected the call. "Shane got hurt, didn't he?"

"He was injured in a house fire this afternoon," Owen told his wife as he pulled her into his arms. "We don't know anything yet. We need to call Taylor, then head up to the hospital."

After talking to Taylor and offering to swing by to pick her up, Owen and Mary headed directly to the hospital. Taylor's parents had been at her house and would take her to the hospital.

Twenty minutes later, Shane's parents, along with Taylor, her parents, and Connor, met Chief Hart and Cody in the emergency room. The chief immediately pulled Taylor into a fatherly hug without saying a word. After subdued greetings, they settled in to wait for word from the doctor while the chief filled them in on what little he knew. After getting the chief's brief update, Taylor walked over to the corner of the waiting room and stared out the window. She brushed away anyone who tried to comfort her, needing desperately to be alone with her thoughts.

About an hour later, the doctor entered the waiting room and greeted the fire chief by name. "Doug," the doctor greeted as he shook hands with the chief and looked around. "Are Shane's parents here?"

"I'm Owen Gallagher, Shane's dad," Owen replied, shaking the doctor's hand. "This is my wife, Mary." Pointing to the others, Owen added, "This is Taylor Wilson, Shane's fiancée, her son Connor, and her parents, Kenny and Stephanie Matthews."

"Okay," the doctor began, "why don't we all have a seat, and I can fill you in."

As they settled in, the doctor continued. "First of all, Shane's a very lucky man. His guardian angels must have been working overtime. The outcome could have been so much worse."

There was a collective sigh of guarded relief among those in the room.

The doctor continued. "After talking to Cody, who was the first one to get to Shane and helped pull the debris off, when the roof collapsed, a couple of the large beams apparently jammed together and protected him to a certain extent. And quite likely saved his life. He's currently in surgery to put a couple of pins and screws in the broken bone of his upper left arm. He has several broken ribs, some minor internal injuries, and what I believe is a mild concussion. I think he's going to recover just fine, but it's going to take some time. He'll be in the hospital for at least a few days as we monitor his head injury. Do you have any questions?"

"Can we see him when he gets out of surgery?" Owen asked.

"Sure," the doctor replied. "Once he's out of recovery and taken to a room, I'll have the nurse let you know, and you can go back to see him. Any other questions?"

"I got a question," Connor said quietly, raising his hand.

Everyone had nearly forgotten the little boy who had been sitting patiently in his grandpa's lap.

The compassionate doctor walked over and knelt in front of the little boy. "What's your question, little man?"

"Do you like firemen?" Connor asked.

"Yes, I do," the doctor replied with a grin.

"Good," Connor said quietly. "My Daddy Shane is a fireman. You take good care of him, 'kay?"

The doctor patted Connor on the knee and smiled. "I promise, I'll take good care of him, okay?"

"Okay," Connor replied quietly. "Thank you."

Walking away with tears in his eyes, the doctor sent

up another silent prayer of healing for the toddler's "Daddy Shane."

* * *

It was approaching dinnertime and the end of a very long afternoon, when the nurse finally came to take them back to see Shane. She cautioned them not to stay too long, then left them alone.

Mary and Owen walked up to one side of Shane's bed, and Taylor went to the opposite side. Taylor's parents stood back a ways with Chief Hart and Cody while Kenny held his grandson. Mary pushed the hair back from her son's forehead just as his eyes began to flutter.

"Mom?" Shane rasped quietly. "What are you doing here?"

"A better question, son," Mary began, holding back tears, "would be, what are *you* doing here?"

Shane didn't try to move his head, which for some reason hurt like he'd been kicked by a mule, but his eyes began searching the room.

"Where are we?" he asked, confused.

"We're at the hospital, son," Owen explained.

"What happened?" Shane asked groggily.

"You were injured in a house fire this afternoon," his father explained. "You got beat up a bit."

Shane was quiet for a few moments as he searched his memory through his pounding head. "Oh, yeah. That could explain the headache. Is the chief here? He's going to kill me."

Chief Hart walked closer to the bed where Shane could see him. "I'm right here, Shane." Then he chuckled before asking, "Why do you think I'd be planning to kill you?"

"Because I ran into the house to find the puppy," Shane said quietly.

"Well, it may not have been one of your smarter moves," Doug grinned. "But I wouldn't expect anything less from you. I would have done the same thing."

"Did someone get the puppy back to the kids?" Shane asked.

"Yeah," Cody answered from the back of the room. "I rescued him from your turnout coat before they loaded you into the ambulance."

"Thanks, bro," Shane replied quietly.

Chief Hart added, "It made them pretty happy. I'm sure getting their puppy back safe and sound is going to be one of the only bright spots in the day for them."

Connor was impatiently bouncing in his grandpa's arms, waiting for a chance to speak, then blurted out, "You ran into the fire to save a puppy, Daddy Shane?"

Shane glanced toward the sound of Connor's voice at the foot of his bed. "Hey, there's my favorite little guy. Where's your mommy?"

Taylor reached out and put her hand on his. "I'm right here, Shane."

"I'm sorry, Taylor," Shane said honestly, searching

her eyes for some sign of what she might be thinking.

"Me too," Taylor replied quietly.

\* \* \*

Shane had been in the hospital for several days while Taylor stayed away and grappled with her emotions. Her absence bothered Shane immensely, but he realized he could do nothing about it until he was released and could speak to her in person. In the meantime, his parents and Taylor's parents stopped by to visit and check on his progress. The chief and Cody also stopped by every day to see him.

After nearly a week in the hospital, Shane was finally scheduled to be released. His parents were going to take him home with them so they could keep an eye on him for a few days. As he was gathering his things, waiting for the doctor to sign his release papers, he looked up to see some visitors standing in the doorway. He didn't recognize the man, woman, and two small children.

Shane looked back at his father, who shrugged, then turned toward the people in the doorway.

"Hi," Shane said with uncertainty. "Can I help you?"

The man glanced at his wife, then back at Shane. "You probably don't remember us. But our house was the one that burned several days ago."

"Oh!" Shane replied. "Come in. You don't have to stand in the hallway. I'm sorry about your house. House fires are devastating for everyone involved."

The man nodded. "Houses can be replaced. That's why we have insurance. I'm just glad the family got out okay."

"Me too," Shane nodded. He then grinned and added honestly, "My mind is still a little foggy about that day. It seems I got knocked in the head."

"I know," the man replied. "You ran into our burning house to save my kids' puppy. You got injured because of what you did. It's not much, but the kids made you a little something."

The man nudged his children forward, and they reached out to hand Shane a homemade card.

"My brother and I made you this get-well card," the little girl began shyly.

Shane accepted the card from the girl who looked to be about six or seven years old. Her brother was maybe five, a little older than Connor. He carefully sat in a nearby chair, favoring his rib cage and his left arm, which was in a cast after surgery.

After catching his breath, he opened the card. The kids had drawn a picture of a house with flames shooting from the roof. Off to the side was a red fire truck with a ladder reaching toward the house. In front of the house, they had drawn a small yellow puppy. Written in crayon at the bottom of the picture were the words "Thank you for saving Toby! Get well!"

"Thank you so much," Shane said sincerely. "This picture is great. I hope Toby is doing okay."

"He's doing just fine," the kids' mother replied. "He's adapting to my sister's dogs. We're staying with her and her family for a while."

"That's good to hear," Shane replied. "If you stop by the fire station someday and ask for Chief Hart, he'll have something for the kids. Tell him Shane sent you."

About that time, the doctor appeared in the doorway with Shane's release papers.

"We'll leave you alone now," the kids' father said, ushering the children toward the door. "Thanks again for everything. I hope you heal quickly."

"I probably won't be fighting fires next week," Shane replied honestly. "But I'm sure I'll be good as new before long. Thanks for stopping by. I love the card. You kids give Toby an extra special hug from Fireman Shane, okay?"

"We will, Fireman Shane," the little girl smiled. "Thanks!"

As soon as the family left, the doctor handed Shane some papers. "Here are your discharge instructions, Shane. Remember to take it easy and give your ribs and insides a chance to heal. You'll probably still have a killer headache for a few days, so don't push yourself. It wouldn't hurt for you to stay with your parents for a couple of days."

"I don't plan to let him out of my sight for the next week at least," Mary stated emphatically.

Shane chuckled. "Gotta love over-protective mothers."

The doctor grinned. "I firmly believe mothers and their prayers are the only reason most of us guys make it to middle age!"

# Chapter Fourteen

Taylor had managed to dodge Shane's phone calls while he was recuperating in the hospital. She justified her actions by telling herself he needed to rest, not talk to her on the phone. Therefore, she always responded with a short text instead of picking up his calls. Now that he was out of the hospital, she didn't think she could postpone talking to him any longer. It didn't help that Connor constantly bombarded her with requests to see Shane. However, she needed time to think without having her emotions pulled in a hundred different directions.

Connor climbed onto the sofa and snuggled against his mom, who had an open book on her lap.

"Busy, Mommy?" the little boy asked, looking up at his mom.

Taylor closed the book she wasn't reading anyway and put it on the end table.

"I'm never too busy for you, Connor," she replied

with a hug. "What's on your mind?"

"You're sad because Daddy Shane got hurt in the fire, huh?" he asked with wisdom beyond his years.

"Yes, I am," she replied honestly. "I would never want Shane to get hurt."

"But, Mommy," Connor began, "sometimes firemen get hurt. Just like policemen sometimes get hurt. They have hard jobs keeping people safe."

"I know," Taylor whispered.

"But, Mommy," the little boy persisted, "don't they need more love when they get hurt? You always give me more love when I get hurt."

Taylor released the breath she didn't realize she was holding and pulled her son onto her lap. She hugged him tightly as a smile finally found her face once again.

"You're a pretty smart little boy," Taylor told her son. "How did you get so smart for being so little?"

Connor smiled. "Grandpa said chocolate chip cookies make us smart."

"He did, huh?" Taylor laughed. "Well, if Grandpa said it, it must be true."

"Mommy, can we go see Daddy Shane?" Connor asked. "I think more love will make him feel better."

Taylor picked up her cell phone and turned it over in her hand a couple of times before finally pulling up Shane's number.

She handed the phone to her son and said, "Push right there, and you can call Shane. Ask him if he's up to having visitors."

Shane answered on the first ring. "Taylor?"

"It's me, Daddy Shane! Connor, remember?"

"Of course, I remember!" Shane replied. "How are you doing, buddy?"

"I miss you," Connor replied sadly. "Can me and Mommy come see you?"

Shane sighed in relief before answering. "I'd love to have you and your mommy come see me. Nothing would make me happier."

"Maybe a chocolate chip cookie?" Connor laughed.

"A chocolate chip cookie would make me happy," Shane chuckled. "But seeing you and your mommy would make me happier."

"I'll bring you a cookie anyway. Can't be too happy!"

"Thanks, Connor," Shane chuckled. "You're pretty smart."

"I know," Connor replied modestly. "Grandpa said it's the cookies."

* * *

Taylor parked her car along the curb in front of Owen and Mary's house, knowing Shane was spending a few days with his parents. She made no move to unbuckle Connor's seat belt. The little boy sat quietly for a few minutes before speaking up timidly.

"Mommy, I think we have to go in to give Daddy Shane his love...and his cookie."

Taylor chuckled and said, "I suppose you're right." She then unbuckled his seat belt, and he immediately scampered from his car seat, waiting for his mom to open the car door.

The moment he escaped the car, Connor ran up the sidewalk and rang the doorbell, jumping up and down as he waited for someone to answer. As soon as Owen opened the door, Connor yelled, "Hi, Grandpa Owen! We brought a chocolate chip cookie and extra love for Daddy Shane."

Owen picked Connor up and asked, "You did, huh? I think he'll enjoy all of it." Before he lowered the boy to the ground, Owen whispered, "Just remember to be careful because he's still hurt, okay?"

"Okay, Grandpa Owen," Connor replied as he walked into the room just as Shane started toward him.

Owen pulled Taylor into a hug as she entered the house. "How are you doing, Taylor?"

"Better, thanks," she replied honestly as Mary stepped up beside her husband.

Without a word, Mary hugged Taylor tightly, then wiped a stray tear from her eye.

Taylor watched her son several feet away as he reached for Shane's right arm.

"Is this arm hurt, Daddy Shane?" Connor asked quietly.

Shane smiled. "No, buddy, that one's good." Then he tapped the cast on his left arm and added, "This one isn't quite as good. But it'll be better before you know it."

"Then you can drive your truck, right?" Connor asked.

"Actually, I can drive my truck now," Shane grinned. "But I'll probably wait a few more days before trying it." Pointing to his mid-section, he added, "Hugging is my biggest problem right now, because of my broken ribs. So I can't give you, or your mom, a hug for a while."

"We'll wait 'til your hugging bones are better," Connor said seriously.

Shane tousled Connor's hair as he looked at Taylor standing a few feet away. She was certainly a sight for sore eyes. *I've sure missed that girl,* Shane thought to himself. *I hope she didn't stop by to give me bad news.*

Shane greeted his fiancée with a smile. "Hi, Taylor."

"Hi, Shane," Taylor replied, smiling warmly. She then walked over, took his right hand in hers, and reached up to kiss him.

Shane sighed audibly in hopeful relief. "It's sure great to see you. I've missed you more than you can imagine. I was beginning to think you were avoiding me."

Taylor smiled apologetically. "I seem to have a history of doing that when things get tough, don't I? I'm working on it."

Shane put his right arm around her and pulled her carefully into a hug before leaning down and kissing her lovingly.

Still standing near the front door watching their son reunite with his fiancée, Owen put his arm around his wife and nodded hopefully.

Taylor patted her son on the shoulder and said, "It took this little guy to point out the error of my ways. He reminded me that I always give him *extra* love when he gets hurt. I wasn't giving you extra love. I was staying away. That was wrong." She then smiled weakly and added, "I also seem to be apologizing to you a lot."

"I knew I loved that boy," Shane smiled. "Why don't we all come in here and have a seat so we can visit?"

Shane sat alone in an easy chair, hoping to avoid accidental bumps to his ribs. Taylor joined his parents on the sofa, and Connor wasted no time climbing onto Owen's lap.

"How long does the doctor think you'll be out of commission?" Taylor asked, watching Shane adjust his left arm so it was in a more comfortable position.

"Probably six to eight weeks," Shane replied. "It'll take that long for the broken bones to heal. Effectively, that keeps me off full-time firefighting for the rest of the summer."

"They're going to miss you down at the station," Taylor acknowledged, trying not to show her relief.

"Maybe. Maybe not," Shane replied cryptically. "The chief proposed an idea when he stopped by yesterday to visit. If I want to, once I feel up to it, I could spend the rest of the summer as the full-time dispatcher."

"But they already have a dispatcher, don't they?" Taylor asked.

"All the firefighters rotate shifts as the dispatcher," Shane explained. "So, if they had a dedicated dispatcher, me, for example, that would free up a firefighter to fill the spot I vacated. It would be a perfect solution. They wouldn't be down a firefighter, nor would they be missing a dispatcher."

"And you'd be okay with just dispatching?" Taylor asked. "It wouldn't make you want to hop on one of the trucks and ride off to a fire?"

"I can't say I wouldn't be tempted," Shane laughed. "But it would keep me involved at the department and would fill a need. So, I'd be helping out. That's what's important to me."

Connor sat on Owen's lap, soaking up the entire conversation. The little boy was deeply interested in anything related to first responders and wanted to learn everything. His fascination with firefighters and police officers often caused Taylor a fair amount of concern, but she reminded herself constantly that he was just a typical little boy.

"Daddy Shane," Connor began slowly, wanting to get the word right, "what's a...a dispatcher?"

"A dispatcher is the person who operates the radio at the fire station," Shane explained. "When a call comes in about a fire or a medical emergency, the dispatcher gathers the information and decides who to send out.

And he keeps in radio contact with the firefighters to give them updates."

"So…you would tell the firemen where to find the fire?" the little boy asked.

"That's right," Shane confirmed.

"But you won't drive a fire truck to the fire?"

"No, the dispatcher stays at the station," Shane explained.

Connor processed this new information for a moment before saying, "But when you aren't hurt anymore, you can drive the fire truck again, right?"

"That would be the plan," Shane chuckled.

"You should be the one to tell them where to find the fire," Connor stated as if that settled the issue. "But only 'til you aren't hurt anymore and can drive the fire truck."

The adults chuckled at the simple logic of a four-year-old boy.

"Daddy Shane," Connor continued, abruptly changing the subject, "are you hungry?"

Shane laughed. "Why, buddy? Are you getting hungry?"

The little boy rubbed his stomach dramatically. "My tummy needs pizza."

Owen laughed, and Taylor shook her head.

"Your tummy *always* needs pizza!" Taylor laughed.

"I think I agree with Connor," Owen smiled as he mimicked Connor by rubbing his stomach. "My tummy might need pizza too."

Mary smiled as she reached for her cell phone. "Well, it sounds like we'd better order some pizza then. We can't have boys sitting around here needing pizza. Taylor, why don't you text your parents and see if they want to come over and join us for pizza?"

"Leave it to my son to start an impromptu pizza party," Taylor laughed as she quickly texted her parents.

While waiting for a reply from Kenny and Stephanie, Shane grinned and said, "Now that Connor woke up my stomach, I think it might need some garlic bread too."

"Yeah, Daddy Shane!" Connor agreed. "We need garlic bread too!"

Taylor's parents accepted the invitation to join the others for pizza, so Mary quickly called in the order. Since they would be out anyway, Kenny offered to pick up the pizza on their way over. Half an hour later, the doorbell rang at Owen and Mary's house.

"I bet that's Grandpa with pizza!" Connor yelled as he ran to the door.

Owen followed the little boy and opened the door to greet Kenny and Stephanie.

"Thanks for picking up the pizza, Kenny," Owen said. "It was probably faster than waiting for delivery, and you have a grandson whose tummy *needs* pizza."

"That boy always needs pizza," Kenny laughed as Connor tugged on his free hand.

"Grandpa," Connor whispered, "be careful with Daddy Shane. His hugging bones are still broke."

"Thanks for reminding us, Connor," Kenny smiled.

Stephanie greeted Shane's mother with a chuckle. "Notice how quickly I become invisible when Grandpa has the pizza?"

"I know what you mean," Mary laughed. "When it comes to pizza or food in general, boys have a one-track mind. And it doesn't seem to matter how old they are!"

Within minutes, everyone gathered around the dining room table and began digging into the pizza. As they enjoyed the food, Taylor's parents got an update from Shane about how his recovery was going.

"I saw the doctor yesterday," Shane informed them. "It's still early in the healing process, but he thinks everything is going to be okay in a few weeks. The headaches will probably hang around for a while, but they seem to be getting a bit better every day."

"That's encouraging news," Stephanie agreed.

"I was just telling Taylor that I might switch to dispatching for the rest of the summer," Shane explained. "Since I'm not going to be ready to fight fires for a while, Chief Hart suggested I take over the dispatching when I'm up to it."

"That might be a good way for you to work back into things slowly as your recovery continues," Kenny acknowledged.

"Yeah," Shane agreed. "It would keep me connected down at the station, and if I can do something to help while I'm recuperating, I want to do it."

By the time they finished eating and had visited for

a while, Taylor could tell Shane was exhausted.

"We should probably get going," Taylor suggested. "It looks like Shane could use some rest."

"Not a bad idea," Shane agreed, standing slowly. "I'm not used to getting tired so quickly."

After helping gather the trash and putting the leftover pizza in the refrigerator, Taylor asked Connor if he wanted to ride home with her or her parents.

"Grandma and Grandpa!" Connor replied.

"Okay, little man, let's go," Kenny said as he put Connor on his shoulders. "Owen and Mary, thanks for inviting us to join you for pizza. Shane, you take care of yourself."

"Thanks, Kenny," Shane replied, "I will. Thanks for stopping by."

Shane followed the others to the door and reached for Taylor's hand when he noticed she had hung back.

"Are we good, Taylor?" he asked quietly.

She reached up and kissed him on the cheek. "Yeah, we're good. I'm still working on turning the worries over to God. It's hard, especially right after you were injured. But I know I'm happier with you in my life than I am without you. So, I've got to get better at letting God handle the big stuff. He's better at it anyway."

Shane smiled. "I love you. Please don't stay away. You and Connor can stop by to visit anytime. I'll probably be here for a few more days anyway. Mom doesn't want me to leave until she's convinced I can drive my pickup without any problem. Dad actually agreed with her on that issue, so she must be onto something." He then laughed, "It's a good thing I didn't break my right arm. I'd have to have Connor shift gears for me."

Taylor laughed. "I'm sure he'd be happy to do that for you. Let me know if you want to hang out at our house sometime. We can pick you up, and I know Connor would be thrilled to have you at the house."

"Even if I can't fight off dragons?" Shane asked, grinning.

"I don't know," Taylor smiled. "With an arm in a cast, that might be just the weapon you need to fight off those pesky dragons."

# CHAPTER FIFTEEN

As soon as Shane felt he could drive his pickup without difficulty, he began working down at the station as the dispatcher. He put in a few shorter days for a while as he regained his strength and stamina. The entire crew was eager for his return and went out of their way to make things comfortable for him. As a joke, some of the guys lined the office chair with pillows to provide extra padding for his broken ribs. Shane laughed when he saw the pile of pillows, then announced he thought he'd probably use every single one of them.

Unbeknownst to Shane, Chief Hart had been conspiring with Taylor to plan a small welcome-back party for the injured firefighter. They gave him time to adjust to his new temporary role before springing the surprise on him.

Shane walked into the station one afternoon and was met with loud cheering and a large welcome-back banner strung from the ceiling.

A little boy, grinning from ear to ear, emerged from the pack of firefighters.

"Did we surprise you, Daddy Shane?" Connor asked excitedly.

"You sure did, buddy!" Shane replied honestly, ruffling the boy's hair. "Did you have something to do with this?"

"Not me!" Connor stated emphatically, holding his arms in the air in surrender. Laughing, he added, "Chief, the guys, and Mommy did it. But I helped pick out the cake."

"Ah," Shane grinned, "so you *were* involved."

"Only a little," Connor laughed.

Shane smiled at Taylor, who was standing beside the chief. He then walked over, kissed her cheek, and took her hand. Together, they strolled to the table along the wall, where he found a cake, ice cream, and a slew of cards.

He grinned at the chief and said, "Well, this is different. A welcome-back party instead of a going-away party. I think I like this better."

Connor joined him along the wall and pointed to the cake. "Do you like the fire truck on the cake, Daddy Shane?"

"I sure do!" Shane replied as he noticed a small yellow puppy on the cake. He looked at Taylor, convinced that it had been her idea.

"The puppy on the cake was the chief's idea," Taylor smiled. "He thought it was appropriate."

"One thing's certain," Shane grinned. "I won't be forgetting *that* puppy anytime soon."

* * *

Shane unlocked the door to his apartment after returning home from his first long shift back at the fire station. He was exhausted. According to the doctor, his recuperation was going well, but he couldn't wait to regain his normal energy. That seemed to be taking a bit longer than he had hoped.

He put the mail on the table and opened the refrigerator door. Shaking his head, he wondered what he could do for dinner when he had no energy to cook. Maybe he'd open a can of soup or fix a sandwich. He had barely talked himself out of both ideas when his phone rang.

Seeing Taylor's name on the caller ID put a smile on his weary face.

"Hey, Taylor," Shane greeted.

Before he could get out another word, Taylor said, "Please tell me you haven't eaten dinner yet."

Shane laughed. "No, I haven't. I just got home and was trying to figure out what to fix."

"Connor and I stopped for Chinese food," Taylor began, "and we're heading your way."

"You're a lifesaver!" Shane said with relief. "Grandma always said the way to a man's heart is through his stomach. How far away are you?"

"Is your parking lot close enough?" Taylor chuckled. "Don't bother coming out to meet us. I'm sure you're exhausted. Just open the door when we get there."

Shane was all smiles when he saw Taylor and Connor walking up the sidewalk with a large take-out bag. He gave Taylor a gentle one-handed hug before kissing her.

"We brought dinner, Daddy Shane!" Connor announced.

"I see that," Shane chuckled. "I'm sure glad you did. Now I don't have to go hungry."

"Silly, Daddy Shane," Connor laughed. "Mommy won't let you be hungry."

They sat down to eat before the food got cold. Shane was partway through his second plate when his phone rang again.

"Hey, Dad," Shane greeted. "What's up?"

"Not much," Owen replied. "Following up on a request from your mother, who seems to think you might starve. Have you eaten dinner yet? We can bring you something."

Shane laughed. "A guy could get used to being spoiled like this. Taylor and Connor brought over Chinese food, so we're eating now. There's plenty if you and Mom want to run over."

"Thanks, son, but we just ate," Owen replied. "I won't keep you since you're eating, but I also wanted to let you know your grandma called this afternoon. It seems she can't take my word for it that you're going to be just fine. She said she needed to see for herself. So, she and your grandpa are flying up tomorrow for a visit."

"All mothers are alike, aren't they?" Shane chuckled.

"Yeah, pretty much," his dad laughed.

"I'm glad they're coming up," Shane began, "it'll be nice to see them. And that will give them a chance to meet Taylor and Connor."

"Yep," Owen said. "Go finish your dinner, son. And tell Taylor and Connor we said hi."

Looking across the table at his fiancée, Shane relayed his dad's message. "Dad and Mom were checking to make sure I wasn't going to starve. They said to tell you both hi. And, it sounds like you're going to be meeting my grandparents. Dad said Grandma doesn't believe him, and she wants to see for herself that I'm recovering from my injuries. So, they're flying up from California tomorrow for a visit."

Before Taylor could reply, Connor asked, "You have a grandma and grandpa?"

"I sure do," Shane answered. "When your mom and I get married, they'll be your *great*-grandparents."

"Wow!" Connor exclaimed. "I'm going to have grandmas and grandpas everywhere!"

Taylor laughed. "You're sure a lucky little boy."

Turning back to Shane, she asked, "I'm just curious. You told me your dad and grandparents were all born in Dublin, but your dad only has a bit of an Irish accent. Do your grandparents still have a noticeable Irish accent?"

"Oh, yeah," Shane chuckled. "Dad left Ireland and moved to the States when he was about twenty, so he's lost much of his original accent. Grandma and Grandpa haven't lived here very long, so I don't think their accents are going anywhere."

"What's accent, Mommy?" Connor asked.

"That's when somebody talks a little differently than we do," Taylor attempted to explain. "Shane's grandma and grandpa spent most of their life living in Ireland, so they talk like people do in Ireland, and it may sound strange to us. If we went somewhere else in the world, the way we talk would sound different to other people."

"Okay," Connor replied, seemingly satisfied with his mother's response. "They hug the same way, right?"

"Yes, they do," Shane smiled. "Hugging is a universal language. Everybody understands a hug. My grandma gives the best hugs. I think you're both going to like her."

"Do you like her, Daddy Shane?" Connor asked, always curious.

"I sure do," Shane replied. "I love my grandma *and* my grandpa. They're great people."

"Then I love them too," Connor decided with an emphatic nod.

\* \* \*

The timing of his grandparents' visit was perfect. Shane

was just going into a four-day-off stretch, so he wouldn't have to juggle work with their visit. Owen picked up his parents from the airport and took them back to the house. Taylor was planning to pick up Shane, and then they would all meet at Owen and Mary's house for lunch.

In typical Connor fashion, by the time Taylor pulled into the driveway at Shane's parents' house, the little boy was tugging at the restraints of his car seat. Even though Shane assured him that his grandparents wouldn't go anywhere without meeting him, Connor couldn't contain his excitement. It was like wrestling a bobcat for Taylor to hold her son's hand until they made it to the front door.

Owen opened the door, and Connor jumped into his arms.

"Hi, Grandpa Owen!" Connor said excitedly as he hugged his grandpa around the neck. "Is your daddy and mommy here?"

"Yes, they are," Owen laughed. "Let's wait until Shane and your mom get inside, then we'll introduce everyone."

Needing no introduction, Shane walked over and kissed his grandma's cheek before shaking his grandpa's hand.

With Connor still in his arms, Owen walked up behind his son.

"Mom, Dad," he laughed. "This bouncing kangaroo here is Connor." Putting his hand on Taylor's shoulder, he added, "And this sweet lady is his mom, Taylor. My dad and mom, Liam and Siobhan Gallagher."

Shane's grandmother smiled warmly as she covered Taylor's hand in hers before patting Connor on the knee. "So, you're the young lady and wee lad who have captured my grandson's heart."

"I certainly hope so," Taylor smiled. "It's nice to meet you both. Shane has told me a lot about you."

Siobhan glanced at Shane and smiled. "You haven't been telling this sweet lass made-up stories, have you?"

"Never, Grandma!" Shane professed. "I only tell 'grandma-approved' stories."

"You're a good lad, Shane," his grandmother proclaimed with a smile.

Standing beside his wife, Liam Gallagher smiled as he pointed out, "See, Siobhan, Owen told you Shane was fine. Why don't we all get comfortable so we can visit?"

Liam led his wife to the sofa, and Connor wasted no time climbing onto Liam's lap like he had known him his entire life. The elderly man didn't bat an eye, simply helped the little boy settle in.

Once everyone was comfortable, Owen looked at his mother and grinned. "Mom, I know how much you love to visit, so I want you to know that you don't have to cram all your visiting into one day. Mary and I have taken a few days off, and Shane has the next four days off. So, we have plenty of time for a nice, long visit."

"So, we have time to get to know Taylor and Connor," Siobhan began, "and still hear about Shane's adventure."

"Daddy Shane saved a puppy from the fire!" Connor exclaimed proudly.

"That's what we understand," Siobhan nodded. "That was a brave thing to do."

"Yep," the little boy agreed. "Firemen are brave, just like policemen."

"I don't know about your grandma, Shane," Liam began, "but I'd love to visit the fire station if that's allowed. Do you think there's a chance we could do that while we're here?"

"Sure," Shane confirmed. "That's not a problem at all. I'm sure Chief Hart and some of the guys would love to meet you."

"Daddy Shane took me for a ride in his big fire truck," Connor announced. "And Cody let me help wash the little fire truck."

"You don't say!" Liam exclaimed with a grin.

"Yep!" Connor nodded. "I'm a fireman just like Daddy Shane. I have a badge and a fireman hat."

"You're pretty little," Liam smiled. "They probably only let you fight little fires, huh?"

Connor shook his head. "I don't get to fight fires. I'm just a little kid. Maybe when I get bigger."

"That makes more sense," Liam agreed, grinning.

The family spent the next hour visiting and getting to know each other. Mary and Owen worked to put together a light lunch for everyone. They were soon gathered around the table to enjoy a selection of sandwiches, salads, and chips while they continued their visit.

As they were finishing lunch, Connor tapped Owen on the hand. "Grandpa Owen, what do I call them?"

"My mom and dad?" Owen asked for clarification.

The little boy nodded.

Owen rubbed his chin in thought. "Well, let's see. You have lots of grandparents, buddy. It would certainly be easy to get them mixed up."

"I know!" Connor said, slapping his forehead dramatically, eliciting a chuckle from Liam and Siobhan.

"What do you call your other grandparents, Connor?" Liam asked.

"Grandma and Grandpa," Connor began. "Grandpa David and Grandma Janet. Grandpa Owen and Grandma Mary…"

When Connor seemed stalled, Taylor helped him out. "That's pretty good, Connor. Then remember my grandparents down in Oregon. You call them Papa and Nana."

"Oh, yeah!" Connor agreed. "Papa and Nana!"

Liam glanced at his wife, then asked, "Would you like to call me Granddad, and Shane's grandma Granny?"

"Hmmm," Connor thought out loud. "Yep. Granddad and Granny. I don't have any of those yet."

* * *

Shane arranged with Chief Hart for the whole family to visit the fire station the next day. They all met in the parking lot, where Connor grabbed Shane's hand to hurry them along.

"Hi, Chief!" Connor announced loudly as he led the group into the station. "We brought Daddy Shane's grandma and grandpa to see the station."

Liam chuckled and whispered to Owen, "That wee lad seems to know his way around."

Owen grinned. "Yeah, he's a favorite down here. Everyone loves him."

Shane introduced his grandparents to the chief and all the firefighters, and then Chief Hart gave them a brief tour of the station. Connor did his part by "explaining" all the fire trucks and pointing out the ones he had ridden in. Liam was intrigued by the differences between firefighting equipment in Ireland and the United States, and was eager to learn the reason behind some of the differences.

Connor took Siobhan by the hand and led her to the small fire truck.

"Granny," Connor began, "this is the little fire truck I helped Cody wash. We did a good job, huh?"

Siobhan had already fallen in love with the little boy. "You sure did! I don't think I've ever seen a fire truck shine quite like this one."

"Chief Hart," Siobhan began, "I'd sure like to sit in one of these fire trucks if that's okay."

"Not a problem, Mrs. Gallagher," the chief replied.

"You just pick which truck you'd like to sit in."

"Mom," Owen grinned. "You're in your eighties. Are you sure you want to climb into a fire truck?"

Siobhan playfully slapped her son on the arm. "Eighty isn't dead, son. Yes, I'm sure. And I want you to take a picture of me in the truck."

Taking her husband's hand, Siobhan said, "Come along, Liam, you're going to sit in the truck too."

Looking around, Siobhan asked, "Where's Connor? He needs to climb up here and sit beside me and Liam."

"I'm right here, Granny!" Connor exclaimed.

Owen helped his mother climb into the fire truck, while the chief assisted Liam. Once they were both settled, Owen passed Connor up to his mom, and he squeezed in between his granddad and granny.

After climbing down, Owen snapped several pictures of his parents and grandson in the fire truck.

Standing beside Shane, smiling, Taylor said, "I'm not sure who looks happier, Connor or your grandparents."

Shane grinned. "The only thing I know for sure is that I'm going to need a copy of those pictures!"

At the end of the visit, Liam walked up to Chief Hart. "Thank you for taking the time to give us a tour, and for humoring my wife about sitting in the truck."

Chief Hart chuckled. "It's been a pleasure." He handed Liam a booklet and added, "Here's a little something for you. It explains the different fire engines and the equipment we use."

"Thank you, Chief," Liam smiled.

Siobhan took the chief's hand and said, "Thank you for letting me sit in the fire truck, Chief Hart. And promise me you'll take good care of my grandson. I know he's a good firefighter, but…"

"I'll do my very best to keep him safe," the chief replied, smiling. "If only I could keep him from running into burning buildings to save puppies."

# CHAPTER SIXTEEN

Shane's grandparents spent several days with the family and dedicated a lot of time to Taylor, Connor, and their family. As Shane expected, they fell in love with Taylor and Connor. He was surprised, however, to see how quickly his grandfather bonded with Taylor's dad. When Kenny mentioned that he restored classic cars, Liam asked if he could see them. So, one afternoon, Kenny picked up Liam and Connor, who insisted he needed to see Grandpa's 'stored cars too, and took them to his garage to see the cars.

"Grandpa, can we take Granddad for a ride?" Connor asked.

"What do you say, Liam?" Kenny grinned. "Shall we go for a ride in the Chevelle?"

"G'wan!" Liam exclaimed.

Kenny laughed. "I'm not up on Irish phrases, but I'm going to take that as a yes."

"Bloody, yes!" the elderly man confirmed.

After driving around town for half an hour, they ended up at Taylor's house, where the rest of the family had gathered, planning to enjoy pizza for dinner later.

The moment they walked in the door, Connor took Liam by the hand and asked, "Wanna see my castle, Granddad?"

"Connor," Taylor reminded her son, "don't monopolize all of Granddad's time. He might want to sit down and visit."

"If the wee lad has a castle," Liam laughed, "then I need to be seeing it!"

Before long, Connor was curled up on the floor next to Shane's eighty-something grandpa and was having the time of his life.

"This is a pretty grand castle you have here, Connor," Liam acknowledged as he inspected the drawbridge. "There are thousands of castles in Ireland, you know. They're quite the sight."

"Thousands?" Connor asked in amazement. "That's a lot!"

"It is, indeed," Liam agreed.

"Mommy said you grew up in Ireland, so your talking might sound funny to us," Connor stated with the bluntness of a four-year-old. "I like the way you talk."

"That's good, Connor," Liam smiled. "I think I'm stuck with the accent now."

"Have you ever seen a *real* castle, Granddad?" the little boy asked.

"Oh, I've seen hundreds of castles," Liam said. "I used to explore castles all the time when I was a wee lad like you."

"Wow!" Connor exclaimed. "I want to see a real castle!"

"Maybe someday you'll visit Ireland," Liam pondered. "Then you'll see castles everywhere."

Still sprawled out on the floor with his granddad, Connor looked across the room at his mom.

"Mommy," he began, "can we go to Ireland to see a castle?"

"Not today, Connor," Taylor laughed.

Connor turned back to Liam and reported, "Not today. Maybe tomorrow."

Liam ruffled the boy's hair and smiled. "Ah, to be a wee lad again with all our tomorrows ahead of us."

\* \* \*

Before anyone was ready for Liam and Siobhan's visit to end, they were gathered at the airport waiting for their flight back to California. Taylor, Connor, and her parents joined Shane and his parents to say goodbye.

Liam and Siobhan hugged everyone in the group before saying their goodbyes. They were extra careful to hug their grandson gently since his ribs were still healing.

"You take care of yourself, Shane," Siobhan admonished with a grin. "Don't make your grandma come back here to pull you off a fire truck."

Shane laughed. "I'll try, Grandma."

"Owen and Mary," Liam began, "thanks for everything. 'Twas great seeing everyone."

Owen hugged his father. "Anytime, Dad. You know we always have a room for you."

"You have a wonderful family, Taylor," Liam stated. "Thank you for welcoming us into your home." He chuckled and added, "Take care of that wee lad. He's a keeper."

"I will," Taylor smiled. "I hope we get to see you both again real soon."

"We'll be back for Christmas or the wedding, whichever comes first," Siobhan smiled.

As the elderly couple walked toward the security checkpoint, Connor waved enthusiastically.

"Bye, Granddad and Granny! I love you!"

Liam and Siobhan turned and waved at the little boy.

"We love you, too, Connor!" Siobhan smiled. "We love you all!"

\* \* \*

By the end of summer, Shane had completed his recuperation and was ready to begin the new school year. He transitioned to a volunteer firefighter role at the fire station and laughed his way through another end-of-summer going-away party. He had no idea that word had gotten around town about his injuries. When he returned to school, his students looked at him as a hero for running into the burning house to rescue a puppy. He did his best to downplay the incident.

A few days into the school year, Shane and Taylor sat at a table in the cafeteria, having lunch with a couple of the other teachers. Two students from his class stopped by and patted him on the back.

"Way to go, Mr. Gallagher!" one of the students said with admiration. "You're the only person I know who's ever run into a burning building."

Shane smiled and said, "No big deal. Just doing my job."

"It's still pretty cool, Mr. G," the second student agreed before the boys wandered off to join their friends.

Shane shook his head and smiled after the students left. "I'll be glad when I'm not a novelty anymore."

"You've got to admit, Shane," Sue said, "rescuing that puppy was an act of bravery." She grinned and added, "The novelty will wear off before long."

"Why don't we discuss something where I'm *not* the center of attention?" Shane laughed. "Help us narrow down a wedding date."

"I can do that," Sue grinned. "Have you two narrowed it down at all yet?"

"Well," Taylor began, "for practical reasons, working around the school schedule, it would make sense to either have it during Christmas break or wait until spring break or next summer."

"Do either of you want to wait until next summer?" Sue asked.

Taylor looked at Shane and smiled. "Not really."

"Then why don't you shoot for Christmas break?" Sue suggested. "That would give you more time off than spring break."

Turning to Shane, Taylor smiled. "According to your grandma, they're coming up for either Christmas or the wedding, whichever comes first. So, we aren't going to want to miss their visit."

"Here's a thought," Shane pondered. "What if we get married right after school gets out for Christmas break? We could stay home for a few days and be here for Christmas with Connor and the family, then leave on the honeymoon shortly after Christmas. That would still give us several days for a honeymoon. Assuming your mom would be willing to watch Connor while we're gone."

Taylor paused for a moment before replying. "I think that could work. We wouldn't miss Christmas with Connor, we'd have time with your grandparents, and we'd still be back in time for school to start back up."

Shane looked at the calendar on his phone and stated, "How does December 20th sound?"

"Perfect!" Taylor smiled.

* * *

Shane found that he had a tougher-than-usual time

transitioning to volunteer status once school started. He spent most of the summer dispatching, so he hadn't fought a fire since the house fire. As a volunteer during the school year, his firefighting would be limited as well. While at the station one afternoon, he overheard Chief Hart take a call about a controlled burn. He hated to admit it, but he felt a bit of an adrenaline rush when he heard about it.

After finishing the phone call, the chief gathered the firefighters to explain the upcoming project.

"There's a large barn just outside of town," Doug began explaining. "It's over on Lancaster Road, and the farmer needs to tear it down. He called to see if we might be able to burn it down for him. It'd be a perfect opportunity for a training exercise. I'll be asking for volunteers from this shift and the next shift. It'd be great if some of you younger firefighters would step up because it would be good experience for you. But, no pressure. Strictly volunteer basis."

Several firefighters immediately volunteered.

"I'm in," Shane declared, raising his hand.

"Are you sure, Gallagher?" Doug asked.

"I'm sure, Chief," Shane replied adamantly. "When will the burn be?"

"After talking to the next shift and getting volunteers," the chief replied, "as long as we have enough firefighters, we'll plan it for Saturday."

Once the firefighters dispersed, Chief Hart walked over to Shane. "You don't have to do this, Shane. We're going to have plenty of volunteers."

"Doug," Shane patted his friend on the back. "It's fine. The first fire after the injury is going to come sooner or later. It may as well be sooner. And what better scenario than a controlled burn? It'll be fine."

"If you're sure," the chief agreed skeptically. "But I don't want you taking any unnecessary chances."

"I won't," Shane assured the chief. "But I've got to get back in there or I'm useless as a firefighter."

By the time Saturday arrived, the volunteer crew was ready, and the younger firefighters were looking forward to the controlled burn. Some of the more experienced firefighters were teaming up with the newer ones to give them support. Cody was one of Shane's closest friends in the department, both with several years of experience, and they partnered up on a lot of fires. Shane was secretly glad Cody had volunteered for this burn, and he admitted to Cody that he was a little nervous about the fire.

"You'll be fine, Gallagher," Cody assured him. "We're a team, remember? I've got your back."

"I know you do," Shane grinned nervously. "Thanks, man."

Once the firefighting equipment was in place, Chief Hart gave some final instructions to the firefighters as the barn's owner stood off to the side. Before long, the fire had been set, and the barn was fully engulfed in flames. The firefighters got to work immediately and did a great job keeping the fire contained to the barn area.

Shane manned a hose, staying well back from the structure as he worked to prevent the flames from spreading into the field. Cody handled another hose not far from Shane. Some of the firefighters entered the burning structure to gain valuable experience working from the inside. Cody watched Shane move closer to the barn several times, but he always backed off. He could tell his friend was being overly cautious as he observed him retreat further away from the blazing structure.

*Why am I backing away from the fire?* Shane asked himself in frustration. *I've been fighting fires for years, and I've never backed away. This is a controlled burn, the absolute best-case scenario.* He shook his head to clear his thoughts. *Get out of your head, Gallagher, and get back in the game!*

Continuing to fight the flames, Cody worked his way closer to Shane. Once he had his friend's attention, he nodded in a questioning gesture to see if he was okay. Shane nodded in return, then began slowly working his way around to the back side of the barn. Suspecting his friend wasn't coping as well as he tried to convince everyone, Cody passed his hose off to another firefighter and headed around the barn. As he rounded the corner of the burning structure, he saw Shane take off his helmet and toss it to the ground in frustration.

Cody walked up behind his friend and put his hand on his back.

"It's going to be okay, Shane," Cody said sympathetically. "Give yourself time."

"I had all summer to recuperate," Shane said, shaking his head in disgust. "I should be ready."

"You gave your body time to recuperate," Cody agreed. "But maybe you haven't given your head time. You were trapped under a collapsed roof in a burning building. That would take a toll mentally on anybody. Give it time. This is your first fire after the accident. A lot of people wouldn't have come back at all. But you're here, and you were manning a hose, fighting the fire. That's a start. The next fire will be a little easier, and the one after that will be even easier. You'll get there."

Chief Hart joined Shane and Cody at the truck while the crew began mop-up duties. He leaned over, retrieved the discarded helmet from the ground, and handed it to the firefighter.

"I believe this belongs to you," the chief stated. "Is everything okay over here?" he asked, looking at Shane.

"Yeah, we're good, Chief," Cody replied on behalf of his friend, who hadn't responded.

The chief nodded and walked toward his truck without saying anything further.

Once all the trucks had returned to the station, Shane and the other firefighters got busy taking care of the equipment.

Chief Hart walked over to Shane and said, "Let's take a walk, Shane."

Shane shook his head and replied, "I need to get the gear squared away."

"There are enough guys here to handle the

equipment," the chief said. "You can sit this one out."

Shane wisely followed the chief out the door and toward the sidewalk in front of the station. They began walking down the sidewalk in silence.

"We've known each other a long time, Shane," the chief began. "I don't plan to stand by and let you beat yourself up over this fire. You did a great job out there today. You showed up, you manned a hose, and you did your job. A lot of people would have quit. But not you. It's only been two months, son. You need to give yourself time. One fire at a time. Allow yourself time to regain your confidence."

"Are you sure, Chief?" Shane asked quietly. "Are you sure I'll get my confidence back? I don't want to let my fellow firefighters down."

"They'll be fine," the chief nodded. "Just don't let yourself down, okay?"

They returned to the station in silence, and Shane stowed his gear.

When he started toward the parking lot to leave, Chief Hart patted him on the back. "One fire at a time, Shane. One fire at a time."

* * *

The next afternoon, Shane took Taylor and Connor to the park. While Connor played on the play equipment with a couple of other young boys, Shane relaxed on the grass beside Taylor.

"You never mentioned how the barn fire went yesterday," Taylor said as she watched her son zoom down the slide.

Shane mulled over his reply before answering. "Let's just say it wasn't my best effort."

"What makes you say that?" Taylor asked, looking at Shane.

"Whenever I got too close to the flames," Shane began quietly, "I backed away. I've never done that before."

Taylor reached for Shane's hand while still keeping her son within eyesight. "You've also never been trapped in a burning building before, Shane. Give yourself some credit. Most people wouldn't have gone back. But you did."

Shane grinned. "Have you been comparing notes with Cody and the chief? That's what they both said."

"They're smart guys," Taylor smiled. "You should listen to them."

"It was a weird experience," Shane admitted. "Even as a teenager when I was training to be a volunteer firefighter, I never backed away from a fire."

Taylor shook her head. "You can't compare anything to being a teenage boy. All teenage boys think they're invincible. Being trapped in that house fire was a new experience," she reminded him sympathetically. "You have to give your body *and* your psyche time to heal. You're dealing with some post-traumatic stress."

Shane looked into the eyes of his fiancée with

wonder.

Taylor smiled. "Yes, Shane, I *do* understand. Let's just say I've had a little experience with PTSD."

Shane nodded. "You're right. I never thought about it that way. I was looking at the difficulty you've had coming to terms with Zach's death as emotional fallout."

"Emotional fallout from a traumatic situation," Taylor nodded knowingly. "Post-traumatic stress disorder."

"Hmmm," Shane replied. He stood and helped Taylor up as Connor started toward them. He pulled his fiancée into his arms and kissed her gently.

"It's a good thing we've got each other," Shane smiled. "We can fight this PTSD monster together."

Taylor chuckled. "Well, you *have* been getting a lot of practice fighting dragons lately."

# Chapter Seventeen

The school year vanished into the abyss of wedding plans while Taylor and Shane tried to keep their heads above water. The ladies were deeply entrenched in wedding plans, while Shane tried to stay out of the way unless needed. As this would be Taylor's second wedding, she didn't want a large, elaborate affair but was open to it if that's what Shane wanted. He was perfectly content with a small, intimate wedding. 'The smaller, the better,' he told Taylor. They decided that Doug would be Shane's best man and Sue would be Taylor's matron of honor, with Connor as the only other attendant. He would be the ring bearer.

The ladies chose a warm fall Saturday afternoon to meet at a local sandwich shop for lunch to discuss wedding plans. Taylor had called Zach's mother earlier and asked if she would like to help with the wedding. Janet was thrilled to be included, so she joined the others for lunch. While Taylor and all the mothers in her life would discuss wedding details, the guys would have a boys' afternoon. Shane and his dad joined Kenny, Connor, and David in Kenny's garage to look at his latest restoration project, a 1967 Chevy Impala SuperSport.

After ordering their lunch, Taylor chose a table in a quiet corner so they could visit. Since the wedding would be a small affair, they didn't have many remaining details to discuss. Mostly, it was a chance to get together for a visit without a lot of distractions. They enjoyed a leisurely lunch and caught up on each other's lives.

"How is Shane doing after being injured in that house fire?" Janet asked Taylor.

"Other than occasional headaches, all his injuries have healed," Taylor replied. "He's still dealing with some PTSD, but that's getting better."

"Chief Hart was right when he told Shane to take it one fire at a time," Mary added. "Besides the first controlled burn, he's been out on three other fires now. Each one has gotten a little better for him."

"That's what he told me the other night, too," Taylor confirmed.

"How are *you* doing with everything, Mary?" Stephanie asked. "I know you've never been comfortable with your son fighting fires."

"I still don't like it," Mary chuckled. "But I'll never convince him to give up firefighting. In a way, getting injured in that fire changed his perspective. When he found himself dealing with some PTSD, it helped him understand my fears about his safety." Turning to Taylor, she added, "And it helped him understand why you had such a struggle getting involved with another first responder."

"Yeah," Taylor agreed. "We've talked about it quite a bit. We've had some really good discussions. He's more aware of my feelings about it now. And it helps me deal with it better knowing that he has some firsthand experience."

Janet shook her head sadly. "Loving first responders is never easy. It doesn't matter if it's your child or your spouse. It's just not easy. But I'm so glad there are people like Zach and Shane who are willing to do those dangerous jobs."

Mary reached over and patted Janet's hand. "We can both be proud of our sons."

The ladies were quiet for a few moments, lost in their thoughts.

"Who wants to go get ice cream?" Taylor asked suddenly.

The mothers all smiled before Stephanie answered. "I think that's a great idea! All the wedding details have been taken care of, so I think we've earned a treat."

Taylor laughed. "Yeah, Mom, it was *real* tough work. We had maybe three things to finalize."

The ladies all laughed, and Janet added, "But they were three *very difficult* details."

Mary wiped her forehead theatrically. "Planning weddings is a lot of work. We definitely earned ice cream."

"As mother of the bride," Stephanie began, "it's my treat. Let's go get some ice cream!"

* * *

Taylor and her entourage ordered their ice cream and settled at a table along the windows facing the parking lot. They had just dug into their dessert when Mary grinned and pointed toward the parking lot.

"It looks like we aren't the only ones who earned a treat," Mary laughed.

Shane pulled his pickup into an empty spot, and Kenny parked his Chevelle beside him. Kenny and David climbed out of the Chevelle before Kenny reached in to unbuckle Connor from his car seat. As Shane and his dad got out of his pickup, Shane grinned and pointed across the lot at Taylor and his mother's cars.

The moment the guys walked into the ice cream parlor, Connor spotted his mom and ran across the room to greet her.

"Mommy!" Connor said excitedly. "Us guys came to get ice cream!"

"I see that," Taylor laughed. "Go have Grandpa order you some ice cream, and we'll pull a couple of tables together so you guys can join us."

"Okay, Mommy! Be right back!" the little boy replied before running back to his grandpa.

With ice cream in their hands, the guys pulled up chairs and joined the ladies.

"Apparently, wedding planning is exhausting work," Owen chuckled.

"It sure is!" his wife replied, grinning.

"Just like restoring classic cars!" Shane laughed.

"Absolutely!" Kenny chimed in. "You have to walk around the car, discuss what needs to be done, think about it, rub your chin a lot, then walk around the car some more. It's enough to wear a man out!"

David had enjoyed his afternoon with the guys. "You know, I never knew so much was involved in restoring cars. I've got to hand it to Kenny and Shane. It certainly isn't a project that you complete in an afternoon."

"Grandpa David," Connor interjected, "it's hard work 'storing cars. You have to walk around the car lots of times. Then," he paused and clapped his hands, "it's all done!"

"So that's the trick?" Owen asked, chuckling.

"Yep," Connor nodded. "Lots of walking!"

"Now here's the important question, Dad," Taylor smiled. "After all the walking around the car, did you finally settle on a color to paint it? You've been debating it for weeks."

"I sure did," Kenny replied with satisfaction. "Connor helped me decide. He suggested painting it red like Shane's fire truck. When I looked at all the original color options for the '67, I decided the Bolero Red was the perfect choice. I should have asked my grandson weeks ago!"

"Do you plan to sell this car after you restore it?" Taylor asked her dad. "Other than the Chevelle and the Mustang, you've sold your other restoration projects."

Kenny looked at his wife and chuckled. "Your mother keeps telling me there's only so much room in the garage, and she won't give up the space for her car. Besides, I enjoy restoring them, but I don't need that many vehicles. If I sell them, it gives me the money for a new project car."

Looking toward the end of the table where his grandson was focused on his dish of ice cream, Kenny lowered his voice. "I think I'm going to keep the Impala for Connor. It'll be a great first car for him."

Shane smiled. "He'll love it, Kenny. That's one boy who sure likes classic cars and trucks."

"And fire trucks…and police cars…" Taylor smiled.

"He came by it honestly, Taylor," Stephanie reminded her daughter. "You grew up helping your dad work on the cars." She laughed and added, "Connor didn't have a chance!"

There was a brief lull in the conversation as everyone finished their ice cream.

"Did you ladies get everything squared away for the wedding?" Owen asked. "The holidays and the wedding will be here before we know it."

"I think so," Taylor replied. "Since it's going to be a small wedding with a low-key reception afterward, there wasn't much left to do. It's really only going to be family and a few close friends."

"We still need to pick up a suit for Connor," Stephanie mentioned. "The ring bearer has to be dressed in style."

"Shane and I talked about that the other night," Taylor said. "We're going to wait until a week or two before the wedding to get his suit and shoes. With my luck, if I buy them too early, that little boy will outgrow them before the wedding!"

"He certainly will if he keeps eating ice cream!" Shane laughed.

"Did somebody say ice cream?" Connor asked, looking up from his empty bowl.

Kenny laughed. "I think we should get this boy home before he has any wild ideas about a second serving."

"I get to ride in Daddy Shane's truck this time, 'member, Grandpa?" Connor reminded Kenny.

"Okay, buddy," Kenny chuckled. "I guess he's all yours, Owen."

"Yay!" Connor screamed excitedly.

Owen settled the little boy onto his shoulders, and Connor immediately began vroom, vrooming his way across the parking lot.

* * *

With Thanksgiving rapidly approaching, Stephanie

talked to her parents in Oregon to see if they planned to come to town for Thanksgiving or wait until the wedding and Christmas. They didn't travel much anymore, but wanted to meet Shane and his family before the wedding.

Taylor walked into her house after another long day at school. Connor was engrossed in fighting dragons at his castle, so she took the rare opportunity to sink into the sofa and put her feet up.

"Tough day at school?" Stephanie asked her daughter as she joined her on the sofa.

Taylor chuckled. "Just trying to keep everyone on task before the holidays sneak up on us. I'm trying to keep the students ahead of the game, so they hopefully won't have to work on school projects over Thanksgiving break."

"I'm sure they appreciate that, or at least they will later," Stephanie smiled. "I know I would!"

"How was your day, Mom?" Taylor asked as she tipped her head back and closed her eyes.

"It was fine," Stephanie replied. "Connor's never any trouble. I talked to Mom and Dad this afternoon."

"You did?" Taylor perked up. "How are they doing?"

"They're doing pretty good," Stephanie informed her daughter. "They're planning to come up for Thanksgiving, then they'll be back for the wedding, obviously."

"Did Grandma say if they're going to stay through

Christmas?" Taylor asked.

Stephanie laughed. "Yeah. While we were on the phone, she told Dad 'By the way, we're staying for Christmas after the wedding.' Dad laughed and said, 'Was there ever any doubt?' So even though your grandma hadn't mentioned it to us *or* Dad, she apparently had already decided."

"That sounds like Grandma," Taylor laughed. "I can't wait for them to meet Shane."

Stephanie patted her daughter on the hand and said, "They're going to love him, just like we do."

Connor suddenly realized his mom was home and ran over to greet her.

"Mommy, you're home!" he said as he crawled onto his mother's lap. "I love you, Mommy."

Taylor smiled as she hugged her son. "I love you, too, Connor."

"Hey, Mommy," Connor began, "guess what?"

"What?" Taylor asked, smiling.

"Papa and Nana are coming to visit," the little boy announced. "They want to meet Daddy Shane...and Grandpa Owen...and Grandma Mary...and maybe Granddad and Granny!"

"That's what Grandma was just telling me. We'll have to talk to Shane to see if his grandparents are coming up for Thanksgiving," Taylor told her son. "We know they'll be here for the wedding and Christmas, but we aren't sure yet about Thanksgiving."

"They'll be here," Connor announced confidently.

"They miss me."

Taylor laughed. "And how do you know they miss you?"

The little boy shrugged as he climbed from his mother's lap. "I know things."

\* \* \*

As if they could read the little boy's mind, Shane's grandparents called Owen and Mary that evening to discuss holiday plans. They decided to come from California for the holidays since, as Siobhan mentioned, 'It's not like our social calendar is booked up. We may as well be with family.' So, the elder Gallaghers would arrive in town just before Thanksgiving and stay until after the New Year.

Before they knew it, Thanksgiving was only two days away, and the family was beginning to arrive in town. Liam and Siobhan were flying in on the same afternoon that Taylor's grandparents were driving up from Oregon. The entire family had plans to meet at a local steakhouse for dinner, then gather at Owen and Mary's house for dessert afterward. Stephanie reserved a banquet room at the restaurant so they could visit without Connor's excitement disturbing the other patrons.

Connor was happily chattering away with Papa and Nana while they waited for Shane and his family. The moment he spotted Shane, he yelled excitedly, "There he is, Papa! There's my Daddy Shane!"

Before he upended the booster seat on his chair, Kenny grabbed his grandson and walked toward the door to the banquet room to wait for Shane and his family. After Connor received all the required hugs, Shane picked him up and returned him to the table.

"Why don't we all find a seat?" Kenny suggested. "Then we can introduce everyone."

Once everyone was seated, before anyone else could say a word, Connor pointed to Stephanie's parents and blurted out, "Granddad and Granny, that's my Papa and Nana!"

Everyone laughed, and Liam chuckled as he said, "It's nice to meet you, Papa and Nana."

"Okay, Connor," Taylor smiled. "Let's let Grandma and Grandpa introduce everyone."

Kenny chuckled as he stood to introduce his wife's parents. "I think I'll start with Stephanie's parents. Peter and Nancy Evans, this handsome young man is our future son-in-law, Shane Gallagher. His parents, Owen and Mary, and Owen's parents, Liam and Siobhan Gallagher." Turning to David and Janet, Kenny continued. "Peter, do you and Nancy remember Zach's parents?"

"Yes, we do," Peter smiled. "Since you moved back to the area, we look forward to seeing more of you."

"We'd love that, Peter," David nodded. "We aren't going anywhere. We plan to stick close to the family. We have a lot of catching up to do."

* * *

Thanksgiving was a happily chaotic day at Taylor's house. Everyone agreed it would make sense to spend the day at Taylor's, where Connor could access his books and toys. They started Thanksgiving dinner early, and everyone pitched in to make the task easier. Taylor talked her grandma into making her peanut butter fudge, a family favorite, and Siobhan announced it was the best fudge she'd ever tasted.

Stephanie relaxed on the sofa next to her husband and sighed. "You know, Kenny, it's great having the entire family together. Shane's family is wonderful, and look how well Mom and Shane's grandma are getting along. They're talking and laughing like old friends."

Kenny nodded. "Even though they came from different backgrounds, being from the same generation gives them a lot in common. Life is changing, honey. But in a very good way. Before we know it, Taylor and Shane will be married."

"I know," Stephanie sighed. "And we'll all become one big family. It's just too bad Liam and Siobhan don't live closer."

"California's not that far away," Kenny said. "They seem to enjoy traveling."

Liam entered the living room from the kitchen after getting another cup of tea. "Who's traveling?"

Kenny chuckled. "We were just talking about how

you and Siobhan appear to enjoy traveling, so maybe you'll come up more often after the kids get married."

"Ah, yes. I'm sure we will," Liam smiled. "Has your family traveled much, Kenny?"

"Not a lot," Kenny admitted as some of the other adults joined the conversation.

Liam glanced across the room, where Connor and Grandpa David were fighting dragons around the castle.

"The wee one wants to see real castles," Liam grinned. "Wouldn't it be grand if the family took a trip to Ireland? The whole lot of you!"

Shane and Taylor got drawn into the conversation as well, and Shane mentioned, "I'd love to go back someday. When we went, I was too little to remember much of it."

"Owen," Siobhan addressed her son, "you really should take Mary back someday. You grew up in Ireland, and it's beautiful there. I agree with Liam. We should plan a trip, and the whole family should go. You know, we still have some family around Dublin."

"I have to admit," Owen pondered, "it would be nice to have a big family vacation. And where better to go than Ireland?"

Siobhan patted Nancy's hand and smiled. "You and Peter should come too. And David and Janet. Everyone!"

Shane's grandma looked at Taylor and smiled. "You two will be getting married before we know it. I think us girls be needing to make the plans for next summer."

She laughed, then added, "We'll make the plans for Ireland and let the lads know when to be packed."

Liam smiled and nodded, knowing that if his wife wanted a family trip, they would find a way to make it happen.

As the aroma of Thanksgiving dinner began wafting into the living area, Connor climbed onto Liam's lap.

"Granddad," the little boy began, "did Granny say we're going to Ireland?"

"If she has her way about it," Liam chuckled, "it sure sounds like it."

"And we're going to explore castles, right?" Connor asked, wide-eyed.

"You can't go to Ireland without exploring castles, lad," Liam smiled.

Connor thought for a moment. "But we're going to eat first, right?"

"It's a long trip," Liam grinned. "You'll need a good meal."

"I better eat *lots* of turkey!" Connor announced as he climbed from his granddad's lap and ran toward the kitchen.

# Chapter Eighteen

Liam and Siobhan were enjoying their time at Owen and Mary's house. They loved spending more time with their son, daughter-in-law, and grandson, taking advantage of the opportunity to get to know Taylor and her family better. As the wedding and Christmas approached, the elderly couple even discussed possibly moving from California to be closer to the rest of the family. Owen was thrilled that his parents were considering the move, but didn't pressure them in any way. Connor, however, wasn't as diplomatic.

"Granddad," the little boy began as they sat on the floor playing with his construction toys. "I like it when you and Granny are here. You should live here forever."

Liam laughed. "Do you think so, Connor?"

Connor nodded without looking up from his dump truck. "Yep. Daddy Shane and Grandpa Owen like it better when you're here. And you can play with my toys whenever you want to. I keep some of my toys here at

Grandpa Owen's house, so you can play with them even if I'm not here."

"Thank you, Connor. You make a pretty strong case, lad," Liam smiled.

"Mommy makes the best chocolate chip cookies," Connor stated. "If you lived here, you can have cookies all the time. Granny, too."

Owen smiled as he worked at his desk in the corner of the room. He and Mary enjoyed it when Connor spent part of the day with them. And his parents were completely captivated by the little boy. If that boy had his way, his granddad and granny would be moving to Washington.

The front door opened suddenly as Shane and Taylor arrived to pick up Connor.

"Hey, Grandpa," Shane smiled, seeing his grandfather sprawled on the floor. "I see you're getting more dump truck training."

Liam laughed as he stood and straightened his stiff back. "As the wee lad keeps reminding me, there's a lot to learn! I'm not sure my old back will survive all the training."

"Don't feel bad, Grandpa," Shane laughed. "I'm still in training, too, and my back is much younger!"

Owen joined them in the living room just as his wife and mother came in from the kitchen.

Siobhan hugged Taylor and her grandson. "Did you kids get the last of your shopping finished? I can't believe the wedding is only two days away!"

"Tell me about it, Siobhan!" Taylor laughed.

Siobhan took Taylor's hand and reminded her, "Just call me Grandma. We're all family now."

Taylor smiled and hugged Siobhan. "To answer your question, Grandma, I think we got everything. Now we can relax and let the pre-wedding jitters settle in."

"It's all going to be fine," Mary smiled. "You two are perfect for each other."

"If that lad gives you any trouble," Siobhan chuckled, "you just let me know. Grandma will come straighten him out!"

Taylor grinned at Shane and said, "I'll keep that in mind, Grandma. I don't know whose idea it was to combine a wedding and Christmas."

"At least they're not on the same day," Shane laughed. "There are four whole days in between. We can do this." Looking around the room, he added, "Besides, look at all the willing help we have."

Siobhan smiled at her grandson. "Willing, you say? I'm willing to entertain the wee lad. But you? You're far too much trouble."

"Oh, great!" Taylor said as she pointed Connor toward the door. "*Now* you tell me he's too much trouble!"

\* \* \*

The night before the wedding, Shane and Taylor enjoyed

an evening to themselves, compliments of Liam and Siobhan. The young couple went to one of their favorite restaurants before returning to Shane's apartment to decompress before the wedding.

Sitting on the sofa together, Shane put his arm around his fiancée and pulled her close.

"So," Shane began, smiling, "are you ready for this? I don't want you backing out at the last minute."

Taylor was quiet for a moment as she pondered her future with this firefighting school teacher.

"You know I'm never going to be completely okay with you fighting fires, right?" she asked.

"I know," Shane replied quietly. "Neither is Mom, and she's had several years to get used to it."

"I honestly thought I had come to terms with it," Taylor began as she rested her head on Shane's shoulder.

Shane kissed the top of Taylor's head and pulled her closer.

"Then, when you got hurt in that house fire..." Taylor hesitated and sucked in a deep breath. "It sent me into a tailspin, and I wasn't sure I could pull myself out."

"I wish I could promise I'll never get hurt again," Shane began, "but you know I can't do that. Every time I climb into a fire truck, that possibility is always there. Just like every time a police officer pins on a badge, there's always a chance of something bad happening. It's a fact of life with first responders."

"I know," Taylor agreed quietly. "Unfortunately, it's an *unavoidable* fact of life." Taylor looked up at Shane and smiled slightly. "How do first responders ever find someone willing to love them?"

Shane grinned. "I don't know about all first responders, but I found someone in the cafeteria at school. Then, of course, there are the moms and dads who love them before they come up with the crazy idea of being first responders. They don't have a choice. You, my dear, had a choice. Yet you fell in love with me anyway."

"It must be your charming personality," Taylor smiled. "Although...it *is* hard to resist a guy with a sweet truck."

"Oh, so the truth comes out, huh?" Shane chuckled. "You actually fell in love with my pickup, and I just happened to be part of the package."

Taylor shrugged, then laced her fingers through Shane's.

Shane looked into Taylor's blue eyes and smiled. He loved this woman completely and was so glad they'd been able to work through this problem.

"But, seriously, Taylor, we'll be fine. As long as we keep the lines of communication open, I have faith we'll get through whatever life throws at us."

Taylor nodded. "I need to remind myself every day that God is in control. I'm not." She chuckled before adding, "It's a good thing because I don't have a clue what I'm doing!"

"That makes two of us," Shane laughed as he stood and reached for Taylor's hand. "Let's get you home so you can get a good night's sleep. You have a wedding tomorrow. If we hurry, maybe we'll get there in time to tuck Connor in for the night."

Taylor glanced at her phone. "It's past his bedtime. That little boy should already be in bed. Unless he talked Grandma and Grandpa into 'five more minutes'!"

\* \* \*

Waiting in the church's foyer with her father and son, Taylor peeked through the window into the sanctuary.

"I didn't think the church would be so full," Taylor whispered in amazement. "I thought we were having a small, intimate wedding."

Kenny followed his daughter's line of sight and grinned.

"It *is* a small wedding, Taylor," Kenny smiled. "Just family and a few friends. And teachers from school…and firefighters…and police officers. Plus, it's a small church, so it looks more crowded."

Taylor shook her head and smiled. "We have too many friends."

She then stepped back with her father as the sanctuary doors opened so the ring bearer could walk down the aisle.

Kenny patted his grandson on the shoulder. "Remember to hold onto the ring pillow, walk down the aisle, and stand beside Shane. Just like we practiced yesterday."

"Okay, Grandpa," Connor replied seriously as he clung to the ring pillow. He looked back at his mom and added, "You're pretty, Mommy." Then he turned and began walking down the aisle before his mother could respond.

Connor looked so grown-up in his crisp new suit. He understood his assignment and was all business as he clutched the ring pillow. However, he still managed to wave at all his grandparents, his firefighter friends, and Sergeant McDonald from the police department. The little boy had a wide circle of friends.

As the wedding march began, Kenny tucked his daughter's hand safely into the crook of his elbow and asked, "Are you ready, honey?"

Taylor smiled as she looked toward the front of the church, where Connor stood near Shane. She scanned the crowd of friends and family and felt secure in her future.

"I'm ready, Daddy," she said confidently.

Kenny beamed with fatherly pride as he walked his daughter down the aisle toward her future husband. When they reached the pulpit, he kissed Taylor on the cheek, then put her hand into Shane's outstretched hand.

The pastor, a family friend, looked at Taylor and smiled.

"Taylor and Shane said they wanted a brief ceremony," the pastor smiled. "In fact, Shane told me I could just skip right to the 'I do' part. So, I guess that means I have to save my long, drawn-out sermon for church."

Everyone chuckled.

"But, I feel compelled to say one thing," he continued. "It's been faith-affirming to watch God at work bringing these young people together. Not only did He have the normal challenges, but some serious healing had to occur as well. But no job is too big for God, so here we are."

After a few more short remarks, the pastor leaned toward Shane. "Okay, Shane, this is the part you wanted."

Shane looked at Taylor with love and smiled.

"Please join hands," the pastor began. "Shane Liam Gallagher, do you take this woman to be your lawfully wedded wife?"

Shane grinned and replied, "I do!"

"Somehow, I thought that would be your answer," the pastor smiled.

"Taylor Ann Wilson, do you take this man to be your lawfully wedded husband?"

Without hesitation, Taylor replied, "I do."

"Okay, Connor," the pastor began, "you've done a great job. Now you can let Chief Hart and Mrs. Jensen take the rings."

"Okay," Connor agreed with a smile.

After the bride and groom exchanged rings, the pastor announced, "I now pronounce you husband and wife. Shane, you may kiss your bride."

"If you insist," Shane grinned just before giving his new wife a loving kiss.

* * *

Immediately following the brief ceremony, the bride and groom posed for photos with family. They took everything in stride when both their grandmothers kept adding special photos they wanted to have taken. Taylor recognized the bond their grandmothers had formed in the short time they'd known each other, so she insisted Siobhan and Nancy have a photo of just the two of them. Soon, the other women in the family joined in a group photo surrounding the bride.

After the photos were taken, Taylor and Shane disappeared to change into more comfortable clothes before the casual reception. While the bride and groom were changing, Taylor's mom cornered Connor. Knowing her grandson well, she quickly helped him change into play clothes. Once the little boy had changed out of his suit and dress shoes, Cody enlisted his help for a small project.

"Come on, Connor," Cody urged. "I need your help."

"Are we going to wash a fire truck, Cody?" the little boy asked.

Cody laughed. "No, we're going to tie strings of tin cans to the bumper of Shane's pickup."

"We are?" Connor asked in confusion.

"Yep," Cody chuckled. "That way, when they drive off after the reception, the cans will rattle over the road and make a lot of noise. Everyone will know they just got married."

"You could just put a sign on the truck," Connor suggested.

Cody ruffled Connor's dark hair and asked, "Have you done this before?"

"Nope," Connor smiled.

"The chief made a sign for the back of Shane's truck," Cody said, pointing to the pickup in front of the church. "But if we tie the cans to the bumper, it will make enough noise for people to look and see the sign."

"Oh!" Connor nodded his head in understanding. "Now I get it. That's pretty smart, Cody."

The fireman smiled. "It must be the cookies!"

As soon as Cody and Connor finished decorating the bumper of Shane's pickup with strings of tin cans, they headed into the reception, where people were lining up at the buffet.

"I wondered where you disappeared to, Connor," Taylor smiled as she helped her son get a plate.

Connor giggled and didn't say anything. Taylor and Shane looked at the little boy and grinned.

"That sounded like a guilty giggle," Taylor noticed. "What have you and Cody been up to?"

Connor giggled again and held his hands in the air innocently. "We didn't do anything."

Shane laughed. "I don't believe that for a minute.

Especially if Cody was involved. Why don't you two hooligans fill your plates and go find a table? Cody, I suspect you're a questionable influence on my son."

"Just showing the boy the ropes," Cody laughed as he guided his young protégé to a table.

Shane and Taylor joined their parents at a table while Connor and Cody sat with some of the firefighters.

"Connor sure likes hanging out with the gang," Owen smiled as he watched the little boy make himself at home among the firefighters, sitting between Cody and Chief Hart.

"They get a kick out of him," Shane grinned. "I think some of them look at him as a little brother. But they all watch out for him."

After eating a quick meal while visiting with their parents, Shane stood and took Taylor's hand. "Well, Mrs. Gallagher, we should make the rounds at the tables, so we can at least say hi to everyone."

"Let's talk to our friends first since we won't see them until after the honeymoon," Taylor suggested as she looked around the room. "I'm glad our grandparents will be here for a while, so we'll have time with them before they go home."

"Me too," Shane agreed. "They're all on their own tonight, then Dad said he'd help me get my stuff moved over to the house tomorrow. It would be nice to have everything moved before Christmas and the honeymoon, so we don't have to worry about it."

"Dad said he'll help too," Taylor informed her new

husband. "Then we can concentrate on enjoying Christmas with the family."

The young couple spent the next hour chatting with friends and family while everyone enjoyed the laid-back reception. Before they realized it, it was time for them to head to the hotel.

As guests followed them outside to where Shane's pickup was parked in front of the church, Taylor cornered her young son.

"Okay, Connor," she began as she knelt before him. "You're going to spend the night with Grandma and Grandpa."

"And Papa and Nana," Connor added.

Taylor smiled. "Yes, and Papa and Nana. I want you to be on your best behavior, okay?"

"I will, Mommy," Connor nodded.

"I love you, my sweet boy," Taylor said, hugging her son. "We'll see you sometime tomorrow."

"I love you, Mommy," Connor replied.

After Shane helped his wife into the pickup, Connor grabbed his hand and whispered, "Roll down your windows before you drive away, Daddy Shane."

"It's winter," Shane laughed. "Why would I want the windows down?"

"I don't know," the little boy shrugged. "You might need to hear something."

"Okay, buddy," Shane agreed with a chuckle. "I'll make sure we roll down the windows. You be good and we'll see you tomorrow. I love you, Connor."

"I love you too, Daddy Shane," Connor replied, giving him a quick hug. "Don't forget the windows."

Shane laughed as he climbed into the truck, rolled down his window, and waved so the little boy knew the window was open.

As Shane started to drive away, the tin cans made quite a racket as they rattled along the road behind him. When he glanced in the rearview mirror, he saw an excited little boy jumping up and down and clapping his hands.

"It worked, Cody!" Connor yelled. "It worked!"

# CHAPTER NINETEEN

After indulging in a leisurely breakfast, the newlyweds pulled into the driveway at Taylor's parents' house. Before leaving the hotel, Shane texted his dad and arranged to meet at his apartment to begin loading things to move to the house. He planned to drop Taylor off and say hi to his new son, and then he and Kenny would head to the apartment.

The minute Shane and Taylor walked in the door, Connor rushed toward them with outstretched arms.

"Mommy! Daddy Shane!" Connor greeted his parents loudly. "You're back!"

Taylor hugged her son tightly, and then the little boy jumped into Shane's arms.

"I only missed you guys a little," Connor admitted. "Grandpa and Papa played with me a lot. And Grandma and Nana helped me read books."

Taylor laughed. "It sounds like you had a good time."

"Yep," Connor nodded.

"Grandpa is going to help Shane move things from his apartment," Taylor began. "And I need to go over to the house to help figure out where to put things. Do you want to go home with me, or stay here with Grandma, Papa, and Nana for a while?"

Connor rubbed his chin as he looked back and forth between his parents and grandparents.

"I can stay here," he decided. "I don't think Papa is done playing with me yet. We haven't played with my fire truck yet. Can we have pizza for lunch?"

"Aren't you tired of pizza?" Shane laughed.

"Nope," Connor replied. "But I could have a cheeseburger."

"I'll tell you what, little man," Shane suggested. "Let us get as much stuff moved as we can before lunch. Then we'll let you know, and maybe we can all meet for lunch somewhere. Give some thought to a cheeseburger instead of pizza. I wouldn't want you to turn into a pepperoni pizza."

Connor laughed. "Maybe a cheeseburger and a chocolate milkshake, where we ate with Grandpa Owen and Grandma Mary the first time."

"Sounds good," Shane agreed. "We'll let you know when we're ready for lunch."

Turning to his father-in-law, Shane asked, "Ready to go move some stuff? Everything's packed up, so it's just moving boxes and a little furniture. Dad's waiting at the apartment, and Cody said he'd probably stop by to help too."

"I'm ready when you are," Kenny replied. "You can never have too much help when you're moving."

When Shane pulled into the parking lot of his apartment complex, he saw Cody's truck parked in the loading zone. By the time Shane got parked, his dad and Cody were adding a small desk to what they had already loaded into the truck.

Shane walked up to his friend and patted him on the back. "Thanks for stopping by to help, Cody. The move will go a lot faster with two pickups."

"As they say," Cody grinned, "many hands make light work. And I'm sure there's something about two trucks being better than one."

Owen patted his son on the back. "Cody borrowed a hand truck from the station. If you and Kenny want to start loading boxes into your truck, I think we can get most of your furniture into Cody's."

"Okay, we're on it," Shane agreed. "Taylor's waiting at the house to help direct where to put things. I'm sure glad the weather is cooperating. Moving would be a lot less fun if it were snowing."

"Don't be tempting Mother Nature, son," Owen laughed.

* * *

By early afternoon, everything had been moved from Shane's apartment and was at least unloaded at the house. Shane was happy they'd been able to get everything in one load using both pickups. Taylor texted their plans to her mom, and the whole family, along with Cody, planned to meet at the diner for a late lunch.

When Connor saw Cody walk into the restaurant with Shane, he waved excitedly.

"Can you sit by me, Cody?" Connor asked.

Cody looked serious before he replied. "You don't plan on stealing my French fries, do you, buddy?"

"No!" Connor laughed. "Grandma's going to order me French fries, a cheeseburger, and a chocolate milkshake. So, I'll have my own fries."

Pulling out a chair, Cody grinned and said, "Okay, then I'll sit next to you."

Once everyone had placed their orders, Mary looked across the table at her son. "How's the move going, Shane? Are you guys almost finished?"

"Yeah," Shane replied. "Thanks to Cody's truck and my willing helpers, the apartment is empty and everything's at the house. So, the only thing I have left is to clean the apartment and turn in the keys."

"Are you two going to start unpacking things this afternoon?" Mary asked. "You've already had a busy day."

"I don't think we're going to do much unpacking of boxes until later, especially since the furniture is mostly in place," Taylor answered. "We've decided we want to be able to spend the next three days getting into the Christmas spirit and packing for our trip."

"Good," Mary agreed. "Why don't the two of you relax for a bit this afternoon? I'll go over and clean your apartment so that's off your plate and out of your head."

"If you'd like some help so it'll go faster, Mary," Stephanie offered, "I can come help you. It shouldn't take long at all."

"Thanks, Stephanie," Mary nodded. "That'd be great."

"Boy," Shane grinned, "all the women in my life are going to spoil me. How many guys can say their mom *and* their mother-in-law cleaned their apartment for them?"

"Don't you go getting a big head, there, lad," Siobhan chuckled. "Grandma will keep you grounded! I just may put you to work helping me wrap a few Christmas presents."

"Are any of them for me?" Shane asked with a laugh.

"Don't you be getting nosy," his grandma replied, "or you'll be getting an empty stocking. Maybe a little coal."

Everyone laughed at the tough little Irish grandma.

"You best be listening to your grandma, Shane," Liam chuckled. "She may be tiny, but she's a wily one!"

\* \* \*

With only a couple of days left until Christmas, everyone made the most of family time. Shane and Taylor's grandmothers were having so much fun together that they had become best friends. Nancy shared her peanut butter fudge recipe with Siobhan, who promised to keep it a secret. It didn't take much arm-twisting for Siobhan to convince Nancy to stay in town until after New Year's instead of going home right after Christmas. The two sets of grandparents were frequently seen huddling in a corner of the room, visiting quietly.

Shane noticed his dad had been watching his parents.

"Those four almost look like they're plotting something," Shane laughed. "What do you think they're talking about, Dad?"

Owen laughed. "I gave up trying to figure my mother out a long time ago. Those Irish women are mysterious. It's great seeing the four of them get along so well, though. Dad and Mom could use some friends their age. As they've gotten older, California isn't really a good fit for them anymore. If they do decide to move up here, Peter and Nancy wouldn't be very far away in Oregon."

"Wouldn't it be great if my grandma and grandpa moved up here, too?" Taylor mused. "They've never talked about it, but you never know."

Shane's mother joined in the conversation. "I heard Siobhan talking the other day about how much Nancy reminded her of her best friend, Maureen, back in Ireland. I never would have guessed Liam and Siobhan would ever consider leaving California, but after seeing how well our two families have blended – and they absolutely adore Connor – I think they want to be closer to the rest of the family."

About that time, Connor came over and climbed onto his mother's lap.

"Mommy," he began, "how much longer before Christmas?"

Taylor hugged her son and smiled. "Are you getting anxious for Christmas?"

Connor shrugged. "I don't know that word. I just want Christmas to be here."

"Tomorrow's Christmas Eve," Taylor explained. "So, that means the day *after* tomorrow is Christmas. Two more sleeps."

"*Two* more?" Connor asked in disbelief. "That's a lot!"

"It'll be here before you know it, buddy," Shane grinned. "You're going to have so many grandparents around here to play with that you probably won't even miss the presents."

The little boy looked shocked. "But there *is* going to be presents, right?" he asked.

"Don't you worry, Connor," Kenny chuckled. "I'm sure there are going to be *lots* of presents. You'll probably have so many presents that you'll forget all about us."

"Silly Grandpa," Connor laughed as he climbed from his mom's lap. "I won't forget you. We work on your 'stored cars together, remember?"

\* \* \*

Even though he never thought he'd survive, Connor made it to Christmas Eve. Everyone gathered at Kenny and Stephanie's house to spend the day playing games and watching Christmas movies. Taylor and her parents typically celebrated Christmas Day at her house because it was easier for Connor to have his things in one place. This year, since Taylor's place was still suffering from post-moving chaos, it made more sense to hold the Christmas Day festivities at her parents' house.

By mid-morning the day before Christmas, Shane's grandparents were engaged in a rousing game of pinochle with Taylor's grandparents.

Owen smiled as he listened to his parents. He turned to Kenny and whispered, "Watch this."

"Hey!" Owen laughed. "Do you people want to hold it down to a dull roar over there? You're making so much noise we can barely hear the siren on Connor's police car."

Siobhan laughed at her son. "Don't make me come over there, Owen Gallagher. You let us worry about how much noise is necessary in a pinochle game. You don't even know how to bid a hand. It requires noise. Lots of noise, lad. That's why you never win. You don't make enough noise."

"Right," Owen laughed. "Like me not making enough noise was ever a problem!"

The pinochle game finished about the same time a movie ended, so everyone gathered in the living room to visit. They had decided ahead of time to graze on light snacks and sandwiches for Christmas Eve since the next day would be a huge feast.

"Is anyone hungry for sandwiches yet?" Stephanie asked. "Or are we still good with snacking?"

After looking around the room, Taylor replied, "It looks like everyone's good, Mom. Why don't you sit down? Everyone already told you they know where the kitchen is, and you told them to make themselves at home. This is supposed to be a relaxing day."

"Taylor's right," Nancy added. "Relax. Besides, your dad and I want to hear where the kids are going on their honeymoon."

Sitting next to his new wife, Shane smiled. "Taylor wanted to do something fun and wintery. So, we've rented a cabin near Mount Rainier for a few days. We're going to rent a couple of snowmobiles and go exploring."

"You're not going into the backcountry, are you, son?" Owen asked with concern.

"No," Shane replied. "I never go into the backcountry alone. This will be Taylor's first time on a snowmobile, so we're going to stick to the groomed trails around the lodge."

"I'm really looking forward to it," Taylor smiled. "I've always wanted to try snowmobiling because it looks like a lot of fun."

Owen smiled knowingly. "You're going to get her hooked, son. Next thing you know, you'll be buying snowmobiles, a trailer, and riding gear."

Shane laughed. "Probably. It's a great family activity. I know Connor would love it too."

"I've seen pictures of snowmobiles," Liam added. "They do look like fun. If you get your wife hooked on them and end up buying one, you'll have to give your old grandpa a ride, okay?"

"Absolutely, Grandpa," Shane smiled. "And Grandma, too."

Liam glanced at his wife and smiled. "When you buy your snowmobile…"

"*When?*" Shane laughed. "Now it's suddenly *when* I buy one?"

Liam just smiled. "As I was saying…*when* you buy your snowmobile, you know what would make it easier to give me and your grandma a ride? If we lived closer."

All other conversations stopped as everyone homed in on Liam's comment.

"Hey!" Peter interjected. "Wait a minute! I want in on these snowmobile rides! And so does Nancy."

Peter threw his hands in the air theatrically. "Well, I guess that means we're going to have to move closer, too."

"Grandpa…" Taylor began slowly. "Are you and Grandma thinking about moving up here?"

"I don't think they really have much choice, Taylor," Siobhan smiled. "It wouldn't make a lot of sense to buy a place and not live in it."

All eyes were on Shane and Taylor's grandparents. Owen and Mary looked at Kenny and Stephanie, and then they all smiled.

"Okay, you four," Owen began with a smile. "Spill it. We suspected you were up to something. What's going on?"

"Nothing much, son," Liam chuckled. "Well, there is the small matter of the four of us putting an offer on a duplex here in town."

"What?" several people asked simultaneously.

"That's right," Peter grinned. "Liam and Siobhan were already thinking about moving up from California to be closer to the family. Then, when the four of us got along so well, it just made sense."

"So, while we were all up here," Liam continued, "we did some checking and found a perfect duplex for sale not too far from here. We put an offer in on it and found out yesterday they accepted our offer."

"You know, Shane and Taylor," Siobhan began, "it's all your fault."

"Oh?" Shane asked with a grin.

"If you two hadn't met," Siobhan smiled, "your grandpa and I never would have met Peter and Nancy. Then there's Connor. He's the cutest lad I've seen in a long time."

Hearing his name, Connor looked up from his toys.

"What about me?" the little boy asked.

"Your granny said you're cute," Taylor chuckled.

"Oh," Connor said, like that was old news.

"Would you like it if your Papa and Nana, and Granddad and Granny all moved closer?" Taylor asked.

"And they'd live here forever?" Connor asked. "And I could see them every day?"

"Well," Taylor grinned. "Maybe not every day. You wouldn't want them to get tired of you."

"They wouldn't get tired of me," Connor stated confidently. "I have lots of toys they can play with. And we can read books…and get ice cream…and eat pizza…"

All the adults laughed.

"Well," Liam chuckled, "it sounds like the wee lad is okay with the plan."

"When is all this going to happen?" Stephanie asked, still amazed that her mother had kept it a secret.

"We've already listed our houses," Peter began, "and we have offers on them."

"So, as soon as we close on the sale of our two homes," Liam continued, "and close on the duplex, then we pack up and move. Our guess is we'll probably be up here sometime in early February."

"And you four did all this without telling us?" Owen shook his head and smiled. "Aren't you the sneaky ones?"

"You've all had a lot going on," Nancy smiled.

"And we didn't want to mention it," Peter added, "in case something fell through. We didn't want to get anyone's hopes up."

Taylor leaned back against Shane's shoulder and sighed. "Isn't this the best Christmas ever? We got married…"

"So, you're stuck with me now," Shane interrupted with a grin.

Taylor picked up her husband's hand and kissed it. "And now we find out our grandparents are moving to town. This has been the best Christmas I could ever imagine."

"Wait a minute!" Connor held up his hand in protest. "You mean Christmas is *over?*"

Shane pulled his son onto his lap. "No, buddy, Christmas isn't over. You didn't miss it."

"It's *tomorrow*, right?" Connor asked his parents for clarification.

"Yes, son," Taylor assured him. "Christmas is tomorrow."

Connor climbed from Shane's lap, shaking his head.

"I'm gonna wake up real early tomorrow so I don't miss it!" Connor insisted as he went back to his toys. "Maybe I'll sleep under the Christmas tree just to be sure."

# CHAPTER TWENTY

Taylor, Shane, and Connor had a Christmas Eve sleepover at her parents' house. When the adults wandered into the living room early on Christmas morning, they found Connor fast asleep – under the Christmas tree, just like he said.

"Hey, buddy," Shane said, shaking Connor's shoulder. "Merry Christmas, Connor."

Connor sat up and rubbed his eyes as he looked around the room.

"Is it Christmas now?" the little boy asked sleepily.

Taylor sat on the floor and pulled her son onto her lap.

"Yes, *now* it's Christmas," she smiled.

"I stayed awake a long time waiting for Santa," Connor said, still rubbing the sleep from his eyes. "But I fell asleep."

"I'm glad you finally fell asleep," Taylor told her son. "Santa couldn't come until you were asleep."

"I thought you were sleeping on the sofa in your sleeping bag," Stephanie mentioned as she glanced at the empty sofa.

"It was too far from the Christmas tree, Grandma," Connor said logically. "I didn't want to miss Santa."

Stephanie laughed. "Well, at least you dragged your sleeping bag and pillow over by the tree, too."

"Were your parents and grandparents planning to join us for breakfast this morning, Shane?" Kenny asked.

"No, I don't think so," Shane replied. "Mom said last night that they'd probably have something light before they head over." Glancing at the clock on the wall, Shane added, "In fact, they should be here any time."

"In that case," Kenny began, "does everyone want to eat breakfast first, or open gifts as soon as the others arrive?"

"Presents!" Connor yelled enthusiastically. "But can I have a donut now?"

About that time, the doorbell rang. "Hold that thought, Connor," his grandpa grinned as he went to the door.

When Kenny opened the door, David and Janet were standing on the front porch as Shane's family walked up the sidewalk. After everyone exchanged Christmas greetings, they settled in to begin opening gifts. In addition to his parents, Connor was surrounded by all his grandparents and great-grandparents, and was soon nearly buried under a mountain of Christmas gifts.

Anticipating that people might not want a big breakfast, Stephanie was prepared with an assortment of pastries, juice, and hot chocolate for whoever wanted it. Connor had finished his second donut and was reaching for a third when his Papa suggested he might want to save some room in his stomach for dinner.

Connor divided his time between everyone in the family as they enjoyed a leisurely Christmas. At various points throughout the day, he had all three grandpas and both great-grandpas on the floor playing with him. The newlyweds were packed for their honeymoon trip in the mountains and were perfectly content spending their first Christmas as a married couple relaxing with family.

Addressing Taylor's grandfather, David began, "Peter, Taylor tells us you and Nancy are selling your house in Oregon."

"We are," Peter confirmed. "When Liam and Siobhan decided to move up here from California, it gave me and Nancy a nudge to move closer to the family as well. So, the four of us decided to buy a duplex together here in town. We hope to close on everything and relocate by early February."

David nodded. "One thing Janet and I learned the hard way is that grandkids make you realize how short life truly is. The best thing we ever did was sell the condo in New York and move back to the Pacific Northwest so we can reconnect with the family and be here for Connor."

"That little boy can certainly worm his way into a person's heart," Nancy added.

"He sure can," Janet nodded. "I truly regret missing the first three years of his life."

Taylor reached for Janet's hand. "That's all behind us now, Janet. What matters is that you and David are here now and will always be part of Connor's life."

Janet smiled. "You and Shane are leaving for your honeymoon tomorrow, right?"

"Yeah," Taylor nodded. "We didn't want to miss Christmas with the family, and we still have several days before we go back to school."

"Did I hear that you're going snowmobiling?" Janet asked.

Taylor laughed. "You heard right. Shane's gone quite a bit before, but this will be my first time."

"Are you nervous?" Janet asked with a smile. "I sure would be."

"No, I'm not nervous at all," Taylor replied as she held her husband's hand. "Shane is an experienced snowmobiler, so I know I'm in good hands."

"We're going to stay on the groomed trails," Shane added. "She'll be fine. My only problem will be getting her out of the mountains without buying a snowmobile!"

Liam laughed from across the room, where he was playing with Connor. "You may make it out of the mountains without one, lad, but you won't make it through the winter without buying one."

"You're not helping, Grandpa!" Shane laughed.

"Liam Gallagher," Siobhan chuckled. "Will you quit pestering the lad? You know full well he's not going to be buying a snowmobile."

"Thank you, Grandma!" Shane chuckled in relief.

"He's going to be buying *two* snowmobiles!" Siobhan insisted. "He'll want one too, you know. His wife won't be sharing hers with him!"

\* \* \*

The newlyweds took advantage of not having a schedule for several days. Connor was in good hands with Taylor's parents and all the grandparents still in town for the holidays. They drove to the mountains the morning after Christmas, reserving snowmobiles and necessary gear upon arrival, even though they didn't plan to use them until the next day. Their first day in the mountains was spent relaxing and exploring the trails around the cabin. The second day, after a lazy morning, Shane and Taylor walked over to the lodge for breakfast before picking up the snowmobiles.

Once they finished breakfast, Shane took Taylor's hand and asked, "Well, Mrs. Gallagher, are you ready to try out the snowmobiles?"

"You bet!" Taylor replied enthusiastically. "I can't wait!"

After picking up the machines, Shane gave Taylor some basic pointers.

"We'll start slow," he began, "and give you time to get a feel for the machine. I'm sure you'll catch on quickly."

Within a few minutes, they strapped on their helmets and headed down the trail. The groomed trails were wide enough to allow Shane to remain beside Taylor in case she got nervous or needed assistance. At one point, about thirty minutes into their ride, Taylor pulled to the side of the trail and stopped. Shane stopped alongside her.

"Is everything okay, honey?" he asked.

"Yeah," Taylor smiled through the shield on her helmet. "I was just wondering if we could go a little faster?"

"Oh!" Shane exclaimed. "Do you think you have a good feel for the machine?"

"I do," Taylor nodded. "It's not like I want to go a hundred miles an hour, but I think it would be fun to go a little faster."

"We can do that," Shane grinned. "You remember where the brake is, right?"

"Yep," she nodded as she squeezed the hand brake.

"Remember, just like a car," Shane instructed, "throttle is on the right handlebar, brake is on the left handlebar."

"Got it," Taylor nodded.

"Okay, then," Shane agreed. "I'll let you set the pace, and I'll stay beside you."

Almost before he was ready, Shane's wife took off

down the trail. He had to hustle to catch up to her.

They spent nearly two hours riding around the trails, stopping occasionally to check out the scenery. At one point, Taylor pointed to some snowmobilers riding down the hill through the trees, throwing a rooster tail of snow behind them.

"Is that something we can do?" Taylor asked, intrigued.

"Maybe someday, but I don't think that's a good idea right away," Shane replied. "It may look easy, but I'm sure they're experienced riders. It's easier to get stuck in deep snow than it is to dig the machine out. I honestly think on this first trip we should stick to the groomed trails. That'll allow you to get comfortable riding and build up some confidence."

"Okay," Taylor agreed readily. "I trust your judgment."

Aside from riding back to the lodge for lunch, Shane and Taylor spent the whole day exploring the groomed trails surrounding the lodge before calling it a day. After checking the snowmobiles in, they walked over to have dinner before strolling along the river back to their cabin.

Curled up in front of the fireplace in their cabin, Shane watched the reflection of dancing flames in his wife's face.

"Did you have fun today?" Shane asked.

Taylor smiled at her husband before replying. "I did. I *really* did. I always thought snowmobiling looked like fun, but I was surprised by just how much I enjoyed it. How did you get so much experience riding snowmobiles? Who do you go with?"

"Some of the guys down at the station ride," Shane replied. "We usually go several times each winter. I go with Cody a lot."

"Does Cody have his own snowmobile?" Taylor wondered.

"Yeah," Shane chuckled. "He actually has two. I usually ride one of his. He says he always needs a spare because you never know when someone may want to go riding and doesn't have a machine."

Taylor nodded, then reached for her mug of hot cocoa. Speaking mostly to herself, she said quietly, "That's good to know."

The couple spent three sunshine-filled days riding around the mountains. They couldn't have asked for better weather, which was unusual for the end of December. Neither of them was ready for the honeymoon to end, but they recognized the need for a couple of relaxing days at home before heading back to school. They also wanted to spend as much time as possible with their grandparents before they returned home.

As Shane loaded their belongings into the car, Taylor looked around the cabin to be sure they weren't forgetting anything. They stopped by the lodge to check out, then began the drive down the mountain.

Taylor settled into the passenger seat and sighed.

"This has been fun. It's nice to get away for a few days to relax. No responsibilities. No schedule. No alarm clock."

"And no fire alarm going off," Shane added.

Taylor smiled. "Yeah, that too."

As he drove along the mountain road, Shane glanced at his wife. "Do you think you might want to come back sometime and rent snowmobiles again? It looked like you enjoyed riding."

Without hesitation, Taylor shook her head. "No, I don't think so."

Shane was genuinely surprised. "You don't think so? But I thought you had a good time."

"Oh, I did," Taylor nodded. "I had a *very* good time."

"But you don't think you want to come back?" Shane questioned. "I'm not sure I understand."

"Oh, I *do* want to come back," Taylor grinned. "I just don't want to rent snowmobiles again."

Shane was confused and didn't respond.

Taylor laughed at the confusion on her husband's face. "When we come back, we'll have our *own* snowmobiles!"

"Oh, no!" Shane roared in laughter. "Grandpa was right!"

* * *

The day after the honeymooners returned home, the

family met over at Owen and Mary's house to visit. Connor requested a pizza party for dinner the first night his mom and Daddy Shane got home. So, pizza, it is.

"Did you kids enjoy your time away?" Owen asked his son and daughter-in-law.

"We had a great time," Taylor nodded. "It was super relaxing. I think we both needed that. It's been a stressful year."

"What about the snowmobiles?" Liam asked, smiling. "Did you enjoy your first time riding snowmobiles, Taylor?"

Taylor grinned. "Yes, I did. We plan to go back one of these days."

"And when would that be?" the elder Gallagher asked with a knowing smile.

Taylor looked at her husband and smiled, without saying a word.

"Apparently, Grandpa," Shane laughed, "it'll be right after we buy a pair of snowmobiles!"

The old Irishman laughed until tears came to his eyes. "What'd I tell you, lad? When your grandma and I get moved up here, and Peter and Nancy, you two can give us all rides on your new snowmobiles."

"Me too, Daddy Shane!" Connor chimed in. "I want a ride on a snowmobile, too!" Tapping Peter on the arm, the little boy asked, "Papa, what's a snowmobile?"

"It's like a really fast sled that zooms over the snow," Peter explained.

"Really?" Connor asked wide-eyed. "Daddy Shane,

I want to zoom on the snow!"

Shane laughed as he picked up his son and settled him on his shoulders. "Right now, little man, I think we need to zoom home so you can wind down for the night."

"Do I get to take the rest of my pizza with me?" Connor asked with concern.

"Yes, Connor," Taylor laughed, "I'll get your pizza for you. Thanks, everyone, for entertaining this little boy while we were gone. We sure appreciate it."

"Connor's never a problem," Shane's mother replied. "We all enjoyed spending time with him."

Shane kissed his grandmother on the cheek. "We'll see you and Grandpa tomorrow before you fly home. And, Peter and Nancy, we'll make sure to see you before you head back to Oregon, too."

"Not a problem," Peter replied. "We'll all meet up before we leave."

"Tell everyone goodnight, Connor," Shane reminded his son.

"Goodnight, Grandpa Owen and Grandma Mary," Connor began. "And Granddad and Granny…and Papa and Nana…"

"Just say goodnight, everybody," Taylor chuckled.

"Goodnight, everybody," Connor parroted. "You have my pizza, right, Mommy?"

"Yes, Connor," Taylor laughed. "I have your pizza."

\* \* \*

Connor had asked Shane to tuck him in for the first night back in his own bed since before Christmas. As Shane was putting his son down for the night, Taylor looked around her living room and sighed. They would have one day of vacation left after their grandparents went home. They needed to spend some of that time organizing and unpacking boxes.

When Shane walked into the living room, he saw Taylor take a framed photo of her and Zach off a bookcase. He knew that was her favorite picture of them. She held it to her chest for a brief moment before pulling it away and looking at it again.

He walked up behind his wife and put his arm around her waist. "What are you doing, honey?"

Looking at her new husband, she said quietly, "I thought I'd pack some of these photos away." She then started to add it to a small stack of framed photos on the end table. Shane noticed all the photos had Zach in them.

He took the framed photo from his wife's hands and put it back in its place on the bookcase before kissing her gently.

"Taylor," he began as he tipped her chin up, so she was looking at him. "Zach was an important part of your life. He was your husband and Connor's dad. You need to know that I'm not here to erase Zach from your life, or from Connor's life. We'll create our own memories and add new pictures to the walls. Add to, not replace."

"Are you sure, Shane?" Taylor asked quietly.

"Yes, honey, I'm sure," Shane said with conviction. "Leave the pictures where they are."

"I love you, you know," Taylor whispered, her voice filled with emotion.

"As you should," Shane grinned mischievously. "I love you, too. Now I think it's time to call it a day. A good night's sleep sounds wonderful. We'll be heading back to school before we know it."

"And you'll be clipping that fire alarm to your belt," Taylor added sadly.

Shane placed his finger on his wife's lips. "Shhh, my dear. Remember, God's in control. Not you. Not me. God."

Taylor smiled, then took her husband's hand, and his advice, and called it a night.

# CHAPTER TWENTY-ONE

Owen and Mary Gallagher were at the airport waiting for the elder Gallaghers' plane to land. Liam and Siobhan were flying in ahead of the moving truck that was transporting their belongings and vehicle to their new home. Owen had flown down to California earlier to help his parents pack up their things just before the sale of their house closed.

At the same time, Peter and Nancy Evans were driving through Oregon on the way to their new home in Washington. Although it was the middle of February, they had been blessed with a relatively mild winter. Stephanie had offered to fly down to help her parents with the drive, but they assured her they would be fine. The moving truck loaded with their belongings was about half a day behind them. Both elderly couples planned to stay with their kids for a few days to allow time for the trucks to be unloaded and their duplex to be functional. In both cases, that would require the assistance of the family.

Since the truck carrying Taylor's grandparents' belongings arrived before the truck from California, the family hoped to make Peter and Nancy's side of the duplex reasonably functional first. Shane managed to recruit some of his firefighter friends to help unload the first truck. Peter and Nancy guided where to place things in their new home while family members unpacked essential boxes. Shane's grandparents wanted to help since their truck wouldn't arrive for a few days. The two sets of grandparents wished to be involved but soon realized they had plenty of help for the heavy lifting, so they were content to supervise.

"Mom," Stephanie began, "could I get you and Dad to do me a favor? If I call in an order for pizza for everyone, would you be willing to go pick it up?"

"Sure," Nancy agreed. "We can do that. We need to feed all these hungry volunteers."

"If you don't mind, Nancy," Liam suggested, "Siobhan and I can ride along with you and Peter. Maybe we could make a quick stop at the ice cream parlor and pick up some ice cream, too."

"You're going to get ice cream, Granddad?" Connor asked excitedly.

"And pizza, lad," Liam chuckled. "Don't forget the pizza!"

"Can I go with you?" Connor asked hopefully.

"Ask your papa," Liam grinned. "He's driving."

"Sure, the more the merrier," Peter replied before

turning to his daughter. "Stephanie, let Taylor know we're taking Connor with us."

"Okay, Dad," Stephanie smiled. "Grab his car seat from my car."

\* \* \*

By the end of the afternoon, Peter and Nancy's duplex was beginning to look more like a home. There were still boxes scattered about in a few rooms, but they were pleased with the progress. Everyone found a place to sit, even if it was on the floor, to enjoy pizza and ice cream.

"How far out is your truck, Liam?" Peter asked.

"It looks like it should arrive the day after tomorrow," Liam replied.

Liam looked at his grandson and grinned. "Any chance we can recruit your firefighter friends to help unload our truck when it gets here? That sure made short work of unloading Peter and Nancy's truck."

Shane chuckled. "Why don't you ask them, Grandpa? I'm sure they can answer between bites of pizza. If it's in a couple of days, I won't be able to help until school releases for the day. But I could run over straight from school."

Liam looked around the room at the handful of firefighters. "Any chance you strong young lads might be available to unload another truck in a couple of days?"

"Alex and I will still be off duty," Cody offered. "We

can come help. I'll give you my cell phone number before we leave. You can call or text me when the truck arrives, and we'll run over."

"Thank you, lads," Liam smiled. "We sure appreciate your help."

"I can make myself available to help, too, Dad," Owen offered. "It shouldn't take long to unload the truck. You and Mom sold a lot of stuff with the house."

"Owen," Kenny began, "if you let me know when the truck arrives, I can run over to help as well."

"Thanks, Kenny," Owen nodded.

"Well, son," Owen chuckled as he looked at Shane, "it sounds like all the heavy lifting will be finished before you get out of school. I think that means you'll need to stop on your way over to pick up pizza for everyone."

Shane laughed. "I guess that's fair. Will everyone want pizza again, or should I pick up some sub sandwiches or something?"

"That can be your call, Shane," Liam smiled at his grandson. "It'll be my treat, but you can surprise us!"

"Got it," Shane laughed. "A box of crackers for everyone else, and a massive cheeseburger for me."

"I want a cheeseburger, Daddy Shane!" Connor chimed in.

"Of course, you do," Shane laughed. "I guess you'll all be surprised when I show up. Will it be pizza? Will it be cheeseburgers? Will he *really* just bring crackers?"

Owen laughed at his son. "You know, Shane, I may need to call your grandma over and have her set you straight."

Shane held his hands above his head and laughed. "I surrender! I promise I'll bring something good!"

"It's a wise lad who knows when to be a wee bit afraid of his Irish grandmother!" Liam chuckled.

* * *

Within a couple of weeks, both sides of the duplex were completely functional, and all boxes had been unpacked. Shane and Taylor's grandparents were settling in nicely and began exploring the town together. The two elderly couples frequently spent their evenings playing pinochle together or visiting with their families. During one of the evening visits, Siobhan again brought up the subject of a summer trip to Ireland. Taylor called Zach's parents to see when they would be free for a get-together to discuss the possible vacation.

With a little planning, the entire family settled on a Saturday afternoon when everyone was available to meet at Shane and Taylor's house. As soon as everyone arrived, Connor took his papa and granddad by the hands and led them to his castle to fight dragons. After playing for a short time, Liam convinced Connor to join everyone in the living room to talk about a trip to Ireland.

"Really, Granddad?" the little boy asked. "Are we *really* going to Ireland to see castles?"

"Well, wee lad," Liam smiled, "let's join the others

and find out."

"I'm with Connor," Shane grinned. "I want to know if we're *really* going to Ireland."

"Shane and I discussed it," Taylor began excitedly, "and we're definitely in. Connor will be five by the time we go. That's about the age Shane remembers being when he went."

"I can juggle clients around to be gone for a couple of weeks," Kenny agreed. "So, Stephanie and I are in. Besides, we can't let our grandson go to Ireland and not take us!"

Owen laughed. "I agree, Kenny! I have plenty of vacation time just wasting away, so I don't have a problem."

Owen turned to his wife. "Didn't you say the other night, Mary, that you have a couple of weeks you can take off?"

Shane's mother nodded. "Yeah, I can easily schedule two or three weeks off."

"David, what about you and Janet?" Taylor asked Zach's parents. "We'd love it if you two could go as well."

"Count us in," Janet smiled. "We'd love to go, and thanks for including us."

"Peter and Nancy?" Liam asked.

"Well, let's see," Peter grinned. "We're done with the move, and our social calendar hasn't filled up yet, you know, with being in a new town and all, so I think we can squeeze it in."

"Nancy," Siobhan laughed, "I wasn't about to let you off the hook. I want you to see Ireland, so you and Peter can start packing your bags."

"Speaking of packing bags," Mary began, "we should figure out when we're going to do this so we can get our vacation time scheduled. Shane and Taylor need to be out of school for the summer."

"I talked to Chief Hart," Shane began, "and it's not a problem for me to take a couple of weeks off from the department anytime this summer. Well, anytime as long as it's after the middle of June."

"Why not until after the middle of June?" Taylor asked. "Not that it matters, just curious."

Shane smiled. "The chief said they need me for the annual Guns and Hoses softball tournament."

"Oh, no!" Taylor laughed. "You do that, too?"

"I look forward to it every year," Shane grinned. "Last year, I missed it because of my injury. That's the only time I've missed it since joining the department."

Taylor shook her head and laughed. "Zach used to play in that every year, too. Those boys take their softball seriously!"

David looked around the room at the other adults and smiled. "Okay, Taylor, you're going to have to bring me and Janet up to speed. What, exactly, is the Guns and Hoses softball tournament? Obviously, I know what a softball tournament is, but why is it called the Guns and Hoses tournament?"

"It's a hardcore rivalry between the police and fire

departments," Taylor explained.

"Wait a minute," Shane laughed. "I wouldn't say it's hardcore. It's a friendly competition."

Owen raised his eyebrow at his son. "I'd have to disagree with you, son. I've been to that tournament every year. I think hardcore is a better adjective than friendly."

Shane laughed. "Well, maybe…"

David chuckled. "I think I'm beginning to understand. But, why Guns and Hoses?"

"Guns are the guys on the police department," Taylor explained. "That's why Zach was involved every year. Hoses are the guys on the fire department, and apparently why my husband participates in this silly rivalry every summer." She laughed, then added, "I wish I had known that before I signed the marriage license!"

"Too late now, honey," Shane smiled.

After further discussion, the group decided on two weeks in mid-July. This would give everyone a chance to book airline tickets and arrange time off from work.

Sitting next to her husband, Siobhan took Liam's hand. "Don't let me forget to post a letter to Maureen to tell her we're coming home. If we're going back to Ireland, she would never forgive me if I didn't see her."

"We'll make sure you have time to visit with her," Liam assured his wife.

"Oh, Nancy," Siobhan said excitedly, "you're going to love Maureen! She's been my best friend back home since we were in secondary school together. You remind me so much of her."

"I can't wait to meet her!" Nancy replied. "Maybe the three of us can meet up for coffee or something."

"Oh!" Siobhan suggested happily. "I'll ask Maureen to make her famous Irish apple cake! It's the best in all of Dublin!"

"Well, we know what the grandmothers will be doing," Shane laughed. "What are the rest of us going to do while the ladies are feasting on Irish apple cake?"

"I'll have to have some Irish apple cake sometime during the trip, too," Liam mentioned. "But I know we have a wee lad who has his heart set on seeing *real* castles."

"Yay!" Connor agreed. "Do we get to explore castles, Granddad?"

Liam laughed. "I think that's a necessity if we go to Ireland."

"Does that mean yes?" Connor looked confused.

"Yes, lad," Liam smiled as he hugged Connor. "A necessity means it's something you *have* to do."

"Oh! That's good!" Connor agreed. "Exploring castles is a…a ne-ces-si-ty. Did I say it right, Granddad?"

"It was perfect, Connor," Liam smiled.

"We all need to think about what we want to see and do while we're there," Siobhan suggested. "And Owen, you and your dad can come up with a list of must-see castles for the wee lad."

"Hey, wait a minute!" Shane protested. "Some of us older lads want to see castles too!"

"Don't worry, son," Owen laughed. "We're all going to explore the castles. But there are thousands of castles in Ireland. I suspect we'll confine our exploration to the handful in and around Dublin."

"We have time to come up with a list of things we want to do," Liam explained. "But we won't want to miss Dublin and Malahide Castles. And we have to take Connor to Drimnagh Castle. It's the only castle in all of Ireland that still has a flooded moat around it."

"That's so dragons can't get in, huh, Granddad?" Connor asked knowingly.

"That's right, lad," Liam nodded. "We have to keep the dragons out."

After getting input and ideas from everyone about what to do in Ireland, the family had a rough plan for their vacation. They would undoubtedly fine-tune their plans over the coming weeks. Since the entire family was all together, Taylor's mother suggested they go out to dinner.

"Where does everyone want to go?" Stephanie asked.

"Pizza!" Connor replied quickly.

Kenny laughed and pulled his grandson onto his lap. "You're going to turn into a pizza, Connor!"

Connor laughed. "That's what Daddy Shane says all the time."

"How about that little neighborhood diner where we all met that one time?" David asked. "They seemed to have something for everyone."

"That's the cheeseburger and milkshake place!" Connor reported.

Everyone agreed that it was a good choice, and Connor began debating who he would ride with.

Once Connor decided he was going to ride with Grandpa Owen and Grandma Mary, he started toward the door.

"Are you going to get a cheeseburger and milkshake, Connor?" Mary asked.

"Yep!" Connor replied. "But maybe I'll get pizza."

Taylor shook her head as she took her husband's hand and whispered. "Whatever you do, don't suggest he get both."

# CHAPTER TWENTY-TWO

School was out for the summer, and Taylor and Shane began settling into their first summer as a married couple. Shane was back to working as a full-time firefighter, while Taylor embraced her role as a full-time mom to an active five-year-old. After hearing the family talk about the summer softball tournament, Connor decided he wanted to play baseball too. So, Taylor signed him up for T-ball, and the family started spending time at the ball field, watching the hilarious antics of four- to six-year-olds learning the art of baseball.

One evening, shortly after dinner, Shane and Taylor were reading a book to Connor when the doorbell rang.

Handing the book to Taylor, Shane stood and offered, "I'll get it."

Shane opened the door to find a police officer standing on the porch.

"Sergeant McDonald?" Shane asked, having only met the man one time.

"Good memory, Shane," the sergeant chuckled.

"Sorry I didn't get a chance to talk to you at the wedding," Shane apologized. "Things were a little hectic with it being right at Christmastime."

"Not a problem," the officer assured Shane.

After hearing the sergeant's voice, Taylor and Connor went to the door.

"Uncle Pete!" Connor yelled as he jumped into the officer's arms.

"How are you doing, buddy?" Pete asked.

"I'm playing baseball, Uncle Pete!" Connor replied excitedly.

"You are?" Pete asked, grinning. "Well, I just happened to stop by to talk about baseball for a few minutes."

"I know all about it," the young boy stated with confidence. "I have a baseball glove!"

"Connor, why don't you hop down?" Taylor suggested. "Let Uncle Pete come in and sit down."

"I'm on duty and was in the neighborhood, so I thought I'd pop in for a minute," Pete explained. "I haven't stopped by in a while, and I have to admit, my curiosity has gotten the best of me."

"Oh?" Taylor wondered.

"Shane, when I met you here that first time, I thought you looked familiar, but I just couldn't place you," Sergeant McDonald stated. "Now that I've put a few things together in my mind, I realize you looked familiar because you play for the Hoses every year."

Shane laughed. "Other than last year, I've played every year since I was eighteen."

"You missed last year because of your injuries, right?" Pete asked.

"Yeah," Shane nodded. "But I'm ready to go this year."

"I heard about the firefighter being hurt in that house fire," Pete began, "but I didn't make the connection and realize it was you until I was talking to Chief Hart recently."

"Don't feel bad, Pete," Taylor chuckled. "I didn't know he played in that tournament until recently myself. Since he didn't play last summer, it never came up."

Pete laughed. "So, Taylor, now you're going to have divided loyalties. You've always rooted for the Guns during the tournament. Now you're married to one of the Hoses. What are you going to do?"

Taylor laughed. "I don't know, Pete. I have so many options. The most attractive one is to stay home and not even go. However, I don't think anyone in the family would allow that to happen. Maybe I'll have a t-shirt printed with Guns on half of it and Hoses on half of it."

"That's not a bad idea!" Pete laughed. "It's too bad Connor isn't older. With him having a vested interest in both the Guns and Hoses, he could be our impartial umpire."

"That's actually a good idea," Shane laughed. "Maybe when he's about thirteen. Since he already 'knows all about it,' he should be an expert by then."

"Well, I'd better get back on patrol," the sergeant announced. He patted Shane on the back and said, "It was good seeing you again, Shane, especially now that I've made the connection."

Pete hugged Taylor and smiled. "Congratulations on the wedding, and thanks for inviting me. I'm happy for you both."

Uncle Pete gave Connor a high-five. "You take good care of your mom, Connor, and I'm sure I'll see you at the softball tournament."

"Daddy Shane takes care of Mommy now, Uncle Pete," the little boy reported seriously. "I'm going to be busy playing baseball."

Pete laughed as he walked toward the door. "Learn everything you can, buddy. I'm counting on you to be our umpire in a few years."

As Sergeant McDonald started down the sidewalk, he heard Connor exclaim, "Yay, I get to be umpire! Daddy Shane, what's a umpire?"

\* \* \*

It was a beautiful summer day in mid-June, and the local softball fields were jam-packed. One field that drew a large crowd was where the annual Guns and Hoses tournament would be starting in a few minutes. It was a popular best-two-out-of-three tournament that pitted the local police and fire departments against each other every year.

Taylor's entire family had already claimed a section of the bleachers they were sharing with the Gallagher clan. Shane and Taylor's grandparents had brought along lawn chairs so they could enjoy the games in a little more comfort than the bleachers provided. True to her promise, Taylor and Connor were both wearing t-shirts that had the Guns logo on the left side and the Hoses logo on the right side. She even had matching shirts made for David and Janet that supported the Guns team. Their shirts had 'In Memory of Zach Wilson' silkscreened across the back.

As the Hoses team ran onto the field, a proud little boy yelled at the top of his lungs. "That's my Daddy Shane!" Turning to Owen, he asked, "Grandpa Owen, what place is Daddy Shane playing?"

"He switched to third base this year to see how his arm does," Owen explained, pointing to his son taking practice throws at third. "He normally plays shortstop, that's between second and third base."

"Yeah," Kenny agreed. "Shortstop might be tougher on his arm. He should do okay, though. It's been nearly a year since the surgery."

"He talked to Chief Hart about it when they started practice," Owen added. "The chief left it up to him, but suggested he might want to give third try to err on the side of caution."

Just before the first batter for the Guns team came to the plate, Connor tapped Kenny on the arm. "Grandpa, can I have a hot dog?"

Kenny laughed. "Didn't you just eat breakfast?"

"That was a long time ago, Grandpa," Connor insisted. "That was before we came to watch baseball."

Taylor passed a sandwich bag over to her dad. "Connor can have a few of these crackers. That boy can't possibly be hungry already. We'll get hot dogs for lunch between the first and second game."

Connor ate a couple of crackers, and then he got wrapped up in the excitement of the game. If he had ever been truly hungry, he soon forgot all about it.

When Shane came to bat for the first time, the whole family cheered for him. Shane's grandma and Connor had a contest to see who could cheer the loudest. When he hit a double and ended up on second base, the little boy yelled, "Good job, Daddy Shane!"

Siobhan gave Connor a high-five and smiled. "I knew he could do it. He's a natural."

The first game was an exciting match-up as the score went back and forth throughout the entire game. After scoring one run in the bottom of the seventh and final inning to break a tie, the Hoses came out winners of the first game.

After the game, Shane joined the family near the bleachers.

"You did good, Daddy Shane!" Connor exclaimed happily. "You won!"

"Well, *I* didn't win," Shane smiled. "Our *team* won. One game down, two more to go. Unless we win the second game. We have a little over an hour before game two. Does anyone want to grab a hot dog from the concession stand and find some shade to relax in?"

Connor instantly raised his hand. "I want a hot dog, Daddy Shane! Mommy said I could have one after the first game."

"That bottomless pit wanted a hot dog the minute the game started!" Taylor informed her husband. "It was barely an hour after he ate breakfast."

"Something about a growing boy?" Shane shrugged. He took his son by the hand and said, "Come on, buddy, we'll get you a hot dog."

Owen asked everyone how many hot dogs and drinks were needed, and then he, Kenny, and Taylor followed Shane to the concession stand, while the others scouted out a shady place in the park.

Some of the other firefighters joined Shane and his family in the shade to relax between games. Before they had a chance to get too relaxed, Chief Hart announced it was time to head back to the field. Taylor kissed her husband and wished him luck before following her family back to the bleachers.

Although everyone played hard in the second game, the Hoses weren't able to clinch the tournament. Sergeant McDonald sneaked in a home run to put the Guns on top, forcing a third game for the championship.

Above all the noise, an excited little boy yelled, "Yay, Uncle Pete!" eliciting a smile and thumbs-up from the police sergeant.

Shane walked across the field and joined the family

at the bleachers.

"How long do you have until the last game, son?" Owen asked.

"About forty-five minutes," Shane replied. "So, I'm going to hang out in the shade, relax, and drink some water." He pointed to a large shaded area under some oak trees. "If anyone wants to join me, I'll be over there."

The elderly family members situated their lawn chairs in the shade, and the rest of the family, along with some of the firefighters, sat or sprawled on the cool grass.

"They sure don't give you lads much time between games, do they?" Liam asked.

"Not a lot," Shane agreed. "But it's not too bad. It gives the players enough time to relax and hydrate, but not so long that their muscles start to cool off and get tight."

Connor imitated Shane and stretched out on the grass beside him, crossing his legs and putting his arms behind his head.

"It's okay that Uncle Pete won this game, Daddy Shane," Connor rationalized. "You and the guys won the first one."

Shane smiled as he glanced over at his son. "That was a nice home run Pete hit."

"Yep," Connor agreed, bouncing the toes of his feet like Shane was doing. "A nice one. But you and the guys will win the next game. And then we'll go eat pizza!"

"Pizza, huh?" Shane smiled. "You think about food a lot, don't you, buddy?"

"Yep," Connor nodded. "I have to grow big and strong so I can be a fireman. Or maybe a policeman. Or maybe I'll fight dragons in Ireland. So, I have to eat a lot."

"That makes sense," Shane agreed, smiling. "It's good to have options."

"Yep," the little boy agreed. "Good to have options."

Everyone had been watching the exchange between Shane and Connor.

Janet had tears in her eyes as she held her husband's hand. "You know, David, since Zach is no longer here, I can't imagine anyone else who would be as good a daddy for our grandson as Shane."

"I agree," David nodded. "He doesn't have to love him like his own son, but it's obvious he does."

Chief Hart walked over to Shane and the others, who were relaxing in the shade. Before he could say a word, Connor jumped up and announced, "Come on, Daddy Shane. It's time to go win a ballgame!"

The chief laughed. "I'm not sure I'm even needed. It looks like Connor's on top of things. You heard the boy, let's go win this ballgame!"

The players on both teams played hard during the last game, each side wanting to take home the championship trophy. The score was close throughout the entire game, with the lead bouncing back and forth between the Guns and Hoses. The players' determination forced the game into overtime when the score was tied at the end of seven innings. The firefighters would have the last chance to bat, so they needed to make sure the Guns didn't score in the top of the eighth inning. Alex caught a long fly ball in left field, preventing a Guns home run and ending the top of the scoreless inning.

"Come on, guys!" Chief Hart yelled as the firefighters prepared for their last at-bat. "All we need is one run. That's it. Let's do this!"

The first two batters each got a single, putting runners on first and second. The next batter, unfortunately, hit into a double play.

As Cody headed toward the plate, Shane slapped him on the back and smiled. "No pressure, buddy. All you need to do is not make the third out."

Cody smiled. "Thanks for the pep talk, Gallagher."

Cody stepped into the batter's box and squared his feet. He looked at the first two pitches, both balls. He sent the third pitch over the right-field fence for a home run. As he approached home plate, he was greeted by his fellow firefighters.

As soon as he stepped on home plate, Shane slapped him on the back. "See, piece of cake."

Both teams lined up to shake hands, with Chief Hart and Sergeant McDonald smiling as they brought up the rear of the two lines.

"Well, Pete," Chief Hart smiled. "It looks like we

get to bring that trophy back to the fire department this year."

"That's only fair, Doug," Pete chuckled. "We've had it down at the precinct since last summer, collecting dust."

"We'll dust it off before you guys get a shot at it again next summer," Doug grinned. "A bunch of us are going to grab pizza at Angelina's if any of you guys want to join us."

"You sure the Hoses don't mind being seen with us Guns?" Pete joked.

"Not at all," Doug laughed. "The tournament's over. Now we're just a bunch of hungry softball players."

The two men shook hands and patted each other on the back. "I'll let the boys know, and I'm sure some of us will meet you there."

\* \* \*

"Cody!" Connor yelled across the pizza parlor, waving his arms high over his head. "We're over here, Cody!"

"I wonder if that boy will ever run out of energy?" Kenny asked his daughter.

"He's five, Dad," Taylor laughed. "I think he's just building up steam."

Before long, all of Shane and Taylor's family, along with several firefighters from the Hoses and a handful of police officers from the Guns, were seated around two long tables.

"Can I sit with the guys, Grandpa?" Connor asked Kenny.

Kenny looked around the two tables and laughed. "Exactly what guys do you want to sit with? You have all your firefighter guys, all your police officer guys, and all the guys in your family. You have more guys than any five-year-old needs, buddy."

"Why don't you come over here and sit with your granddad?" Liam asked. "That way you can show me what your favorite kind of pizza is."

"Okay, Granddad," Connor agreed. "Pepperoni is the best!"

"Okay, lad," Liam grinned. "I'll make sure we have some pepperoni pizza right in front of us. How does that sound?"

"Sounds good, Granddad," Connor agreed.

Siobhan looked around at all the softball players and smiled. "I'll bet you lads will sleep good tonight. So, it looks like the firefighters get to take the trophy home today, yeah?"

"Yes, ma'am," Chief Hart replied with a smile. "The police officers captured the trophy last year, so I guess it was our turn."

"It's nice of you lads to share," Siobhan smiled.

Shane laughed. "I'm not sure we share, Grandma. We all fight pretty hard for the trophy each year."

"Didn't the chief just say the police officers had the trophy last year?" Siobhan began with a smile. "And this year, the firefighters get the trophy?"

"Yes, but…" Shane started.

"Then that means you lads are sharing the trophy," Siobhan stated with conviction. "Next year, the police officers get to have it back."

Liam laughed. "Just say 'yes, ma'am,' Shane."

Laughing, Shane agreed. "Yes, ma'am, next year the trophy goes back to the Guns."

"But that's *next* year," Taylor smiled. "An entire year away before we have to worry about this madness again."

"Madness?" Shane asked innocently. "What madness? Just a little friendly rivalry."

Taylor looked at Shane's father and raised her eyebrow.

"Hardcore rivalry, son," Owen corrected, as he winked at his daughter-in-law. "Hardcore."

"Friendly," Shane insisted. "See, we're all sitting together getting ready to eat pizza."

"I have to agree with your dad, Shane," Chief Hart laughed. "Eating pizza is friendly. Playing softball is hardcore."

"And speaking of eating pizza," Cody began, "here it comes!"

"Yay, pizza!" Connor shouted.

And just like that, the softball rivalry fell into a friendly evening of enjoying pizza together.

# CHAPTER TWENTY-THREE

Liam shook his great-grandson's shoulder to wake him. "Connor, wake up, lad."

The little boy stirred slightly before opening his eyes and looking at his granddad.

"Are we still on the airplane, Granddad?" he asked sleepily.

"We are, lad," Liam smiled. "And you're going to want to be seeing this. Look out the window."

Suddenly, the little boy's eyes were wide open as he stared out the plane's window.

"Is that a castle, Granddad? A *real* castle?" Connor asked in disbelief.

Taylor, Shane, and the rest of the family were straining to see out the windows of the plane as well.

"Yes, lad," Liam confirmed. "That's an honest-to-goodness real castle. That's Malahide Castle."

"Can we go see that castle, Granddad? Please?" Connor begged.

"Probably not today, lad," Liam smiled. "But we'll be sure to see it while we're here."

"Have you ever explored that castle, Granddad?" Connor asked.

"Oh, lad," Liam began as he reminisced, "I explored that castle hundreds of times when I was a lad. It was one of my favorite castles."

Connor turned slightly to see his mother in the seat behind him.

"Mommy!" he said excitedly. "We're going to explore that castle down there. Do you see it? Do you see it, Mommy?"

Taylor and Shane chuckled at their awestruck little boy. Although, if they were to admit it, they were every bit as amazed as he was.

"Yes, we see it," Taylor smiled. "I'm sure by the time we head back home, you'll be an expert on castles."

Connor returned his gaze to the scene outside his window as the plane approached the Dublin Airport.

"This is Ireland, right, Granddad?" Connor asked.

"It is, indeed, lad," Liam replied happily. "That city below us is where your granny and I were born. Your Grandpa Owen, too."

"Really?" Connor asked. "Wow! You were born by castles!"

Everyone settled in for the approach, eager to finally touch their feet to the ground again. They had no plans for their first day in Ireland, other than to check in at their hotel, rest up, and have a good meal. Castle exploration and other sightseeing would begin the next day.

* * *

Even though everyone in Shane's family had been to Ireland at least once, including his dad and grandparents who were born there, no one in Taylor's family had ever set foot on Irish soil, nor had Zach's parents. Therefore, they decided before the trip that there would be times when the group would split up. Siobhan didn't have much desire to go sightseeing. Her primary focus was visiting her best friend and catching up on their lives, especially knowing that Maureen's husband Patrick had passed away the previous year. Zach's parents, Taylor's parents, and her grandparents wanted to see some of the old cathedrals in and around Dublin, and they all wanted to escape the city for a day in the Irish countryside.

The one thing they all wanted to do together was visit the castles. Everyone was interested in seeing the Irish castles, even those who had seen them before, but no one wanted to miss out on sharing that experience with Connor. Liam was nearly as excited as Connor, eager to relive that part of his childhood through the eyes of an enthusiastic little boy.

Connor was up and about early on their first full day in Ireland. As the family enjoyed breakfast in the hotel's restaurant, he had a difficult time sitting still in his chair.

"Grandpa Owen," Connor began, tapping his

grandpa on the arm, "are we going to that castle today?"

Owen grinned. "What castle? I didn't know we were going to a castle today."

Mary laughed at her husband. "Owen, don't tease the boy. Yes, Connor, we're going to see castles today. Maybe more than one. We'll have to see. Your granddad is in charge of castle exploration."

"Oh," Connor nodded, turning his attention to Liam. "Granddad, are we going to the castle we saw from the plane today?"

"That's the first thing on the list, lad," Liam smiled. "Right after breakfast."

Connor pushed his plate away. "I'm done. Can we go to the castle now?"

Taylor laughed. "You may be done, little boy, but the rest of us need to finish breakfast. And you might want to finish your waffle."

"I'll eat fast," Connor announced, pulling his plate back toward him. "Then we can go."

\* \* \*

Before they knew it, the family was standing in front of Malahide Castle. Not realizing he was leaving his family behind, Connor slowly walked up the pathway toward the castle, completely mesmerized.

"I guess we should probably follow him," Shane laughed.

When everyone caught up to the little boy, he had

stopped and was quietly staring up at the massive fortress.

"Whoa," Connor barely whispered in awe. "It's really a castle. I'm standing by a real castle."

Liam walked up beside Connor with tears in his eyes. He remembered that feeling the first time he saw a castle when he was about Connor's age.

"Do you want to go inside, lad?" Liam asked quietly.

Connor simply nodded and took his granddad's hand.

The old Irish gentleman, with the little boy's small hand tucked safely in his, led the group toward the entrance to Malahide Castle.

Once inside the stone building, the family spent a couple of hours exploring, allowing Connor to immerse himself in the experience. For many in the family, this was their first time seeing a castle as well, and they made the most of the visit.

Taylor turned around to say something to her son and didn't immediately see him.

Turning to her husband, she asked, "Shane, where's Connor? Is he with your grandparents?"

"He was right here a minute ago," Shane replied, looking around. "I'll ask Dad."

Taylor, with panic slowly rising, followed Shane over to Owen and Mary. When the entire group was reassembled, everyone looked around, and several mentioned that Connor had just been with them.

"Daddy!" Taylor began in a panic, "Where's

Connor? We have to find him!"

Kenny pulled his daughter into his arms. "We'll find him, honey. He couldn't have gone very far."

Everyone spread out and spent the next ten minutes scouring the immediate vicinity before Taylor's mom alerted one of the security guards.

Taylor's panic was in full gear at this point as the group huddled together while Stephanie talked to the security guard and provided Connor's description.

Suddenly, Liam gave his son a knowing look, and Owen nodded.

"The tower!" Liam and Owen announced simultaneously.

"The what?" Taylor practically screamed.

"Owen, I can't climb those stairs anymore," Liam admitted. "You and Shane go. I'd bet money the lad found his way to the stairs leading to the tower."

Not sure where they were headed, Kenny and Taylor quickly followed Owen and Shane to a nearby stairway.

"If he finds his way to the tower, the lad will be fine," Liam assured the rest of the family. "I used to disappear to the tower nearly every time we went to a castle when I was a lad. It was my favorite place. You can see for miles. I admit it caused no small amount of grief for my mother."

It took every ounce of restraint Taylor possessed not to push ahead of her husband and father-in-law, who were hurrying up the narrow stairway. Once they reached the top of the stairs, she heard Owen let out a huge sigh of relief, followed by a chuckle.

"There he is," Owen said, pointing toward the little boy who had inadvertently joined a tour group.

Taylor rushed up to her son and pulled him into her arms. "Connor, you scared me half to death!"

Oblivious to the stress he had caused his mother, Connor pointed out the tower window to the surrounding area, which included the Irish Sea.

"Isn't it pretty, Mommy?" Connor asked, still gazing out the window. "You can see forever!"

Connor finally noticed Shane standing behind him, along with both his grandpas.

"Grandpa Owen, can we go see that water when we're here?" Connor asked, still completely captivated.

Owen smiled at this curious little boy, remembering his own childhood in Ireland.

"That's the Irish Sea, Connor," Owen explained. "There are some wonderful places along there for a picnic. I know we have it on the list to get out of the city and enjoy the countryside for a day. I'll suggest we picnic along the banks of the Irish Sea. But now, my curious little wanderer, I think we need to get you back to the rest of the family before they send out another search party for all of us!"

* * *

Over the next several days, the family explored Dublin

Castle in the heart of the city and Swords Castle north of Dublin. Allowing Liam and Siobhan to be their unofficial tour guides, they were able to see many other sights in the area while avoiding the more touristy locations. The elder Gallaghers also contacted a few relatives who still resided in the Dublin area and made arrangements to visit with them.

One evening, after another full day of exploring, Liam addressed the family.

"While we're here," he began, "Siobhan and I would like to see some family who are still in Dublin. Most of the family has moved on to other parts of Ireland, and a few to Scotland, but we still have a couple of nephews and their families in town, and Siobhan's younger brother. Obviously, none of you are obligated to go see them, but we'd like to visit with them a bit tomorrow."

"I'd like to see them too, Dad," Owen replied. "Who knows when we'll get back over here?"

Connor looked around the group, then raised his hand. "Granddad, you and Granny are going to see some more Irish people?"

Liam smiled at this young boy he had come to love in a very short time.

"Aye, lad," Liam confirmed. "Some very nice Irish people."

"Can I come see them too?" Connor asked.

"You certainly may," Liam agreed. "Anyone who wants to come along can. I'm sure we'd all be welcome."

Zach's parents scanned the group, then David

suggested, "I think we all should go. I'm sure there's more to Ireland than simply seeing the sights. Getting to know some of the people is important, too. And what better people to get to know than family?"

Siobhan smiled as she saw all the heads nodding in agreement. Soon, arrangements were made for the entire group to meet up the next day.

Connor walked over and climbed onto Liam's lap. For a moment, he studied the old man's face without saying anything.

"Granddad," Connor began, "do these other Irish people have any...what do you call me...a wee lad? That's a little boy, right?"

Liam hugged Connor tightly. "Yes, Connor, a wee lad is a little boy. And one of the families has a wee lad about your age."

"Do you know him, Granddad?"

"No," Liam admitted. "He was born after your Granny and I moved to the United States. But we'll all meet him tomorrow."

"What's his name, Granddad?" Connor asked. "I want to be able to call him his name."

Liam smiled. "His name is Sean. I think you'll love him."

"Me too," Connor agreed without hesitation.

* * *

Siobhan was able to spend the better part of a day

visiting with her dear friend Maureen, who had been missing her terribly. When Siobhan mentioned the family would be taking a day to escape the city, see the Irish countryside, and have a picnic along the Irish Sea, she invited her friend to join them for the day. Maureen agreed and insisted on packing the picnic for the entire family.

With many sets of eyes on the adventurous little boy, there wasn't much danger of Connor disappearing while on their picnic. Shane and Taylor took him down to the water so he could put his hand in the Irish Sea that he had seen from the castle tower.

Swishing his hand back and forth in the water, Connor exclaimed happily, "I'm touching Ireland water, Mommy!"

Connor had always been a curious child, but Ireland had completely captivated him. Everything held such wonder for him that his parents hoped he wouldn't be too disappointed when it was time to go home.

As they gathered the remnants of their picnic lunch, and Siobhan said a tearful goodbye to her dear friend, Liam looked at Connor, who was fascinated by a butterfly near their picnic blanket.

"I have one more castle I want you to see, Connor," Liam grinned. "Tomorrow we'll go to Drimnagh Castle. That way, you can see what a castle looks like that has a moat around it."

Connor clapped his hands in excitement. "I bet *they* don't have any dragons!"

Liam laughed. "No, lad, I don't believe they do."

"Why didn't the other castles have water around them, Granddad?" Connor asked.

"Most of them don't anymore. There aren't many dragons left, I suppose," Liam grinned. "In fact, Drimnagh is the only castle left in Ireland that has a moat."

"I'll watch for dragons anyway," Connor nodded. "Just in case."

"Always a good plan, lad," Liam grinned.

The next day, after strict instructions from his mother to always hold onto someone's hand, Connor and the family headed up the path to Drimnagh Castle.

As they approached the castle and the stone bridge, Connor pointed to the moat.

"There's the water, Daddy Shane!" Connor exclaimed. "That keeps the dragons out!"

Shane looked around the area seriously. "It must be working, buddy. I don't see any dragons."

The family spent nearly two hours exploring the castle and the surrounding grounds with its beautiful gardens. Taylor and Shane took some time to stroll through the gardens hand in hand while Shane's parents showed Connor the castle a third time.

"Tomorrow we pack up to head home," Shane mentioned quietly. "Have you enjoyed Ireland, honey?"

Taylor leaned her head against Shane's shoulder. "Yes, I have. It's been a wonderful experience. Well, everything except losing my son in a castle!"

Shane laughed. "Yeah, that wasn't a lot of fun. It's a good thing Grandpa knew where a little boy would disappear in a castle. I think this trip was important to Grandpa. I hope it's not the last time he can come back."

"Your grandparents are in great shape for someone in their eighties," Taylor reminded her husband. "If they want to come back, they'll be back."

Shane nodded. "Do you think your parents and grandparents enjoyed the trip?"

"I do," Taylor smiled. "I heard them talking to your grandparents about it the other night. I wouldn't be surprised if your grandparents don't drag mine back here again, just the four of them."

"What about Zach's parents?" Shane asked. "We all tried to make sure they were included in everything. I hope they never felt like outsiders."

"I don't think they felt that way at all," Taylor assured him. "They were happy we included them, and they seemed to enjoy everything. I even saw David showing Connor a picture of a knight on the wall at one of the castles. I'm really glad they're back in Connor's life."

Shane hugged his wife. "Me too. Well, honey, as much as I've enjoyed our time alone, we should probably find the rest of the family and see if they're ready to go."

Taylor reached up and kissed her husband. "Or, we could hide in the garden and wait for them to find us."

Shane laughed as he led his wife out of the garden,

where they found their family patiently waiting in front of the castle.

* * *

Connor wasn't the only one who covered their ears to block out the loud noise of the engines as the plane prepared to take off. Once they were in the air, Liam tapped Connor on the shoulder and pointed out the plane window.

The little boy smiled widely when he saw several castles growing smaller as the plane climbed higher into the air. When the plane reached cruising altitude, everyone sat back in their seats to settle in for the long flight. Connor continued staring out the window until they were above the clouds.

With a small wave, he whispered, "Bye, castles. Bye, Ireland."

Liam pulled his great-grandson close and said quietly, "We'll be back."

Connor looked up at his granddad and nodded. "Yep, we'll be back."

# Chapter Twenty-Four

A week after returning from Ireland, Taylor followed her son into the fire station. Chief Hart was talking to Shane and Cody just outside his office when Connor ran over to say hi.

"Hi, Chief! Hi, Cody!" the little boy greeted with a smile.

"What?" Shane asked, feigning disbelief. "I don't even get a hello from my son?"

"Hi, Daddy Shane!" Connor laughed.

Taylor kissed her husband and smiled. "I'll say hello to you, honey. You know how that little boy is when he gets around 'the guys'!"

Chief Hart chuckled as he gave Connor a high-five. "Where have you been, buddy? We haven't seen you around since the softball tournament."

"We been in Ireland, Chief!" Connor announced proudly.

"Ireland, huh?" the chief asked. "Did you see any

castles?"

"Yep!" Connor replied excitedly. "They were cool! We went in towers and everything!"

"Well," Taylor interjected, "we weren't *planning* to go into the towers. A certain little boy went exploring on his own."

"Boys will do that!" the chief laughed.

"Did you get to see any dragons, Connor?" Cody asked with a smile.

"Nope." Connor shook his head sadly. "Granddad said there aren't many dragons left anymore. So, most of the castles don't have water around them now. Granddad said there's only one castle in Ireland that has water around it."

"Did you get to see that castle?" Cody wondered.

"Yep! We got to explore inside," Connor explained. "No dragons in the castle because of the water outside."

Cody nodded. "That makes sense."

"If your son is finished talking about dragons," Taylor smiled, addressing Shane, "I can tell you why we stopped by. We were running a few errands, and I thought I'd see if you guys were out on a fire. If not, I can go pick up pizza for everyone."

"At the moment," the chief began, "we don't have a lot going on. Of course, as you know, that's always subject to change. We're going to have some training exercises later this afternoon. Pizza might be a good way to get some extra carbs."

"Okay, I'll hurry!" Taylor laughed. "We can't have

you guys running out of energy partway through training."

"Mommy, can I stay here with Daddy Shane and the guys?" Connor pleaded.

Taylor looked at her husband for his reply.

"It's okay," Shane agreed. "He can hang out with us for a few minutes while you grab lunch."

On her way out, Taylor whispered to Cody, "Don't let him talk your ears off about castles. That's all we've heard since we got back."

Cody grinned. "That's what Shane said. Maybe I'll show him some of the new equipment we got in. That should distract him for a few minutes."

"Hey, Cody," Connor began as he walked up, "did you know you can see forever from the tower in a castle?"

"You can?" Cody asked in amazement. "I didn't know that. I've never been in a castle."

"You should go to Ireland!" Connor suggested. "Granddad said they have *thousands* of castles!"

"I may have to do that someday," Cody nodded.

"You can come with us next time we go," Connor invited his friend. "Granddad said we'll be back."

"That'd be awesome, buddy," Cody agreed. "Hey, have you seen the new gear we got in? We got in some pretty cool masks and helmets the other day."

Connor was instantly intrigued. "You did? Will you show them to me? Do you think I can try on one of the new helmets? And maybe a mask? What else did you get?

I'm going to be a fireman someday, you know. Or maybe a policeman. Or maybe something else. I might fight dragons in Ireland. Not sure yet."

Taylor smiled as she walked toward the parking lot, leaving her son and his thousand questions to the firefighters.

* * *

By the time the family returned from their vacation in Ireland, summer was slipping away quickly. Taylor felt a mix of emotions about the upcoming school year. On one hand, she was relieved because it meant Shane would transition to volunteer firefighter status once again. On the other hand, her little boy would be starting kindergarten this fall, and she wasn't sure she was ready for that. One significant advantage of her teaching at Mountainview Christian now is that it means Connor will be attending her school. The three of them will be able to ride to and from school together.

"Connor, are you about ready to go?" Taylor asked as her son played with his castle in the corner of the room.

"Where did you say we're going, Mommy?" Connor asked as he raised the drawbridge.

Taylor grinned. "We're going to pick up Grandma and go shopping for school clothes."

"Why does Grandma need school clothes?" Connor asked, obviously distracted.

"Grandma doesn't need school clothes," Taylor explained, smiling. "*You* do."

Connor jumped up. "Oh, yeah! I get to go to school now with you and Daddy Shane."

"That's right," Taylor laughed. "But only if we get you some clothes that fit!"

Connor smiled and shrugged as he ran to the door. "What can I say? I'm a growing boy."

"Don't I know it!" Taylor exclaimed as she grabbed her purse and keys.

Taylor was glad her mom agreed to go shopping with them. It was at least a two-person job keeping Connor focused on picking out and trying on suitable clothes for school. Convincing little boys to try on clothes was no easy feat, but between Taylor and her mom, they managed to get him to try on enough jeans and tops to determine his size. Trying on shoes was a bit easier. The most challenging part was having him decide on a shoe style he liked, since he couldn't find anything with dragons on it. Finding the correct size was simple.

Once that task was completed, the three met up with Taylor's dad so Connor could collect on the promised cheeseburger for lunch.

That evening, Shane's shift allowed him to join them for dinner as he was about to enter his last cycle of four days off from the department. After that, he would work ten days straight, and then he'd be done for the summer.

"Were you able to find everything Connor needs to

start school?" Shane asked Taylor as they cleaned up the dishes after dinner.

Taylor laughed. "For the time being. If that boy would quit growing, maybe his clothes would fit him for more than a month."

"Don't count on that happening," Shane laughed. "On another note, I was thinking earlier that since I'm off for a few days before my last stretch, why don't we have the family over for dinner? Maybe we could barbecue or something."

"The whole family?" Taylor asked. "That would be fun. I don't think we've all been together since we got back from Ireland."

"Let's do it then," Shane smiled. "You call your family, and I'll call mine. Let's plan for Saturday. I happen to know Mom has that day off this week."

"Wow," Taylor whispered as she watched her son playing in the living room. "A dinner with the whole family that doesn't involve pizza. How will we ever survive?"

Shane grinned. "I'll make sure to grill some hot dogs too, then all will be right with the world."

* * *

The barbecue grill was fired up on the back deck, a couple of canopies were set up in the yard, and tables and chairs were arranged beneath the canopies. The entire family had gathered for the end-of-summer cookout. Connor had convinced his Grandpa and Grandpa Owen to shag balls for him as he practiced his T-ball skills. Grandpa David had offered to help Shane man the grill, so he was relieved of T-ball duty. Fortunately, the food was ready just as Kenny was about to call a halt to the T-ball game. A couple of Connor's wild hits bounced off the table where the boy's great-grandparents sat visiting.

"Oops! Sorry, Granddad and Granny!" Connor yelled.

"No harm, no foul," Liam laughed.

"Actually, Dad," Owen chuckled, "I believe that *was* a foul ball."

Shane and David added trays of hamburgers and hot dogs to the tables already loaded with food. "Okay, everyone, it's time to eat!" Shane announced.

Connor dropped his baseball bat and ran to the tables.

"I want a hot dog, Grandpa," he told Kenny. "And a cheeseburger, and some chips, and some macaroni salad…"

"Whoa there, buddy!" Kenny laughed. "How about if you start small? Let's get you a hot dog and some macaroni salad to get you started. If you're still hungry when you finish that, we'll discuss a cheeseburger."

"*If* he's still hungry?" Taylor laughed. "Dad, that boy is *always* hungry. I'd be willing to bet that within an hour after finishing dinner, he'll be asking for some of the leftover pizza in the fridge!"

"We have pizza?" Connor asked as he quickly swallowed a bite of hot dog.

"Eat your hot dog and macaroni salad," Taylor laughed. "We'll worry about the leftover pizza later."

Kenny laughed. "He did tell your mom the other day that he was a growing boy, and that's why you always needed to buy him new clothes."

"Six months," Taylor said, shaking her head. "All I want is six months where I don't have to replace all of his jeans."

"He's a boy," Owen laughed. "If he weren't growing out of the pants, he'd be wearing them out. Either way, you two are in for the long haul when it comes to supplying your son with clothes."

Shane patted his dad on the back as they went to join the others at one of the tables. "I can think of a lot worse problems to have."

\* \* \*

Connor had been put to bed for the night after several pleas for one more story. Taylor had laid out her son's clothes for the first day of kindergarten and finally managed to quiet the excited boy enough to hopefully fall asleep. After multiple back-and-forth 'I love you' and 'I love you more' as they worked their way down the hallway, Taylor and Shane were finally able to relax on the sofa for a while, mentally gearing up for heading back to school in the morning. Taylor tipped her head back and closed her eyes, neither of them speaking for several minutes.

Shane reached over and pulled his wife into his arms, and Taylor wasted no time snuggling against her husband.

"Well," Shane began quietly, "it's back to school tomorrow."

Taylor didn't reply; instead, she simply nodded.

"It's hard to believe it was only two years ago when we met over lunch trays in the cafeteria," Shane smiled. "A lot has happened in the past two years."

Taylor sat up and looked at her husband. "So much."

Shane watched his wife's face cloud over. "The last *three* years for you have been kind of a whirlwind," he said sympathetically, kissing her forehead and pulling her closer.

"Do you think I'll ever get to the point where I don't look at life as before Zach's death and after Zach's death?" Taylor asked quietly.

Shane thought for a minute before replying. "I've never lost a spouse, so I honestly can't say. All I can say is that I'll always be here for you, and you can always talk to me. If you're having a bad day with memories, talk to me. If you remember good things about your life with Zach, tell me about them. I want to hear. I want to hear about anything that makes you happy or sad."

Taylor looked into Shane's eyes and saw nothing but love and compassion.

She sighed. "When Zach was killed, I honestly thought my life was over. I couldn't believe I was a widow at twenty-six. I was suddenly a single mom with a two-year-old boy. That wasn't what my life was supposed to be like. Zach and I were supposed to grow old together and raise Connor – together. I was completely devastated and had no clue what life was supposed to be like."

Shane didn't interrupt, knowing she still needed to work through things in her own way.

"Then I met this handsome math teacher who drove the coolest pickup I'd ever seen," Taylor continued with a smile. "And I fell in love."

Shane grinned like a schoolboy. "With the handsome math teacher or with the cool pickup?"

"With the cool pickup, of course," Taylor replied playfully. "At first. The handsome math teacher grew on me."

"Hopefully not like a bad chemistry experiment," Shane laughed.

Taylor smiled. "More like the oil and water don't mix experiment. But a handsome man with a cool pickup is hard to resist.

"Then I found out you were also a firefighter," Taylor continued sadly. "I had already convinced my heart, so I thought, not to fall for another first responder. I talked to my heart over and over again. I begged. I pleaded. My heart didn't listen."

"Go, Team Heart!" Shane added with a smile.

Taylor returned his smile and took his hand in hers. "Yeah, go, Team Heart," she repeated quietly. "I couldn't believe my heart dared to ignore me. Completely and totally ignore me. I was very explicit in my demands. 'Do not fall in love with another first responder.' Very simple. However…"

"Ooh, can I finish the story?" Shane asked excitedly.

Taylor laughed. "Well, you can give it a try. Just remember, *I'm* the literature teacher. *You're* the math and science teacher."

"No problem," Shane replied with confidence. "I've got this. Then you fell madly in love with the *extremely* handsome math teacher who just happened to also be a firefighter. An extremely handsome firefighter, I might add."

Taylor laughed and shook her head.

Shane continued the story. "The handsome math teacher slash firefighter with the very cool pickup had already fallen madly in love with this beautiful English teacher. She didn't have a cool pickup, but her dad had an amazing 1968 Chevy Chevelle, so that gave her bonus points. And…she had this totally awesome little boy who also fell in love with the math teacher's pickup, and kind of liked the math teacher too. So, the very wise math teacher…"

"Oh," Taylor interrupted, "so now you're not only extremely handsome, but very wise too?"

Shane grinned. "Well, of course! Anyway, the very wise math teacher started giving the beautiful English teacher and her awesome little boy rides in his cool pickup. They went for ice cream and pizza. And the little boy was hooked. He fell in love with the cool pickup…uh, I mean, the wise math teacher."

Taylor laughed as Shane continued his story.

"And the very wise math teacher, who just happened to be a firefighter, was hooked for life. He realized he had not only fallen in love with a beautiful school teacher, but he had also fallen in love with her awesome little boy."

"Not bad," Taylor nodded. "But why don't you let the English teacher finish the story?

"At the end of the story, the beautiful English teacher realized that maybe, just maybe, her life wasn't over after all. Maybe her new life was just beginning. It wasn't going to replace her life before Zach's death. It was going to *add* to it. And it was going to be a wonderful life."

Shane leaned over and kissed his wife lovingly. "And they all lived happily ever after."

# EPILOGUE

*Eight Years Later*

The bleachers surrounding the softball field were quickly filling up as people awaited the start of the Guns and Hoses tournament. The annual event, which pits the local police and fire departments against one another, always attracts a large crowd. This year, the crowd was even larger than normal since it was the twenty-fifth anniversary of the local Guns and Hoses tournament. Shane and Taylor Gallagher's entire family was present for the game, as they were every year.

Along the third baseline, several feet away from the freshly chalked diamond, a dark-haired teenager played catch with his younger sister. Thirteen-year-old Connor Wilson had waited eight years for this day. He was an energetic five-year-old when he attended his first Guns and Hoses tournament with his newly extended family. He was told then that when he was thirteen, he could umpire the friendly rivalry.

Connor was friends with many of the police officers and most of the firefighters. The coaches of both teams unanimously agreed that the young boy would be a fair and impartial umpire since he had a vested interest in both teams. From the time he began playing T-ball, Connor concentrated on learning everything he could about the game of baseball. He was ready.

"Hey, Kylie," Connor motioned to his six-year-old sister after he caught her last throw. "We need to stop now so I can get ready for the game."

Decked out in shorts and a custom t-shirt supporting both teams, the young girl, with her blonde hair in a ponytail, ran up to her older brother.

"So, you're really going to be the umpire, Connor?" Kylie asked in wide-eyed admiration.

"Yep," Connor replied proudly. "This will be my first time."

"Are you nervous?" the young girl wondered as she watched some of the players warming up along the sidelines.

"Not really," her brother answered honestly. "I know all about softball, and I've been coming to the Guns and Hoses tournament since I was younger than you."

"Do you want me to take your baseball glove, so it doesn't get lost, Connor?" Kylie asked. "I won't let it out of my sight, I promise."

Connor patted his sister on the shoulder. "Yeah,

that'd be great, Kylie," he replied, handing her the glove. "I know you'll take good care of it. You always do."

Kylie held her brother's prized glove close to her chest.

"Good luck, Connor," Kylie smiled. "You'll be the best umpire ever!"

"Thanks, Kylie," Connor replied as he hugged his sister. "Grandpa is standing over by the bleachers waiting for you," he added, pointing toward the bleachers.

Connor and Kylie waved at their Grandpa Kenny, who returned the wave.

"Go straight to Grandpa, alright?" Connor instructed his little sister.

"I will," Kylie nodded as she gave her brother one last hug. "Good luck!"

\* \* \*

Connor had been correct; he wasn't nervous at all. Most of the players on both teams were his friends, and he had known them for years. He strapped on the umpire's chest protector, turned his ballcap around backward, and pulled on his mask, leaving it perched on top of his cap.

He gestured for the coaches of both teams to meet on the pitcher's mound for the coin toss. Chief Doug Hart was the coach for the Hoses, and Captain Pete McDonald coached the Guns. Connor had known them both since he was a small boy. Both men patted him on the back.

"Are you ready to go, guys?" Connor asked, smiling.

"Ready whenever you are, Ump," Captain McDonald grinned, shaking his head. "You've come a long way from the first time we met, the day you were born."

Connor grinned at the family friend he had referred to as Uncle Pete since he was old enough to talk.

"Who wants to call the coin toss?" Connor asked, getting down to business.

Pete smiled at Doug and replied, "We'll let the Hoses call the toss. They're going to need every break they can get today. Remember, Shane's grandma said the trophy has to come back to the precinct this year."

Doug laughed. "Only if you Guns promise to keep it dusted this time."

Dusting the traveling trophy had become an inside joke between the firefighters and the police officers, with Chief Hart making a point of shining it up before it was presented to the Guns.

Connor grinned at his two friends. "If you two are finished, let's toss the coin and get this game started."

"Okay," Doug began, "we'll call heads. No, wait, we call tails."

"Are you sure, Chief?" Connor laughed.

"Yep," Doug laughed. "We call tails."

Connor flipped the coin and showed the men that it landed heads up.

"Okay, Uncle Pete," Connor grinned. "Do the Guns want to bat first or take the field?"

"We'll take the field," Pete chuckled. "You should have stuck with your first answer, Doug."

"I had a fifty-fifty chance," Doug laughed as he walked over to his waiting team. "You can call the toss next year, Pete!"

The first batter for the Hoses came to the plate, patted Connor on the back, and wished him luck.

The Guns and Hoses fought hard during the first half of the game, with the Hoses leading by one run. Throughout the game, Connor could hear Kylie wishing him luck. Each time, it brought a smile to his face. He truly loved his kid sister. At times, he had to tune out the cheers from the bleachers to avoid distraction. He could hear his mom and all the grandparents cheering for both teams, but they seemed to yell loudest for their favorite umpire.

At the end of the first half of the final inning, Shane hit a long home run, putting the Hoses two runs ahead.

As he crossed home plate, Connor signaled him safe, then said, "Nice hit, Dad!"

Shane smiled. "Now we just need to make sure the Guns don't score in their last at-bat."

"That's your job, Dad," Connor grinned. "I'm impartial, remember."

The Guns only scored one run in their last chance at bat in the first game, relinquishing the first win of the tournament to the Hoses.

The two teams had about an hour break between the first and second games, so many of them hit the concession stand to fuel up.

"Hey, Dad!" Connor yelled as Shane headed toward the concession stand. "Can you grab me a hot dog and a drink?"

"Sure, buddy," Shane replied.

Captain McDonald heard the request as he, too, headed for a snack. "You're not bribing the umpire, are you, Gallagher?" Pete asked, laughing.

Shane laughed. "Nope, just feeding my son."

Pete slapped him on the back as they placed their orders. "That was a nice homer you hit. But, you realize you Hoses are going to have to win another game."

"True," Shane grinned. "But you Guns have to win two in a row! Good luck!"

After a short break, game two began with the firefighters taking the field and the police officers batting first. Much like the first game, both teams played well, and the lead bounced back and forth. Connor was secretly glad he didn't have many close calls in his debut as an umpire. He was fairly confident in calling the balls and strikes, although he knew he had messed up on one. Luckily, it didn't affect the batter's time at the plate. So far, all his calls with runners coming in to score had been clear, so there were no debates.

By the end of the second game, the Guns came out on top. The third game would decide who would be taking home the trophy this year.

Since most of the police officers and firefighters had been friends for years, the tournament truly was a friendly rivalry, even though they put on a show of it being a life-or-death contest. During the break before the final game, several players from both teams joined Shane and Taylor's family in the shade to relax.

Shane's ninety-year-old grandma sat in a lawn chair beside her ninety-three-year-old husband.

Siobhan shook her frail finger at Captain McDonald and smiled. "Remember, Captain, it's your turn for the trophy this year. Those firefighters have had it down at the station all year. So, you guys need to win this last game. Understand?"

Pete laughed. "Yes, ma'am, I understand. We'll do our best."

"As long as your best takes the trophy back to the precinct," Siobhan nodded. "I don't want to have to go take it away from the lads at the fire station."

Shane's dad laughed at his mother's response. "I'd take her at her word, Pete. Those old Irish women are tough and sneaky!"

"Who are you calling old, Owen Gallagher?" Siobhan asked her son.

"Certainly not you, Mother!" Owen smiled contritely.

About that time, Connor stood and announced, "Okay, guys, time to get the final game started."

Owen stood and patted his grandson on the back. "Thanks, Connor. Saved by the umpire!"

The third and final game of the Guns and Hoses tournament was more relaxed. At times, it appeared that none of the players wanted to explain to a certain elderly Irish woman why the police officers wouldn't be claiming the trophy. The Guns won game three by two runs, thus taking possession of the prized trophy and saving Siobhan a trip to the fire station.

Both teams gathered their softball gear and began heading toward the parking lot.

"Hey," Connor began before everyone got too far away. "Can we go to Angelina's for pizza?"

Several of the players looked around, considering the offer.

Chief Hart shrugged. "It sounds to me like the umpire has spoken. Shall we all just meet over there?"

"Yes!" Connor pumped his fist in the air and then gave his sister a high-five.

As they walked across the field, Kylie laughed. "Connor, don't you ever get tired of eating pizza?"

Connor shrugged. "Not in the last thirteen years or so!"

* * *

Between Shane and Taylor's family and most of the Guns and Hoses players, along with some of their families, the group managed to fill three long tables at the pizza parlor. The tables were soon loaded with trays of pizza, salad, garlic bread, and drinks.

"Hey, Connor," Cody waved at the teenager from the end of the table. "I just wanted to let you know you did a great job umpiring your first tournament out there today."

"Thanks, Cody," Connor smiled. "It was a lot of fun. Maybe I can do it again next year?"

"You've got the vote of the Hoses," Chief Hart nodded.

"No objection from the Guns," Captain McDonald added. "You may have yourself a permanent gig, Connor."

"Thanks, guys!" Connor replied proudly as Kylie gave him a high-five.

The tired softball players and their families visited and enjoyed pizza for over an hour before the gathering began breaking up. It had been a long day.

Taylor followed her parents and grandparents to the door and was nudged by her daughter, who ran up behind her.

"Mommy," Kylie began, "can I ride in the pickup with Daddy and Connor?"

Taylor smiled. "What if I wanted to ride with your dad?"

Kylie held her hands together and pleaded. "Please?"

"Okay," Taylor laughed. "I guess I'll ride with Grandma and Grandpa and hope they take me home!"

Once they got to the parking lot and everyone began going their separate ways, Connor looked at Shane with mischief in his eyes.

"Hey, Dad," he began with a grin, "can I drive your pickup home?"

Shane raised his eyebrow. "Let's see. Are you fifteen yet?"

Connor grinned and replied hopefully, "Almost."

"Yeah, thirteen's almost fifteen," Shane laughed before continuing his interrogation. "Do you have a learner's permit?"

Connor smiled, knowing his dad's answer before he even asked the question. "Not quite."

Shane laughed as he pulled his son into a hug. "Well, then, son, I guess you can't quite drive my truck yet."

Connor ran his hand along the side of the restored 1954 Chevy pickup. He and his mom had both fallen in love with this truck the first time they met Shane when Connor was only three years old.

The optimistic teenager smiled. "One of these days, Dad, I'll be driving this sweet truck."

"I have no doubt, son," Shane laughed. "You've been telling me that since you were about four years old."


~ The End ~

# ABOUT THE AUTHOR

After nearly thirty years of crunching numbers, Joyce Byers Hill retired to pursue her dream of writing. Joyce enjoys writing fiction from a Christian perspective, interlaced with a bit of humor. In all her books, you'll find happily ever afters, delicious food, and days that are sunny with a chance of baseball.

*First Response* is Joyce's first standalone novel, following the completion of the *A Place Called Hope* series.

Joyce lives in Central Washington with her incredible daughter and son-in-law, and her overly bossy dog.

For information on upcoming events
and the latest novels by Joyce Byers Hill,
visit **www.joycebyershill.com**